Take Control of Your Life

A Story of Wrestling with Personal Growth

THIS BOOK, *TAKE CONTROL OF YOUR LIFE*, DOES NOT PROVIDE LEGAL, FINANCIAL, PSYCHOLOGICAL, OR MEDICAL ADVICE ("PROFESSIONAL ADVICE"). ALWAYS SEEK PROFESSIONAL ADVICE BEFORE CHANGING ANY PHYSICAL OR MENTAL HEALTH PRACTICE OR MAKING ANY INVESTMENT.

Take Control of Your Life

A Story of Wrestling with Personal Growth

―

Steve G. Vogel
Sanguinity LLC Press
Frenchtown, New Jersey, USA

Cover Design: J.R. Bale, Balefire Communications,
www.balefirecom.com

Graphic Concept: Tom Pfaff and Pat Dickson

© 2005 Steve G. Vogel. Printed and bound in the United States of America. All rights reserved. No part of this book may be reproduced or transmitted in any form or by any means, electronic or mechanical, including photocopying, recording, or by an information storage and retrieval system – except by a reviewer who may quote brief passages in a review to be printed in a magazine, newspaper, or on the Web – without permission in writing from the publisher. For information, please contact Sanguinity LLC at 1-408-887-5127.

Although the author and publisher have made every effort to ensure the accuracy and completeness of information in this book, we assume no responsibility for errors, inaccuracies, omissions, or inconsistencies herein. Any slights of people, places, or organizations are unintentional.

First Printing 2006

ISBN 0-9769387-0-7

LCCN 2005928151

Sanguinity LLC Press books and products are available for purchase, special promotions, and premiums. For details, please visit our Web site at: www.sanguinity.org

FIRST EDITION

TABLE OF CONTENTS

	Dedication	vii
	Preface	ix
Chapter One:	The Stranger	1
Chapter Two:	Wrestling Practice	7
Chapter Three:	Developing Goals at the Library	18
Chapter Four:	Anger Recognition and Forgiveness	24
Chapter Five:	Overcoming Fear Through Visualization	33
Chapter Six:	The Visualization Unfolds in the Bethlehem Valley Scrimmage	43
Chapter Seven:	The Words Worked	49
Chapter Eight:	The New Phase	58
Chapter Nine:	The Study Date	64
Chapter Ten:	Wrestling and the Doctor	72
Chapter Eleven:	Canyon Creek High – The First Big Test	82
Chapter Twelve:	The First Real Date	92
Chapter Thirteen:	The SAT and The College Decision	103
Chapter Fourteen:	Pam Meets with Greg's Parents	111
Chapter Fifteen:	Christmas Break	121
Chapter Sixteen:	Pam's Return to New Jersey	130
Chapter Seventeen:	The Funeral	137
Chapter Eighteen:	Wrestling with Weight	139

Chapter Nineteen:	Facing Faith	148
Chapter Twenty:	Gurist the Coach	151
Chapter Twenty-One:	Accept Death and Face Fear	156
Chapter Twenty-Two:	Getting Back on Track	160
Chapter Twenty-Three:	Districts and Regions	164
Chapter Twenty-Four:	Planning for States: The Seven Steps and the Ten Keys	166
Chapter Twenty-Five:	States	192
Chapter Twenty-Six:	College Bound	209

Appendices:

Personal Growth Index	211
The Seven Steps of the Personal Growth Cycle and the Ten Keys	212
The Seven Steps of the Personal Growth Cycle	213
The Ten Keys	219
The Seven Steps of the Personal Growth Cycle (Symbol Meanings)	229
The Ten Keys (Symbol Meanings)	230
Glossary (Word List)	231
Order Form	243

Dedication

This book is dedicated to my poetry writing mother, Anne Meredith Vogel, and my father and fellow logophile, John Joseph Vogel, whose personal library, to my mom's chagrin, approaches 10,000 volumes. These spry octogenarians support me in all I do: I love them both. It is equally dedicated to the three dearest loves of my life: my brilliant, beautiful, and bold spouse, Šárka, and our two wonderful sons, Jakub Gregory Josef (Kubi) and Benjamin Franklin Patrik (Patrik). They are my world. Šárka, who valiantly relocated from the Czech Republic, keeps me loved, motivated, and grounded, while Kubi keeps me honest and sharp, and Patrik keeps us all smiling. Love to my sister, Donna, for she would have admired the wisdom of Anthony. To all twelve siblings who have had a positive impact on me: Carol, John, Suzy Rita, Sandra, Mark, Donna, Maria, Paul, Fred, Janice, Thalia, and Sharon. To Šárka's parents, Josef Novák, a Czech governmental funds consultant, and Helena Nováková, an author of Czech real estate textbooks: Děkuji.

Special thanks go to my business partner, author, lawyer, Web site creator, powerlifter, and dear friend, John Patrick Dickson. I so admire him that I named Patrik after him. His constructive feedback, unbridled praise, tolerance of my impatience, and diligent oversight motivated, inspired, and contributed immeasurably to this work.

My editor, Denny Diehl, has exhibited rare traits for an editor. He has been patient, caring, and timely while carefully cloaking all well-deserved criticisms in sagacious suggestions. For her passionate and accurate insights I thank Marylu Horkowitz who helped the manuscript "Live in the Present." Thanks also to

Margaret Gallos and Vivian Fransen for consistency and critical errata reduction.

A great leader and inspiration: Coach Gregory Strobel, Olympic coach and NCAA Outstanding Wrestler, I thank him for taking valuable time to peruse the full manuscript and offer valuable insight and much appreciated plaudits. Lastly, I would like to add thanks to those teachers and professors who epitomize the Socratic ideal and helped make an average student less average: Lehigh University Psychology Professor Emeritus and Associate Dean William Newman, Arizona State University Law Professor Dale Beck Furnish, New York University Law and Business Professor Joseph W. Bartlett, New York University Law and Accounting Professor Abraham Stanger, Wharton School of the University of Pennsylvania Marketing Professor F. Stewart DeBruicker, and University of California Berkeley Boalt Hall Law and Economics Professor Jesse M. Fried.

Preface

Five o'clock on a Friday afternoon, while reading a law assignment in torts, the phone rang. A fellow student urgently requested my presence to join our study group at a favorite watering hole. Neither the call nor my response came unexpectedly. I eagerly departed, gladly leaving my legal tome behind as I braced for the Pittsburgh winter. Only after starting the car, engaging the clutch, and pulling away from the curb did I glean the magnitude of the event. I had answered the phone, listened, said yes, grabbed keys and coat, unlocked my car, jumped in, started the car, shifted gears, and pulled away. I had reacted. Not for one second had I *consciously* responded. Not for one second was I *mindful* of my actions. I was on automatic pilot heading directly towards bad grades in law school. How did this happen?

This Gestaltian "aha" moment revealed one thing with perfect clarity. While my conscious self may have wanted good grades, my unconscious self only knew of my desire to be among classmates with a bottle of Rolling Rock in my hand. Recognition of this unconscious act done so effortlessly, painlessly, and unknowingly created the "aha" moment. How did my conscious and my unconscious become so misaligned? And how could I instruct my unconscious mind to do what my conscious mind wanted? How could I become mindful of my actions?

Therein began my quest for an answer. After several years and much struggling I developed a patent-pending solution that is the heart of Sanguinity and *Take Control of Your Life*. Be it weight loss, improvement in school and test scores, exercise, goal setting, or stress reduction, Sanguinity has a proven track record of helping me and others achieve their dreams.

By aligning my unconscious mind and conscious mind, the breadth and scope of my abilities have expanded. My scores on the GMAT improved from the 51st percentile to the 98th. I graduated cum laude from a law school that had initially rejected my application. This success has in turn caused my view of human limits to expand exponentially. Having wrestled briefly in high school and college, I could not help but wonder what high school would have been like had I found Sanguinity earlier. This question led to writing *Take Control of Your Life*.

Sanguinity helps you take good ideas, like dieting and exercise programs, and make them work. Many self-help works may present good ideas. This book is meant to help you apply those good ideas that you find. As a student of personal growth, I marvel at the ancient master Socrates who gave us the wonderfully salubrious process of questioning that has lead to the Socratic Method used in law school. The question mark in one's mind herein used to denote **Learn Who You Are**, one of the Sanguinity **Ten Keys**, was surely best lived by Socrates whose explanation to Crito of his decision to stay and die versus flee and live provides a deadly account of self-knowledge.

Dale Carnegie's *How to Win Friends and Influence People* has influenced me since attending and becoming a teaching assistant in the basic Dale Carnegie training course in Buffalo, New York. His basic tenets are no less viable today.

Important recent works in self-development include Victor E. Frankl's *Man's Search for Meaning* and Robert Ellsberg's *The Saint's Guide to Happiness*. Frankl attests to the fact that meaning can be found anywhere; even in hell on earth. Ellsberg's impressive work thoroughly explains how being good and living right may be more associated with happiness than suffering.

Benson and Proctor's *The Break-out Principle* presents an

advanced self-help work. His discussion of the triggering of nitric oxide explains a scientific basis for *Endorphins Corral Frissons*, one of Greg Gurist's affirmations. He shows how nitric oxide may be the magic secretion that helps optimize performance and turn fear into constructive action.

On exercising, I have learned from books by the aerobic masters like Kenneth Cooper and Lance Armstrong. Using interval training ideas I put together a training program that has helped me achieve a sub-6-minute treadmill mile; something I hadn't been capable of since high school. This shows that ideas for personal growth can come from anywhere, but the goal setting and motivation program that can help you effectively apply them centers around the work presented in this book, the companion book, *Walk and Talk it Off: The Sanguinity Approach to Diet and Exercise,* and the **Personal Commercial**. All are available through the Web site at: www.sanguinity.org.

Take Control of Your Life

A Story of Wrestling with Personal Growth

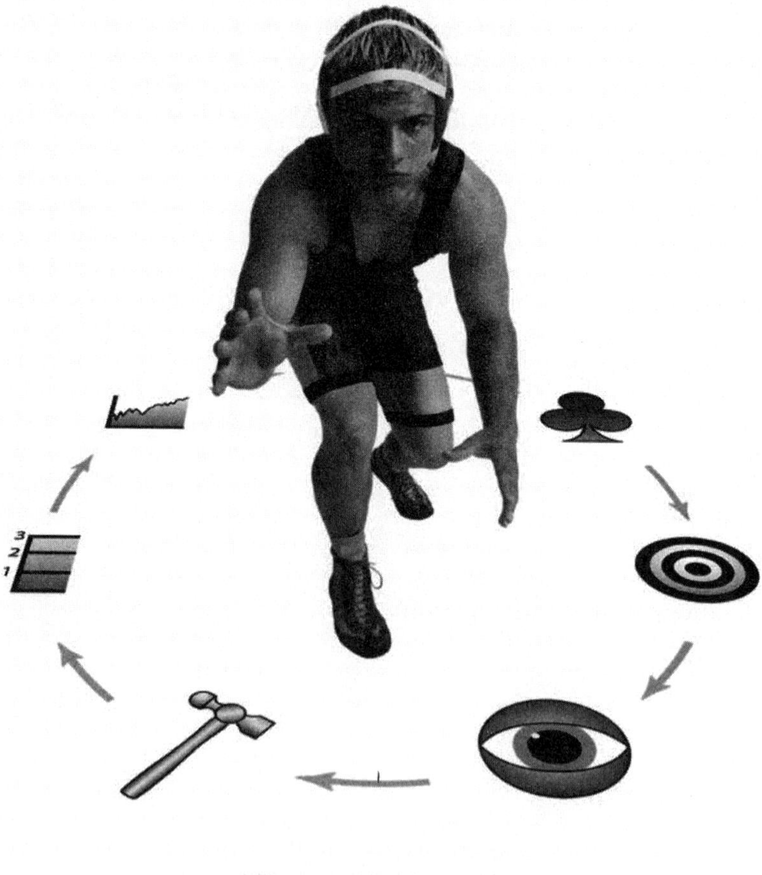

Steve G. Vogel

Chapter One
The Stranger

Zzzzzzzzzzzzz. The alarm sounds. Greg turns and squints at the luminous dial. 6:06 a.m. Today is the day.

"Today I start," thought Greg. "1-2-3. Success," he thought, "is *as easy as 1-2-3. Push, pull, turn. 1-2-3.*"

Cutting weight isn't supposed to be easy. But what about those Herrinsburg guys? They balloon to 180 summers and wrestle 130, or so the story goes. With a turn and a touch, the alarm relinquishes its fleeting hold.

Not today.

After school Greg attends wrestling practice. What was he thinking? Getting up at six-o-six?

Coach Gallo calls out, "Gurist, get over here!"

"Yes, Coach?" obliges Greg.

"Get on that mat, Gurist. It needs rolled. Gurist?"

"Sure, Coach. I'm there."

Greg had hoped the coach would be praising him for his wrestling skills or maybe making a suggestion about his stand-up escape or his set-up for a takedown move he drills: the *push and pull* of the push, pull, turn.

Not today.

No morning sprints.

No afternoon kudos.

Practice ends. The crisp fall air first invigorates and then chills. Somehow when cutting, the cold feels colder, thought Greg, as he zipped up his jacket collar to his chin. Actually... "It's warmer than a varsity jacket," he said, unconscious of his soliloquy. "I'd still rather have one," he thought out loud.

"Have one what?" said a stranger also walking down Main Street just feet away.

Greg, more embarrassed than startled, replied, "What?"

"You said you still want one. One what?" the stranger asked again.

"Oh, sorry, sir. I was just talking to myself."

"About what?"

Greg paused. Flemington was a pretty friendly place. I don't fear much, he thought. Nothing except perhaps failure in wrestling, especially when wrestling a Herrinsburg guy, he thought.

He again reassured himself with just an ever-so-fleeting doubt.

But I don't fear anyone on the street. He mentally noted the incongruity and reengaged the stranger.

"Well, to be honest, I was talking about a varsity jacket; a varsity jacket in wrestling, sir." Greg caught himself saying "sir," although the man was not very old. Looking a little closer at the stranger, he saw a well-groomed, dapperly dressed man with an unusually bright complexion and pleasant smile.

"So why do you want the wrestling jacket?" inquired the stranger.

"Not to be impolite, sir," said Greg, "but who are you?"

"Please call me Anthony. And you?" asked Anthony.

"Oh, sorry, sir, I'm Greg," he said, turning and facing Anthony. Both gave the other a firm handshake and made direct eye contact. Greg's dad always told him you could measure a man by his firm handshake and simultaneous eye contact or lack thereof. He was sounding like his attorney dad now, he thought.

"No need to be sorry and I didn't mean to pry, but you spoke and I thought perhaps you were speaking to me."

"That's okay. I suppose I was asking – or complaining – or something. I said I wanted a varsity jacket because I wrestled for our team last year, Flemington Central, but I only wrestled the last four bouts. While I did wrestle Districts, I didn't qualify for a jacket. You need to start five, maybe six, varsity bouts to earn one."

"So, you're coming from practice now?" Greg nodded. "And you want to do better this year and get a jacket?"

"Well, actually, yes, I want a varsity jacket. And I really want more than that. I want to beat..."

"You want to beat?" asked Anthony.

"My Herrinsburg guy," responded Greg.

"Doesn't he have a name?"

"Yes. Mulino. John Mulino. And actually, I don't even need to beat him. I'd be happy to score on him and mostly not get pinned," said Greg.

"Not get pinned? That doesn't sound very inspiring."

"Actually," countered Greg, "this guy…"

"Mulino?" asked Anthony.

"Yes, Mulino, is really good. While he makes weight at 123, he looks like 150. By match time he probably weighs 135. Summers, they say he weighs 175, maybe more," complained Greg. "At last year's States, against the best in New Jersey, Mulino pretty much stood still, arms in a pancake ready motion, just taunting his opponents. He pins almost everyone. He could have pinned in Finals if the guy hadn't stalled using a smeltsly."

"What's a smeltsly?" queried Anthony.

"Oh, that's where you grab a guy's leg and just hold on, making sure nothing happens. This move can stop most attacks. It's a defensive strategy that seems to work well in high school, even college, but in Freestyle it could cost you back points when the guy tips you as you hold his leg. I know. I saw the Olympic Trials. It was unbelievable!"

"So, Greg, you're telling me Mulino is good?"

"Actually, he's the best I've ever seen, at least in high school. He has won States twice, and short of serious injury, he will win three. Had they let him wrestle as a freshman, I...oh...sorry, sir, I'm rambling."

"Anthony is fine."

"Yes, I mean, sorry *Anthony,* but that Mulino guy really gets to me. I've got to find a way to beat him – or at least not embarrass myself – but of course I have to make it to States in order to meet him."

"You will make States?" asked Anthony.

"Maybe. I surely could. I'm stronger and I'll be carrying a lot less fat this year," answered Greg.

"Tell me, Greg, how did Mulino get so good?"

"I'm not sure," answered Greg. "But I do know he pumps iron and does some serious cutting. They say he weighs over 175, off-season. Did I tell you?"

"Greg, if he reduces his bodyweight by 50 pounds, do you think Mulino is serious about wrestling and his goals?"

"Yes, sir, I do," answered Greg.

"How do you know?" asked Anthony.

"Well, he is so good. I just kind of think he must be," answered Greg.

"So, what can you learn from Mulino?"

"Learn from Mulino? I'm still learning the fundamentals. I can do a pancake, but I'm not going to sit there like a wind-up pinning machine and hope guys just let me flip them to their backs," replied Greg.

"No, not about his technique. What can you learn from his mental approach?"

"I don't know. Do you know wrestling? Because a good pancake can be really effective to counter most leg shots. And you're just skipping over Mulino's best takedown and pinning combination. Are you a coach?" asked Greg.

"Why's that?"

"You talk sort of like my coach and sort of like my dad. And for a second it sounded like you understood wrestling," replied Greg.

"I work quite a bit on improving performance and goal achievement, so I do get involved with sports," said Anthony. "I usually do this as a part of my personal coaching. Of course, the people I help must want my help and must specifically ask for it."

"Do you make them sign a contract or something? My dad and I often enter into contracts. I promise something and he promises something. Quid pro quo, you know, something for something. Is it like that?" asked Greg.

"No, I don't ask for a contract as I demand neither money nor performance. But I must admit I do seek performance," said Anthony.

"I sure could use some help."

"What kind?" asked Anthony.

"Well, someone to make me a better wrestler for starters," responded Greg.

"I come by here about seven o'clock each evening and walk this way, usually to the Tally Joe Diner for dinner. Just farther up Main," said Anthony. "If you ever need some assistance, I can spare a little time each day. But first be advised my instruction will help you first as a person and second as a wrestler."

"Sure, but I can't afford much," said Greg. "My coach at

school barely talks to me. The truth is I'm not sure how I'm doing, but practice just started so maybe he'll notice me."

"If you need me, I'll be here," smiled Anthony.

Chapter Two
Wrestling Practice

"Greg!" called Coach Gallo. "Get in there and show Ken an inside single-leg trip."

Greg complied, eager to get the coach's attention and approval. Greg made a sweet flowing move, driving low, hooking one foot around Ken's leg and maneuvering his arm under his other leg. It was a strong move to the mat, a solid takedown creating a great position for back points while maintaining control.

Greg stood and looked around for Gallo. The coach didn't seem to be watching. He was working with one of the District champions. Two and a half weeks and that leg trip request represented their entire dialog. Two and a half weeks and Greg noticed his dream slipping away. He felt weaker, not stronger, and Mulino now seemed more daunting in his mind than ever.

"I'm tired, frustrated, and, yes, weaker," he thought. The wrestling practice workouts and dieting hadn't hardened his resolve as it had hardened his midsection. He couldn't see himself challenging Mulino.

"Not this year," he thought. "Maybe not ever." As he began walking towards the showers he heard his name, "Gurist. Gurist!"

It was the coach!

*Well finally...*thought Greg.

"Roll the mats!" demanded Gallo.

Greg rushed to help roll and carry the mats back under the seat stanchions in the gym. It had slipped his mind: only lettermen are exempt from the now demeaning task of rolling the mats. Greg recalled how last season, when joining the team, the task had seemed an honor.

"Ugh," said Greg aloud, but no one seemed to hear or care. *If I were a District champ this wouldn't be happening. I could be a District champ. I could challenge him.* He couldn't bring himself to even think Mulino's name.

I want to do it. I need to do it. But I'm not exactly kicking butt out here. I need to get better. A lot better. He thought all this as he watched last year's lettermen casually walking by and talking without noticing him. Thankfully they weren't gloating as they passed Greg and the others rolling the mats.

Later, as Greg walked home, he spotted the man he had talked to before. He was walking in Greg's direction, just ahead. Greg hesitated. *The personal coach, er Anthony. He doesn't exactly know wrestling, but he did offer to help. Maybe he knows someone who could help me?*

Greg instantly wondered why the team couldn't help, but then reflected that the best guys on the team were much heavier and their styles and approach wouldn't help him. If only the coach thought he had potential maybe he would help him. Now he had a question for... *Anthony*, he thought. *Yes, I'll ask Anthony.*

"Hi, sir," said Greg, remembering Anthony's name but still not being comfortable enough to say it.

Just relax...

"Hello, Greg," said Anthony. "How is wrestling practice?"

"Whew," thought Greg, happy to know Anthony remembered both his name and their conversation.

"To be honest, sir, not too well."

"Sorry to hear that," said Anthony.

"I guess I'm not projecting a lot of confidence," said Greg.

"No, it wasn't that," replied Anthony.

"Regardless, you're right," replied Greg. "I'm not getting better. The coaches don't care and the wrestlers around my weight can't really help me."

"You are asking for my help?" asked Anthony.

"Yes, I am," said Greg, surprising himself. A few seconds ago he had decided to only ask Anthony if he knew someone who could help, not for help.

"Greg, I can help you, but I want to caution you. I may sound impassionate and theoretical. At times I may sound like your father. But you will need to have a little patience, trust, and faith. Give my ideas a chance. If you don't have faith and attempt to follow my ideas carefully, I assure you I won't bother you further," explained Anthony.

"That was the friendliest threat I have ever heard," replied Greg curiously, adding, "What do you mean ideas? It sounds like, if I don't listen you won't continue to teach me?"

"No, I'm giving you more of a heads-up. I can only intercede where I am wanted. Should you choose to ignore my recommendations, I must assume you are no longer interested in my help. I only work where wanted, needed, and heeded. What good is unwanted advice? In fact, good advice unwanted is not good at all. And good advice unheeded helps no one. I will offer you ideas that will develop your greatest wrestling muscle," explained Anthony.

"What muscle? What ideas? And where will we train? You're sure you can help my wrestling?" asked Greg.

"For goodness sakes, Greg, yes!" smiled Anthony. "But wrestling's not just about wrestling. I was talking about faith. I was talking about your brain. I will help you prepare your body and mind for wrestling and life."

"How can I have faith in someone I don't know?"

"Only you can answer that question."

"Well," pondered Greg thoughtfully, "I could trust you one idea at a time?"

"Excellent," said Anthony. "This is all I can expect and all we need. But since the ideas work, if you find they haven't, you should first check to be sure you applied them to the best of your abilities. I ask no more of you than that."

"Anthony, will we ever talk about wrestling?" posed Greg.

"Not today. Not yet."

Not today?

"Well, okay, but when?" queried Greg.

"It is up to you, actually. You have much work to do. The mental and physical preparation that you must undertake will prepare you for wrestling," said Anthony.

"OKAY. I'm ready. What is the first step?"

"I think you already know. In fact, you were talking about Mulino. He certainly took the first step."

"By cutting a huge amount of weight?"

"Yes, that is a reasonable assumption, but it isn't what I was looking for," said Anthony, adding, "But you are close."

"I know then. One must be committed!" exclaimed Greg.

"That's extremely close. Greg, the path to growth starts with a positive attitude. When you told me that Mulino stood with his arms poised as to pin his opponent, I knew that Mulino was planning to win. This is great evidence of a positive attitude."

"Is that where we start with a positive attitude?"

"Precisely. **Think Positive** is the first step to take when attempting to change ourselves for the better."

"Remember, *good things happen to good people who do good things*. Greg, in order to **Think Positive,** you must believe you can and will succeed. This positive attitude doesn't require the apparent swagger of Mulino, but still one must have self-confidence and one must be positive about his environment. This view of your environment as positive leads to step two: You must **Accept Fate**. You must recognize your present reality and accept it," said Anthony.

"This sounds like a fatalistic viewpoint. It doesn't matter what I do? I might not beat Mulino," shrugged Greg.

"I see where you might get that Greg, but **Accept Fate** is more like going out and buying a map to first see where you are and then accept it. Where you are doesn't matter as much as accepting where you are. If you woke up one day in Denver, it wouldn't do you much good to think you were in Dallas or Detroit," explained Anthony.

"So, be realistic?" asked Greg.

"Precisely," said Anthony. "You must be realistic and honest with yourself. Recognize exactly where you are. This means recognize who you are and what you have and don't have. Then accept the facts. But you needn't view these facts and your acceptance of them as a limitation. They are more of a starting point."

"In terms of wrestling, what does it mean?"

"Before we get to wrestling, remember you must **Think Positive** and accept your fate, surroundings, and yourself. Be happy with who you are and what you have. **Accept Fate** and **Think Positive** are the first two steps in what we call the **Personal Growth Cycle**. These are critical. People with serious problems never get help until they are able to stop and realize where they are. Take the person who has a problem with drugs. Few people cure their problem without first recognizing it. Then they need to acknowledge their lack of success in tackling the problem. Then they are in a position to do something about it."

"But can't people do it by themselves?" questioned Greg.

"Greg, they do much of the fix by themselves, but without acknowledging the true depth and nature of their problem, they can't begin the change process. Commonly, people blame their circumstances, family, friends, foes, and fate. But once people understand and recognize they have a problem, once they see where they are and accept it and take responsibility for their part in it, they can begin the healing process."

"If they accept personal responsibility, accept where they are and accept that whatever they have been doing hasn't worked, they can move on. Then they may reach out to God, loved ones, and others for help."

"I understand a positive attitude and accepting my fate are necessary. I think I do those two things, er, steps. But what is the **Personal Growth Cycle**?"

"The **Personal Growth Cycle** is a paradigm of the process for personal growth: First you **Think Positive** and **Accept Fate**; then you **Set Goals**. You then **Visualize Success**, **Work Hard**,

Measure Results, and finally, you **Analyze Results**. These are **The Seven Steps** in this ongoing cycle. The cycle then begins anew. Let me draw it for you. Please follow the steps around the cycle. The **Personal Growth Cycle** shown is diagramed as an oval. At 12 o'clock high is **Think Positive,** followed by **Accept Fate,** etc., and the **Personal Growth Cycle** continues. You must maintain the positive attitude and continue to recognize and accept where you are and reset goals as necessary. You actually reset goals based upon the information gleaned from your measurement and analysis. The strength of the process will become abundantly clear as you follow the steps."

THE SEVEN STEPS OF THE PERSONAL GROWTH CYCLE™

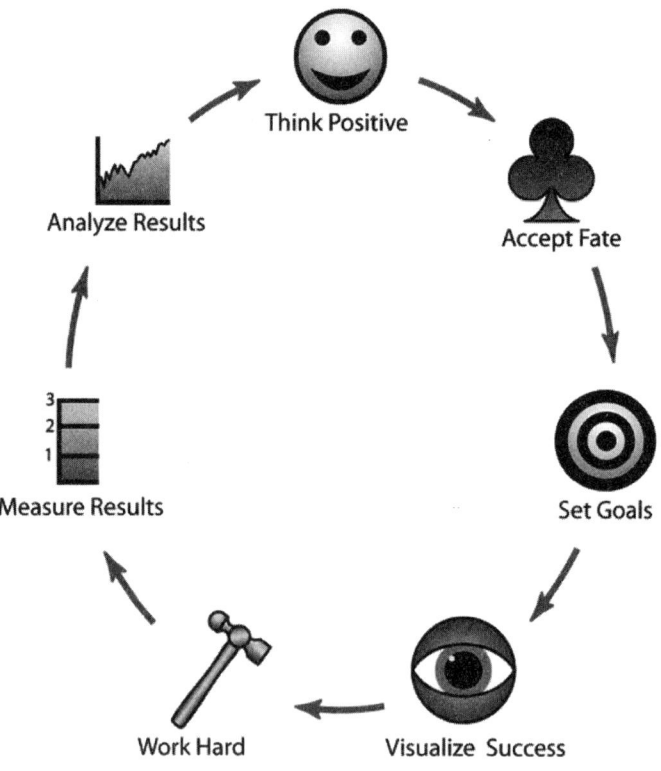

"Well," observed Greg, "I am way committed to improvement, so where do I start?"

"Great, Greg. The relevant question remains: Are you willing to do what it takes to achieve your goals? This question will be evaluated in detail when we go through the process of goal setting."

"Of course I will do what I need to do!" exclaimed Greg, who then instantly winced as he said the words. He stared at Anthony contritely and let his head and eyes slowly lower from Anthony's face. Greg's thoughts went back to his alarm clock set for 6:06 a.m. He had set it numerous mornings only to tap the snooze alarm and return to his slumber. His mother would wake him by 7 a.m. in plenty of time for school but without time for sprints, jogging, and free weights.

"Okay," said Greg. "I haven't given 100%. I'm not sure why. I really want to get to States. That's it!" exclaimed Greg. "I want to get to States."

"Precisely," said Anthony.

"I don't just want a varsity jacket and I don't need to beat Mulino but I do want to get to States. I need to finish first, second, or third in Regions to go to States," said Greg.

"I thought you wanted to beat Mulino?" said Anthony.

"He can be beaten."

"Greg, I'm impressed."

"Why?" asked Greg of his new friend and personal coach.

"I am impressed you have begun to think through your goals. As we say, 'the divine is in the details.' You have begun the step of **Set Goals**."

"I am ready!" exclaimed Greg. "I am ready to get up each morning for sprints, weights, and whatever else I need to do. I am nearly down to weight so I can concentrate on getting in shape and improving my wrestling technique."

"I'll ask you again, Greg."

"What?"

"Are you really prepared for the serious work?" questioned Anthony.

"Well, how will I know?"

"Greg, once you begin the process, including the formulation of your goals and motivation program, you will know. You will know because you will need to decide how best to reach your goals and what you will do to meet them."

"Wow! This sounds so formal. I feel like 'Greg Gurist, Inc.' a company – like one my dad works for – he's a corporate lawyer. I feel like my products are being inventoried and next year's budget is being developed. Do I need all this?"

"Greg, I am impressed. Actually, I find it quite interesting that very intelligent adults, who understand how to run a company by using state-of-the-art budgeting, planning, and measurement systems, rarely think to apply these same techniques to their personal lives. They act as if a company deserves better attention than a human. The thought nearly makes me shudder and I haven't shuddered in eons," said Anthony. "Greg, we need about three or four hours to go through the exercises. That will allow you to complete the **Set Goals** step of your **Personal Growth Cycle**. We can put these together with an inventory, planning, and motivational program."

"Well, I have school, then wrestling practice, so maybe Saturday. Sunday, I go to church, so that doesn't work," explained Greg.

"Saturday, at the Hunterdon County Library, at say 8:30? Does that allow you enough time for your morning workout?" queried Anthony.

"Precisely," said Greg with a little chuckle to himself, realizing he was using Anthony's favorite word.

"Precisely it is," said Anthony with a broad and satisfied smile.

Chapter Three

Developing Goals at the Library

"How many pages do I need to complete?" asked Greg.

"The inventory part is just that, Greg, an inventory. So read the questions and fill in the blanks. I can't tell you what to write or even how much to write. I can give you some general guidelines, however:

- ✠ It is vital to be perfectly honest, specific, and detailed.
- ✠ Write as quickly as the thoughts come to you.
- ✠ Be completely open-minded and relaxed as you write.
- ✠ Search deep inside yourself for the real truth.
- ✠ Feel free to be personal. You have my confidence.
- ✠ As you let your thoughts flow smoothly, remember there can be no wrong answers."

"Wow, that's a relief," interrupted Greg. He had already completed a few pages. At the top of each page was a topic. The first page, titled ***Accomplishments,*** Greg completed and quickly set it aside. Another page, titled ***Happiest Moments,*** caused him to hesitate.

"What do you mean *perfectly honest*?" asked Greg.

"You need to tell the complete truth. For instance, if you beat a District champ because he withdrew due to an injury, this wouldn't really be an accomplishment. And if you had done well in school last year as a junior, don't merely say you *did well* but say, *you received a 3.4 which put you in the top five percent of your junior class.*"

"How did you?" asked Greg, a little spooked by Anthony's accuracy.

"How did you know?" asked Greg again nervously, as he glanced down at his completed ***Accomplishments*** page. It was in plain view to Anthony. They both laughed, and Greg felt some relief.

"Sorry, Greg, but I do need to read your completed pages as I need to give you feedback on the process. Keep in mind each of these exercises help you learn about you. The happy, thankful, proud moments, the accomplishments and regrets all say something about you. Think of them as evidence to prove who you are. The specifics of each tell you much about yourself. A further review of weaknesses and strengths can lead you to your ultimate purpose."

"Wow, please slow down, sir," said Greg. "Am I out to find my true purpose in life?"

"Precisely," said Anthony. "The **Personal Growth Cycle** conscientiously applied will ultimately lead you to your purpose. It cannot be otherwise. You will come to see this for yourself. I could explain why, but nothing will replace your own experience, so I won't try."

Greg knowingly smiled. He sensed Anthony had much to teach and he knew he had much to learn. It was like receiving a precious gift he would unwrap over time.

"Why do I need to list my regrets? I don't want to be reminded of my failures," explained Greg.

"That's true. To be reminded of your failures can be unsettling. But often in failure one finds the clues to success. If you lost a big match because you were winded, you would put conditioning into your goals. One great wrestler said, 'The best wrestler never fails. He only runs out of time on his path to victory.' "

"Cool, wrestling," said Greg. "Did I say that?"

Anthony continued, "When you have finished listing events and moments, then please review your lists. When complete, you should observe its trends and your proclivities. This analysis will help test your goals. This becomes critical as you attempt to develop efficacious strategies, tactics, and action plans to achieve them."

"How does this help, Anthony?"

"Let's say your goal is to be a trial attorney. Successful trial attorneys in general are comfortable speaking in front of people. If you reviewed your favorite moments and you were most proud of your solo wilderness adventure, an archeological dig, and other non-people encounters, you may wish to rethink your goal. Maybe you should become a scientist or an athlete. Likewise, a person whose hands shake chronically should think twice before attempting to become a neurosurgeon."

Greg completed all the exercises and began the next step of listing his desires and goals. He listed his hopes and dreams, his wish list, and his "got to" list. He then prioritized his goals.

"I'm done," said Greg, "and I feel good. I know my goals fit who I am. But, Anthony, I am a little concerned. Not many of these goals have to do with wrestling and that's why I thought we were doing this — to help my wrestling?"

"Are your wrestling goals included?" asked Anthony.

"Yes, but now I realize something very important. College and career are my top priorities. I am not exactly sure of my major, but I am really sure I need to focus on the SAT to get into the right school and I think I need to start right away. I take the exam in three months and this presents my last chance to take it."

"Greg, we will do a detailed analysis of your top goals. Let's take a look at your SAT goal and your wrestling goal," instructed Anthony.

"Anthony, I noticed under both goals, I had to list why I might fail to achieve either goal. Both reasons point back to my family. In one case, my parents may fail to support me and in the other, my brother may sabotage my studies. It seems that without their support I won't be able to do well in either. To make things worse, life at home has not been easy."

"Greg, it sounds like you have a third goal that may be worth analyzing."

"Making peace at home?"

"Precisely," said Anthony.

"Great," said Greg. "Say, Anthony, I feel much lighter already. I'm not talking about getting down to weight. I must have been stressing about the SAT or about my brother or both."

"So Greg, it's not all about wrestling?"

"Well, it's all about wrestling alright, but it's all about everything else, too. I am more like an ecosystem. I require that many things be done simultaneously to meet my goals. This must be why we analyze a goal. We can't always go straight to the goal. I see now that if I don't get along with my brother, my parents won't let me wrestle. So I need to fix that. If I don't do well on the SAT, I won't be able to get into my top choice schools, which also have wrestling programs. I also want a program likely to get me into med school or law school," explained Greg.

"You understand the most important part of improving your life, Greg. All things are connected. You don't live in a vacuum. Greg, you said it best when you said you were like an ecosystem, a delicate one at that. Most people's goals work the same way. That is why, in addition to the **Personal Growth Cycle**, I will emphasize a list of the **Ten Keys**, Greg. They are critical constructs that you should strive to make a part of your life. They will help you reach your goals. Without them, achieving your goals and living well may be impossible."

"I see, Anthony, balancing things may be the hardest thing I do. But without all these things happening at once, I won't be successful at any one!" exclaimed Greg.

"Precisely. So let's finish. Once you complete the exercises today we will have enough information to record your daily goal reminder and motivational program I call the **Personal Commercial**."

"And now?"

"Now Greg, you continue to complete the sheets in front of you to help you understand and verify your goals."

"What's in the recording, I mean **Personal Commercial,** and what do I do with it?"

"I use your accomplishments, short-term and long-term goals, action plans, and other pieces of information from your inventory, and I make a short recording. You will listen to the recording daily. You may listen each morning when you exercise."

"What's in the recording?"

"Your ideas in my words combined with appropriate motivational wording. It will remind you of what you want to do and why. It will help convince you that you can achieve your goals and it will remind you what they are. Greg, you told me of your reminder: *1-2-3. Push, pull, turn. 1-2-3.* This expression I will include in your recording verbatim. A short, pithy phrase such as this, which I call the **Personal Commercial *Jingle*,** provides a summary reminder of your goals. Keeping your goals in your head and heart at all times will allow you to perform miracles. But please listen to it each day and record the results in your Personal Journal. You will learn the power for yourself."

"I use a planner to keep track of my weight loss and exercises. Can I use it?" asked Greg.

"Yes," said Anthony. "Thanks for reminding me. As the critical step in the **Personal Growth Cycle**, one must **Measure Results**; any convenient log can work as a Personal Journal. As long as there's ample room for goals, action plans, and the recording of comments and accomplishments, it can work."

"Sure. My planner has every week on two facing pages and additional pages where I save all my good ideas," observed Greg. "My dad gives me one each year just before year end. He bought me the letter sized one as I entered Flemington Central. Now I use the next smaller size because it fits into my gym bag. Should we set up our next meeting now?"

"Good idea, Greg."

Chapter Four
Anger Recognition and Forgiveness

"Anthony, tell me why my brother, Allen, does whatever he can to drive me crazy? My mother accuses me of 'being mean' to him but I think I'm doing a great job not punching him every day. I know it's not good for either of us to be this angry."

"Why are you angry?" asked Anthony.

"I don't know. He always bothers me," said Greg.

"What does he do that bothers you?" asked Anthony.

"He is always in the way."

"How?"

"He comes into my room when I'm studying or attempts to follow me when I visit my friends," said Greg.

"So why does this bother you?"

"I deserve privacy. I need time to study and I need my own friends and he doesn't need to pester me. It makes me angry and I tell him to leave. But as soon as I do, my mom is in the middle accusing me of mistreating him."

"Greg, it just sounds like your brother wants to spend some time with you. You are his big brother. He needs you."

"Well, that makes no sense. If he needs me, why does he do anything he can to make me mad? I'll never forgive him for what he did to my bike."

"What did he do?" asked Anthony.

"The low gear is wrecked. My three-speed is now a two-speed, and he knows better."

"So why did Allen wreck your bike and why haven't you forgiven him?"

"Why should I? He hasn't even apologized and my parents won't do anything. Actually, my mom blames me for his breaking my bike. Talk about unfair."

"Why does she blame you?"

"He borrowed my bike because his was broken. I know you're going to ask why. I was supposed to fix his bike but I tried and I couldn't. Dad should have taken it to Billy's Bikes in town."

"Did you tell your mom you tried to fix it? Did you tell your dad you couldn't fix it and it should go to the shop? Did you ask your brother to apologize?"

Greg was silent for a moment and then said, "Why do I have to do everything? Fix the bike. Tell my mom. Tell my dad. Ask my brother to apologize?"

"Greg, are you asking or just commenting? Someone has to do the right thing. Why not you? You do believe in the power of forgiveness?"

"What do you mean?" asked Greg.

"Forgive your brother and start to be nice to him and see what happens," said Anthony.

"But forgiving him when I am so angry; that's not going to be easy," explained Greg.

"Greg, listen to what you are saying. Your pride is causing you to hang onto your anger and your anger is preventing you from forgiving your brother. Now you can't be nice to him: you ignore him, so then he irritates you because he wants your attention. You can't give him attention because you're angry with him because he won't apologize. This further prevents you from being nice which can lead to more of the same..."

"Okay, Anthony, I get it. Someone has to start being nice and acting right, otherwise my brother and I could continue at odds, ad infinitum?"

"Or at least ad nauseam," said Anthony. "Greg, forgiveness is smart and healthy. Medical research has proven the value of happiness and positive thinking. Harboring hatred by not forgiving is counter to the Universe. For those who believe, the Bible is clear: we must forgive."

"Yes," said Greg. "I remember reading something, or maybe it's a prayer that says, 'forgive so that you may be forgiven.' It makes sense."

"Maybe it works that way, Greg, or maybe one can't receive forgiveness until one has forgiven. Perhaps God wants to forgive but you aren't able to receive His forgiveness. An angry heart may not be open to forgiveness. Forgiving can be the right step in starting something good. Greg, what is the worst part of anger?"

"Sometimes I am so angry at my brother that whatever he does bothers me. In fact, my anger can be so bad that sometimes I literally can't see straight."

"That's the point," said Anthony. "If you are so angry you can't see straight, anger has control over you. Do you like giving control to anger?"

"No, but how do I rid myself of it?" asked Greg.

"One way is to forgive," said Anthony.

"Forgive who?"

"Forgive everyone that you have any reason to be unhappy with," said Anthony.

"My brother certainly needs my forgiveness," said Greg.

"Can you forgive him?" asked Anthony.

"He did wreck my bike and he does irritate me to no end, but I suppose I could."

"Do you want God's forgiveness?"

"Sure I do!"

"Would you expect His forgiveness if you failed to forgive Allen?" asked Anthony.

"I know. I get it. But that doesn't make it easy."

"It isn't necessarily easy, but hating may be harder. If you just let go of the hate it will leave," said Anthony. "You could also reflect on how you got where you are. You're probably just a little frustrated at the unfortunate events that may have been avoided with just a little more effort and communication. You may not even be angry with Allen."

Greg thought for a moment about the escalation with his mom, dad, and Allen. He had been properly held to a higher standard than Allen.

"I can forgive him," said Greg. "I have to. I have been disagreeable. But Mom and Dad – they have been totally on Allen's side. Wait, Anthony, what are you thinking? You look a little disappointed in me."

"Greg, is there anything else?"

"Well, actually, yes. I did hit Allen a few weeks ago."

"Care to elaborate?"

"Well, he wanted to join me and my friends and I didn't want him to come."

"Why?"

"I didn't know what else to do."

"Greg, you hit your brother because you didn't know what else to do?"

"The truth is, I hit him so hard on the chin, he dropped like a sack of potatoes."

"Greg? I don't understand."

"I was going to go out with my friends. They or *we* were going to be drinking. I couldn't let my brother get exposed to it. Anthony, I could have stayed home. I didn't have to punch my brother. I didn't have to get drunk."

"What happened?"

"Now I see I was pretty immature. I didn't expect to drink but once we all started we kept drinking. We all had the worst headaches the next day. Now I know why my parents don't drink anything but a glass or two of wine. It really hurts. The next day at school I looked and felt green."

"It sounds liked you learned something?"

"Well, I know I didn't have to slug my brother. What I did to him was much worse than what he did to my bike. I realize now, I could have stayed home."

"Lots of people get drunk once, don't they, Anthony?"

"Some do, Greg. But that doesn't make it right. Did you ever reconcile with Allen?"

"Not exactly."

"Does that mean no?"

"Yes, that means no. I didn't. I will."

"Everyone deserves forgiveness because to do otherwise is against God's law. In order to be angry, we must condemn, and in order to condemn, we must judge. To do this requires a depth of knowledge and understanding of events few may ever possess. It is logical to avoid hate because it entails an unproductive use of time and energy."

"What you're saying, Anthony, is that hate is not a very useful emotion. It can only get us in trouble. I wonder why we have it at all?" pondered Greg.

"The initial anger instinct isn't necessarily bad. The threat a ferocious animal may pose could rightfully cause anger and send noradrenalin for life saving self-defense into your system. Fortunately those days are mostly past," said Anthony.

"I hope so," added Greg. "However, I could use a little of that caveman bear-wrestling instinct! I am sure my ancestors wrestled a few."

"I'm sure they did. The problem is those same instincts that did well to protect us now stand in the way of our progress. Man needs to use the same approach to personal growth as we did to putting man on the moon. If we did, perhaps schools of self-improvement would be as ubiquitous as coffeehouses."

"But I have you," said Greg.

"Thank you for the vote of confidence," said Anthony. "Let's go back to our discussion on hatred. I think if you use the The Whys Approach you will come to understand *why* you are angry."

"What is the The Whys Approach?"

"Greg, The Whys Approach says to ask *why* as many times as necessary until you uncover the real issue or the root cause of the problem. You may have noticed: I use it a lot. It's called The Whys Approach because typically after a few *whys* you often get to the bottom of things and can become *wise* as to the problem. In this case, Greg, with enough whys asked you may come to realize there was no merit to your anger. This may in turn allow you to move on to forgiveness. Greg, think of the anger emotion as an *old instinct that should be extinct.* You can learn a technique that may diffuse an unwanted emotion."

"This is a technique beyond The Whys Approach?" asked Greg.

"The Whys Approach is an approach to use after the anger has made its way in. The technique I'll now discuss is the one that will hopefully *keep the anger from coming in.* I'll explain: Once you feel any negative emotion, recognize it, feel it, acknowledge it, and let it go."

"I don't get it," said Greg. "In fact, I don't always even know I am angry. Sometimes I just feel aggravated and sometimes a little confused. Sometimes I just get really, really steamed."

"All of these feelings can be associated with anger. The first step to releasing anger or fear or any emotion you wish to release requires you to first recognize the feeling."

"You make it sound so easy."

"Greg, you will be surprised how quickly anger can be released once you recognize it and practice letting it pass."

"Then what do I do once I recognize it?"

"Once you recognize it, things get easier. Begin by attempting to trace the original source of the anger. Usually the thing that triggers anger becomes readily apparent if we recognize anger as it begins. Then you just follow the path backwards. You may not always find the source immediately but you may often discover enough to eradicate the cause or accept the event as unavoidable and undeserving of your anger. Anger rarely makes sense except in times of impending physical crisis. Remember that unbridled anger needn't occur. Releasing anger requires you to treat it like you would a message."

"Like a message? I don't understand…," said Greg.

"Think about it for a second, Greg. Assume you are on your morning run and you feel your calf tense from a cramp. Would you ignore it?"

"Of course not," said Greg.

"Why not?" asked Anthony.

"An intense pain in my calf could lead to a muscle tear. I would normally stop running, massage it by hand, and walk it off. I would start running when it felt better."

"Precisely," observed Anthony. "A cramp or a fit of anger or jealousy or hatred must be treated in much the same way. You treat the cramp like a message. Your body is telling you something. Like any message, don't ignore it. Read the message. Then just as you would do with any message, respond appropriately. With a pain you may stop and assess your body for physical injury. With a mild stitch in your side from running you may ignore it."

"With anger it may be as easy as taking a deep breath and letting the feeling pass. Some people visualize the emotion passing through them. Some may take a walk or exercise or divert themselves until it subsides. Perhaps the only bad thing is to deny the message, to pretend you don't hear it and avoid reacting to it. Don't deny it or chase it. Denial has a way of compounding the problem. Once held inside, it can fester like an infected wound."

"The next step after understanding the message is relaxation. Many emotions can be controlled rather quickly through relaxation. Listen to the message, understand the source so that you can respond, and then relax and let it go."

"Am I supposed to remember all of this?" asked Greg.

"Yes, please, remember these fundamentals," answered Anthony.

"Emotions that are negative: anger, hatred, revenge, and jealousy are all ancient instincts that you should make extinct. You treat them like other messages that come into your head. Treat it like you would a pain when you run. You *read the message,* which is acknowledging the pain. Trace its source and take appropriate action in response. Then relax and *release it.* Relaxation works well. A simple walk around the block or exercise will help. But don't deny the message," instructed Anthony.

"Okay, I get it. Recognize, analyze, take positive action, and forget your anger. Always ask 'why?' " restated Greg.

"Precisely," exclaimed Anthony.

Chapter Five
Overcoming Fear Through Visualization

Wednesday, three weeks later.

"Anthony?"

"Yes, Greg, how are you?"

"Can we meet after practice?"

"Sure, Greg, what's the urgency?" asked Anthony.

"Well, I am wrestling my first bout and I need your help."

"I thought wrestling team eliminations were a couple of weeks away?"

"They are but we have a scrimmage and about twenty wrestlers from BV will be wrestling against us. I will wrestle at 133."

"So why do you need my help?"

"Can we can talk about it tonight?"

"See you at the library."

Greg walked in a bit more tired than usual, his head down and his smile more a pained grimace. It wasn't his usual, sanguine smile.

"What's up?" asked Anthony.

"I am just sick about Friday's scrimmage."

"Why?"

"To start, I don't feel prepared. I'm tired. I feel slow. I've got to make weight. I've got a bunch of studying to do. I'm stressed about the match but worst of all, I'm nervous."

"Are you listening to your **Personal Commercial** each day?"

"Yes."

"Are you working out each morning at 6:06?"

"Yes."

"Did you carve out the study time agreeable to your mom and Allen?"

"Yes."

"Are there clues in your Personal Journal?"

"Mostly my notes reveal I am tired and, well, drained."

"What does this tell you?" asked Anthony.

"It says I need a break?" answered Greg. "Maybe I've been getting too much of a good thing?"

"Greg, what things do you do for you?"

"I enjoy everything I do, but I don't have much free time."

"Greg, rest and leisure time are important and can't be ignored for long. Remember the key, **Have Fun**? It sounds like you haven't been having a lot of fun lately. I think you can fix that without me. May stress be tiring you?"

"Maybe, I get tired just thinking about the match."

"I sense you need to **Think Positive** as well. What else are you feeling?"

"I haven't wrestled in front of a crowd since last year," answered Greg hesitantly. "I felt in better shape last year. Now I feel I may lose. I hate losing. If I am going to lose, I'd rather not compete at all."

"Greg, let's use the fourth step on the **Personal Growth Cycle**, **Visualize Success**, to alleviate your fear."

"Greg, visualize the match now."

"The scrimmage Friday?"

"Yes," answered Anthony. "Visualize the scrimmage. Advance yourself two days. Do you know where it will be? Do you know the uniform, singlet, you will wear? The placement of the wrestling mats? Who will referee the bouts? Who you wrestle? Have you been to their gym or is it in yours?"

"How will this help?" asked Greg.

"Greg, if you can mentally create the event in advance you can prepare for winning. The more thoroughly one visualizes, the better the preparation. Visualizing the match through to your victory will help your mental powers and enlists the power of God and the Universe to ensure your success. How many times do you think great athletes, actors, and performers imagined the real event in preparation for it? While Mr. Clutch, Jerry West, has made the game winning shot perhaps a *hundred* times, he has imagined making them *thousands and thousands* of times."

"Will this work?" exclaimed Greg.

"Remember our agreement? Trust me. Try it and see. Make it as real as possible. If you have trouble imagining parts of your match at the scrimmage, investigate the truth so that you can fill in the gaps. Get over to BV at lunchtime if you need to and see their gym."

"Okay. I'll get there," said Greg. "Then I'll imagine the bout."

"Visualize the match and don't forget to win!" chuckled Anthony.

Anthony knew many people had trouble when first attempting to visualize. He also knew this same difficulty one has attempting visualization provides a learning experience. He had no doubt that Greg could imagine a match in great detail, from inside single or power trip to a cement mixer, so he suggested, "Greg, before you start I want you to remember your successful bouts last year as you enter your Visualization. The positive impact of these wins can continue. So tell me, were you afraid when you wrestled Easton?"

"Anthony, I told you I had almost no fear against Krause and before that match I was even more afraid than I am now."

"Why was that?" asked Anthony.

"I don't know," said Greg as he thought back to the match. "My team had just lost three straight bouts to Easton that night and I wasn't about to make it four."

"Was the team afraid before the meet began?" asked Anthony.

"We were all afraid."

"Why?"

"Easton was beating everyone. Nearly half of their team had gone to States the prior year – and that's Pennsylvania, which is usually even tougher than Jersey. Krause was ranked in the state," explained Greg.

"So how did you overcome your fear?" asked Anthony.

"I remember watching our wrestlers making some very basic mistakes they would never have made in practice. As I saw Easton's intimidation break our wrestlers, I felt a calm overcome me. Maybe I relaxed because there was nothing to lose, with no pressure to win and no stigma to losing. But I wasn't going to allow their mere reputation to win my match. If Krause defeated me, he would have to do it on his own. The crowd wasn't going to help him because I stopped hearing it. I also thought if I showed some courage maybe the rest of our team would have courage. And it worked! We did well after my bout. Even though we lost, we felt great about the match."

"Greg, let's turn back to your bout. What specifically allowed you to drive away your fear?"

"It's hard to describe, as many emotions and logic worked together. I thought it would be foolish to let my fear hamper my wrestling. I knew we had a better team than we showed and I wanted to prove it. I knew that Krause was tough but not invincible. And finally I wanted to do something for my team. I could no longer stomach their hubris and I began to calmly plan my wrestling strategy," said Greg.

"Precisely," said Anthony.

"Precisely, what do you mean?" lamented Greg, sensing an important moment.

"Why weren't you thinking about your fear?"

"I was too busy warming up and planning my takedown!" eructed Greg.

"Too busy?"

"That's right. I was thinking about my takedown."

"*So, do that again*. Learn from it."

"I can't always come up with a great strategy for each match," countered Greg.

"Why can't you? Visualize every match so that you are too busy to let fear into your heart. When you work hard to prepare for a victory and gain it, you keep fear at bay. So what happened with Easton's Krause, at home as you said, and highly favored to beat you?" inquired Anthony. Anthony was eager for Greg to relive the success and thus reinforce his fear fighting preparation through the careful attention to details. Anthony patiently waited as Greg thought deeply, going back to last year's face-off with Krause.

"I knew Krause would shoot a single leg. It was his best move and the other Easton lighter weights had opened strongly with singles. As I thought about his best move, I mentally worked on my counters. I pictured my well-timed sprawl. Then I thought of several counters, from a snap down and spin to an arm drag. I knew he would be very pumped and ready to dive at my legs. I decided then to begin backing away so he would have to begin his single farther away and with more momentum. I could picture him lunging at me, flying low and flat. I would keep him flat for an instant then snap and spin as we often did in drills. I believed that if he really thought I was afraid and backing away he would commit to his single and my counter would be effective."

"Then what happened in the visualization, Greg?"

"Then I saw him stand-up and escape."

"And then?"

"I thought he would stand up bringing his left foot forward, nearly to his chin. Then I would quickly clamp under the leg and around his neck; sticking the cradle. I sensed he was too strong to hold long, so I planned to immediately rip him backwards. In my thoughts, it would flow so well that Krause wouldn't have time to counter," explained Greg.

"Did it work in the match, Greg?"

"Did it ever! Krause was so flat when he lunged for the single I think he burned his chin on the mat. I spun and the ref signaled two points after I got behind and in control and we went off the mat. Then he popped his foot up and I clamped the cradle on hard and quickly pulled him back. I held him on his back for thirty seconds during the most eerie silence you can imagine. He finally wiggled out for an escape and the crowd cheered but you could tell that everyone knew they weren't going to witness the continued decimation of our team."

"Greg, that is excellent. What was the score?"

"I won, 9-5. We traded takedowns and escapes after that. He never again tried a single on me. He was so shaken by my takedown and cradle that his confidence and rhythm were destroyed."

"Greg, again, that's excellent. You already know the important basics of visualization. Use your victories to reinforce your confidence. Success begets success. Repeat the things you did to achieve the success in the first place. Notice that your preparation in visualizing the match and your victory also involved meditation and relaxation during warm-up. A great form of meditation and relaxation occurs as we merely go about our daily activities, fully focused on what we are doing. The Zen masters call this *mindfulness*. I refer to it as the key: **Live in the Present**."

"*When you stay in the moment there is no room for fear.* 'Just do it' may sound trite but the importance of staying in the moment and taking action cannot be over-emphasized. Remember as you visualize the bout: continue the match through to victory. Even if the visualization doesn't complete the match, jump to the moment when the referee raises your hand. Feel that moment. Enjoy it. Make it real. Just as you must believe you can succeed when you complete the first step of **Think Positive**, the Visualization step requires you to see yourself succeed, to visualize the success so accurately you see yourself as the winner. And don't be afraid to bask in the glow of success."

"Anthony, will you be there Friday?"

"In spirit, Greg, I will. You'll do fine. I do hope to come to a match or two this year."

"That would be great, Anthony."

Anthony nodded.

Greg continued. "If you change your mind, we haven't sold out a wrestling meet. You can still get a good seat Friday, or anytime. You can see my parents there, too."

"I would look forward to it," Anthony replied.

"Cool," said Greg.

"Keep on task the next two days and Friday's bout will come and go smoothly. In fact, other than the visualization exercises and the meditation warm-up this week, you can remain focused on the SAT. You have been throwing some big moves with words lately, from 'hubris' to 'decimation'; your vocabulary seems to improve each day."

"Thanks, Anthony. I hope I haven't been too obvious in trying to impress you."

"I am flattered, but it isn't necessary."

"Actually it helps me," said Greg. "I feel uncomfortable using the sesquipedalian words, you know, big words in class or even at home."

"Why?" asked Anthony.

"I don't want to seem pompous or condescending. In class, if I use a word the teacher doesn't know, the class either gets on my case, or worse yet, the teacher's case. I feel guilty," complained Greg.

"Greg, if you do it in a sentence that allows everyone to guess correctly at the word, then you get to use it and others get to learn and no one feels intimidated. What if you said, *our team won 45-10, decimating the competition*. Or *braggadocio is for braggarts?*

While they may not understand completely, you have helped them without embarrassing anyone."

"Maybe," said Greg. "But I think I'll restrict my audience to you."

"Why not use vocabulary words with your parents? I would surmise your parents are well-read and possess sizable vocabularies. Perhaps they are being polite to you by not talking over your head? Maybe if you show an interest they will unleash a fusillade of, what did you say, Greg, sesquipedalians? Maybe they will throw in a sesquipedalian word or two worthy of a neophyte logophile."

"Come to think of it, Anthony, maybe I should stick to the easy ones like provincial and parochial (not worldly, unsophisticated) and catholic and ecumenical (universal in scope)?"

"Precisely," exclaimed Anthony. "The SAT words offer adequate challenge. The big words can wait for word games."

"I can do that."

"Using the words with your parents may be a good idea. I am curious to hear how they react."

"I bet my mom just rolls her eyes," said Greg.

"Let me know," said Anthony in a way that seriously led Greg to wonder what *would* happen. Each of Anthony's ideas or even whimsical-sounding suggestions had led to something favorable. Greg would verbally accost them tonight. *No, not tonight, today*, Greg thought, preferring the equally correct "today" to match his recording. *Today*, he thought. *As easy as 1-2-3. Push, pull, turn. 1-2-3.* That Jingle within his highly motivating **Personal Commercial** popped up numerous times each day just as the word *today* had prompted him to stay in the moment. He was making the most of each day; completing his *To Do List* each day; listening and logging each day in his Personal Journal. This time his **Personal Commercial Jingle** reminded him of the pancake move that he had recently begun using as a set-up for a single or double leg takedown, when he penetrated his opponent deeply enough. It looked a little like a shrug or a duck under. The pancake move just lifted an opponent's arms enough to go under for control. This move capitalized on his upper body strength, while recognizing that many of his top opponents were training to defend against the pancake. *Not mine*, thought Greg, *Mulino's*. It didn't matter. Greg was using the pancake as a set-up for a single or double, or just a duck under to get behind his opponent and bring him to the mat for two. In his vivid Visualization, Greg heard the two-point award called out just as he realized Anthony had gone without a sound or goodbye. *He usually says something...*

Chapter Six
The Visualization Unfolds in the Bethlehem Valley Scrimmage

Friday's scrimmage:

Greg brought himself back to the mat as he pulled up his kneepads and began a few drills on a side mat. Everyone had weighed in and the coaches from both teams were planning a "friendly" scrimmage. These two teams, although geographic neighbors, rarely met in the regular season and never at States, an indirect benefit of their mutual existence near the Pennsylvania / New Jersey border on opposite sides of the Delaware River.

Today, the coaches were hoping to match up their wrestlers by weight and experience. This only worked if both coaches understood their own wrestlers' abilities and mental preparedness. A wrestler needing a confidence boost might be paired with a less skilled wrestler or lighter wrestler that he would beat handily. The lesser skilled opponent had a chance to test his wrestling skills or mettle in the face of great odds. Each opponent would hopefully be at the stage where he could benefit from the planned mismatches. At least this was the logic. Sometimes star wrestlers would get their butts kicked by heavier and stronger though less skilled opponents, risking the star's pride. Outside the wrestling room, developmental matches like these were rare.

But these two coaches usually made them work. Of course many wrestlers met wrestlers with similar skills so there were plenty of exciting *normal* matches.

"Greg!" called Coach Gallo. "I am setting you up with Bethlehem Valley's State guy at 109."

"Coach, I'm 133 and I know the guy — he's their star. He won at 106 last year. I'm more than 20 pounds heavier than he is. I could pin him quickly if he decides to wrestle and a little later if he decides not to wrestle. I won't even break a sweat much less get in a good workout. I won't feel good about it." Greg quickly realized the coach wasn't really asking him; he was politely telling him. Greg felt humiliated by the no-win situation. He pins him and no one cares. If he eases up a little, wishing not to embarrass the BV star, he may be embarrassed or hurt. He had learned that wrestling less than all out caused more injuries than it avoided, unless it was a friendly bout. A friendly bout — usually called going takedowns or rolling around – was what wrestlers did in a warm-up when they each alternately allowed the other to take them down. This looked much like a choreographed action scene out of a Kung Fu show. Greg then had a rush overcome him. He felt profoundly foolish. Just two days ago he feared this scrimmage, worrying about winning and losing. What a change of events. All that fear and worry for nothing, he thought, trying to assuage his vexation.

"Worry is worthless!" Greg thought, nearly out loud.

"Coach," asked Greg, "will this be friendly?"

"Friendly? If you let him win it will be. Coach Lurner says his guy expects to beat you."

"Coach, can I get in a real bout?"

"I think it will be real. I think you are stronger this year but remember last year's scrimmage. You didn't even wrestle with our first team against BV. I think they expect the Greg Gurist of last year."

"Coach, I can only go all out or just friendly."

"Then I suggest you go all out, Greg."

"You mean I should neither seek nor cede quarter?"

"You better worry more about getting hurt and less about your big words. This guy has caused more bloody noses with his wicked crossface in a season than most teams do."

"Yes, but he needs to get behind me or over me to use a crossface. That won't happen."

"Sounds like you're ready."

"But Coach, if I pin him, can I wrestle a good 130- to 140-pound guy?"

"What? You want a second bout? If you stack 'em you'll deserve another shot."

"I could get a good workout and they could extract revenge, assuming I win and then their bigger guy wins."

"Thinking pretty far ahead, Greg. Don't underestimate this guy. He's as tough as they come and quite talented. I wish we had a dozen like him here."

"Maybe you do, Coach," muttered Greg under his breath.

"Greg, I can set you up with their 150-pounder. He's a solid wrestler, very strong. He's slotted to wrestle Mike at 167. I expect Mike will get all he can handle. I am sure they would let him go again later with you. You each would get an hour's rest, but I don't want to set it up unless you commit to go now. I can't very well reschedule bouts based on your pin or loss."

"Loss? Coach, do you think he can beat me?"

"I bet he's taking the match a lot more seriously than you are. I'd be a little less confident. Sure, I think you can take him, but you probably will have to get heavy on him. This won't be too easy because we're wrestling 2-1-1. Four minutes can go by quickly and favors this guy. He's faster than you. He's more skilled, and don't take that badly. I bet he has wrestled for more than eight years. Greg, you were playing junior varsity basketball when he was winning a State wrestling title. I know you can beat him, but you may get a good workout and he will fully test your reaction time. I recommend you grab him and hold on. Drive him to the mat. But don't let go or he will score on you. So you want the second bout for sure? You will be taking on two very tough guys. If you control the action on the little guy you shouldn't have a problem. If not, you're in for eight minutes of wrestling hell. Still want to go?"

"Sure, Coach. Set them up."

The teams were pretty well matched although the set-ups often preordained a win or loss. Greg liked the idea of wrestling the 150-pound guy; he would have to wrestle a lot more defensively than he had visualized he would need to. He now had to think about how he would wrestle the light guy. The heavy guy would wait. *Hopefully our 165-pounder will push him much harder than the 109 guy will push me,* he thought. Then he replaced the thought with a more positive one, thinking, *I am conditioned for anything, even the full eight minutes.* Greg then remembered what the coach said about the star, "control the action." Then he caught the thought, *Star. Okay, he is a star,* thought Greg, but a *109-pound star*, thus *mere fodder for a 133-pound stud!*

Greg began his visualization. He visualized his opponent as being quick, which would require him to be more cautious in setting up his takedowns. When he tied up he would lock him up and convert to a lateral drop or a power like pancake and put him on his back for good. One good double under hook or even double over hook will give me the match, visualized Greg. His comfort and concentration were interrupted as the coach signaled him to the mat.

Greg took a deep breath and looked at his opponent. He was extremely cut for any weight and looked strong. Greg still knew his own strength, combined with his wrestling skills, would carry him comfortably, but he no longer believed this guy was an easy mark. Greg moved in to tie-up immediately, but the *Star* wouldn't tie-up. He was comfortable taking his shots without tying up. Greg hadn't plan on his refusal to tie-up. *Did I think he was stupid?* wondered Greg.

In order to control him, I have to tie-up. If I can't grab him, I can't pin him. "Make him wrestle, ref!" yelled several spectators. But the ref made no call as the *Star* was continuing to shoot on Greg, always staying in motion. He moved quickly. He even shot a Russian single takedown that left Greg looking for a tie-up that never happened. *Wow,* thought Greg, as he looked up. 0:55 and no takedown. He had planned a pin by now. Greg had to change his strategy or at least alter it to get the bout started. He decided he had to go straight at him and accept whatever contact occurred. Seconds before the *Star* was a whirling dervish, going left then right then spinning. Now Greg rushed forward with a double-leg takedown, looking like a football tackler, as the *Star* backed up.

Greg kept stalking with more and more intensity. The *Star* kept out of his reach. At 1:15 the ref called the *Star* for stalling, actually backing off the mat. As Greg continued, the *Star* continued to back off and was called again. *This time I get a point*, thought Greg. *Now he'll wrestle.* And he did. Just as Greg relaxed, the *Star* swept in for a pretty single leg and gracefully yet decisively tripped Greg down to the mat for two.

Whew, thought Greg, *he is fast. When I switch, I'll be on top for the pin.* Greg popped out and reached his arm around for the switch but the *Star* let him go and now was driving forward to regain control and potentially back points. Greg was surprised when the *Star* surged forward, driving Greg to his back. He was able to fend off the attack and turn to the mat. As the *Star* attempted to throw in the legs, Greg stood up and turned into the *Star*. Not much of a move, but effective enough to get into a double-leg takedown position, as the *Star* attempted a late crossface block. Greg picked him up and held him as he flailed. The coach watched as Greg juggled him to get the half in as they came to the mat. He sunk it deep and the match was quickly over by fall, leaving but six seconds on the clock.

Greg was pleased but little had worked as planned, yet he had pinned his opponent. He felt good. His team was pleased as he had been behind and still won. Greg spent over fifteen minutes of his warm-up for his second match, visualizing as he moved. The second match went more as planned. Greg wanted to work takedowns and he did. The Bethlehem Valley guy also seemed to want takedown practice as they both appeared to automatically let each other up after each takedown. First Greg went up 10-8 on the strength of four versus two takedowns. As he tried different moves the heavier guy caught up and won 17-15. Greg felt great as he had assessed and effectively determined which of his moves had worked best on a stronger wrestler.

Chapter Seven

The Words Worked

Two weeks later.

Anthony begins by asking Greg about the Bethlehem Valley scrimmage.

"How did you do?"

"Fine, but my visualization didn't work. It didn't really fit as I had envisioned a guy my weight. I ended up meeting this light guy, their *Star*, and then a 150-pound guy."

"So the visualization didn't prepare you for the match? It didn't reduce your nervousness? It didn't put you in the right frame of mind?"

"Actually it did do those things. It just didn't prepare me for those two guys."

"Did you use it with these two guys before the matches and remember to visualize your victory?"

"I did. But I received a surprise by wrestling outside my weight class."

"Did it help you adjust to the change? With visualization often comes the ability to better adapt to change."

"Now that makes some sense. I am not sure that what I envisioned worked so much as it kept me focused on the task at hand. It kept my stress level down and helped me get into the zone."

"Greg, that is exactly what Visualization is meant to do. It should keep your stress level down. It should prepare you for the match so that there are few surprises. It should help get you into the zone."

"Okay. That makes sense. I feel a little better. Somehow I thought or hoped the match might turn out exactly as visualized. That didn't happen and probably with those guys it couldn't have."

"That's right. Visualization prepares you just like exercises and drills. Greg, please keep it forever in your repertoire. Visualization won't always perfectly mirror a match but it conditions you and conditions the environment."

"Conditions the environment? Maybe the ref then believes I will win?"

"At the very least the ref will see your self-confidence. He may see you are trying to gain a takedown and maybe he won't call you for stalling. Regardless of the result on others, the greatest and most profound effect is on you. So, **Visualize Success** for that reason alone. If other things happen, even better."

"Anthony, may I ask you something? I have begun, as you said, and worked to understand how my brother and mother drove me crazy. Surprisingly, they have both been quite flexible. Once I made it clear to them that I cared about them and that I wanted to make them happy, they responded to my request much more favorably."

"This should work with most people. What's the question?"

"The technique doesn't really stop me from getting angry, although it does stop me from getting *really* angry. I find that I recognize anger as my *improper response*. Does this make sense? I thought that once I became good at recognizing my anger as a message, then acknowledging it, that I wouldn't ever feel it."

"Greg, this statement shows the solid progress you are making. You are on the right path. Stick with it. Was that your question?"

"Well, sort of. I still get angry with my brother and mother. Mostly when I am busy and don't have time to deal with things."

"Greg, they may face the same problem. People never seem to take the time to deal with problems head-on. Instead, they end up taking much more time later, after the minor problems balloon into galactic proportions. I would work on solving problems as they occur. And please, never let a highly emotional issue go unresolved, only to fester."

"This was my problem. I was looking to save time by dealing with my problems on a weekly basis."

"Greg, that's very hard to do. I would strive to solve them as soon as possible. Weekly may work if the problems are simple and emotions are not flying high. But Greg, you haven't spoken about reconciling with your brother."

"Anthony, I didn't want to get into it, but I owe you."

"No, Greg, you owe yourself to forgive. You don't owe me."

"No, I mean it. I owe you an explanation and apology. I did think I was doing the right thing when I hit my brother. I actually thought I was saving him in a *Holden Caulfield - Catcher in the Rye* style. It sounds ridiculous because it is. Cold cocking him wasn't my only choice. I had the choice to *just stay home*. I was too self-centered to see another choice. It scares me how little remorse I had for hitting him. It wasn't until I told you that I recognized the convoluted way I had rationalized my deplorable act."

"Greg, have you reconciled with Allen?"

"That's the worst part. He wasn't very upset I hit him. He hated me for leaving him at home. He stood up so quickly after falling, whatever happened, was over fast."

"Greg, did he forgive you?"

"Well, that's the best part. He even honored me with several SAT words. He said, 'I will consider a rapprochement despite your faux pas if the denouement includes a coup de grâce if ever you don't include-moi.' Which means, in Allen speak, in anglicized and butchered French, that we can return to friendly terms after my mistake, as long as he gets to punch me out if I don't include him. Anthony, I couldn't believe it. I even checked that neither Mom nor Dad put him up to it. So yes, he has forgiven me and I now see he is such a good sport, next time I plan to include him. But we won't be drinking."

"Great, Greg. Great," said Anthony. "How are you progressing with your other goals?"

"My vocabulary and word usage are cascading to improve my practice scores *and* my parents, just like Allen, are helping. They quiz me at dinner and sometimes by phone. They try to make the words SAT words. They both bought SAT vocabulary builder books. I think I've become an excuse for them to study and improve their own use of words: lexicology. They also seem to be reading more. After it worked, I told them it was your idea. Now they want to meet you. They even asked me a bunch of questions about you that I've never thought to ask."

"So, they did like it?"

"It's as if it gives them a good excuse to talk to me. It is helping my home life and maybe even my personal life."

"How is that?"

"It may get me a date with Pam."

Anthony looked quizzically at Greg.

"Yes, Pam Dega. Do you know her?"

"So what happened?"

"In Western Civilization, I used a word that few, but the teacher, Mr. Thomas, knew. I talked about the 'celerity of the advancing troops.' Pam smiled and asked after class if I wanted to study Western Civ with her. I don't think she had ever noticed me before, although my desk juxtaposes hers. I've been trying to find an excuse to talk to her and ask her out, but she seemed to be with this guy. I don't like interfering."

"Oh, she's engaged or serious with someone?"

"Well, no, Anthony. To be honest, maybe I just fear rejection."

"Greg, you haven't heard my screed, my long discourse, on dating?"

"If the recommendation revolves around visualization, I'm afraid I'm way ahead of you there, Anthony."

"Touché. No, Greg. Healthy visualization can be appropriate, but what I was going to say was a bit more general. You have been and will be attracted to many women. Candidly, your self-confidence and success will attract even more women than you may suspect. But it's more important you choose dates like you choose your close friends. Be sure they are good people. Be sure they have a good influence on you. Most importantly, you should have no fear of dating women, setting aside the normal trepidations and anticipation accompanying early dating. To start, you should not fear rejection."

"That doesn't sound like a technique that will reduce my fear."

"You're right. I didn't explain. So let me ask you why you fear dating? Was it just the fear of rejection?"

"Yes."

"Why fear rejection?"

"Rejection means I am not worthy."

"Does it, Greg?"

"Well, rejection means she doesn't like me."

"Maybe or perhaps she's busy, seeing someone else, tired, frustrated, or shy or…?"

"I get it."

"Maybe you do. There are many reasons, but let's go back to the fear of rejection. Do you expect every woman to be attracted to you?"

"Sure. Why not? Well, okay. Yes, or well…okay, no. I can't expect everyone to want to go out with me."

"Precisely. It is perfectly natural for some women to like you and some to prefer others."

"But rejection still hurts."

"Look at dating as if you have a key that fits some doors and not others. Should you be angry or disappointed with the key? Not everyone will like you or prefer you to others. Accept it now. It will make your life easier."

"I'm the key?"

"Precisely."

"I should accept that I won't always open the door to their heart?"

"Precisely."

"This will make my life easier?"

"Yes, and the lesson is greater still. Things happen for a reason. Sometimes people like you and sometimes they don't."

"**Accept Fate,** Greg. Dating simply represents one way in which accepting your fate allows you to maintain your sanity and optimize your chances."

"Wait, how does accepting that someone doesn't like me, optimize my chances?"

"Greg, the flip side of this is to be sure not to assume the most beautiful, intelligent, and wonderful woman won't like you. That's how it may vastly expand your opportunities. Not to mention, if you are mourning because someone doesn't like you or you are busy chasing the one who rejects you, you might miss noticing the right woman as she passes by."

"Anthony, this all sounds good, but accepting defeat still feels wrong."

"That's the point, Greg. In love there can be no defeat. Love that starts from afar only progresses to true love once both people begin moving together. There is nothing at all lost when two people don't click."

"So when someone rejects me – or what if I lose a match? I should just accept it? Should I just accept defeat? I don't ever want to accept defeat!" cried Greg, displaying a verbal outburst that surprised them both. *Dating failure may embarrass me but wrestling failure would devastate me,* thought Greg. "I don't want to accept failure. I never do and never will!"

"Accepting a wrestling loss and accepting a date rejection are different, Greg. A date that wasn't meant to be frees you to find the one that was meant to be. A loss in wrestling should be accepted as a tool to help you become a better wrestler — sometimes a better person as well. But don't accept failure going in. Doing so is to waste your time. But failing doesn't make you a failure. Let's look back at the scrimmage, Greg. Did you beat the 150-pound guy from BV?"

"No."

"So you failed to beat him...You were a failure?"

"I was practicing takedowns, and I wasn't too concerned about the score. *I was wrestling to learn.* You taught me to do that. It wasn't a failure. It was actually a victory of sorts. I went even-up with a bigger, stronger kid."

"So not all failures are failures? You can then accept some failures and not others?"

"Wait, Anthony, you're confusing me. It sounded like you were saying failure was just going to happen, so accept it."

"No, Greg. The point is in order to move on you must accept *reality*. Many times what appears to be failure may as easily be a stepping-stone to something better, as was your match at BV. But moving forward is what must happen regardless. Learning from failure is a great thing, but in order to learn you first have to accept that you lost. Once this is accepted, you can move on. This is much like the message pain or fear may deliver. Read the message, accept, and move on."

"At the risk of sounding single-minded, how about my problem. What do I do with Pam?"

"Greg, she asked you to study with her, right?"

"Yes."

"You want to be with her and I assume this includes studying with her?"

"Yes."

"Then go study. You do have plenty of work to do on the SAT and your grade in Western Civilization means something as well?"

"Yes, I won't be wasting study time by being with her. She did make the National Honor Society so she's smart enough. It is hard to make it."

"Studying would appear to be a good way to learn both about Pam *and* Western Civilization. So what's the problem?"

"Well, I almost expected a sermon about how a woman could reduce my focus on school or the SAT or reduce my wrestling effectiveness."

"Will she?" asked Anthony.

"No, of course not. No way. I won't let it. I believe Pam will help me feel better about myself. With her, I think I may have avoided the down feeling I had before the BV scrimmage. Remember, Anthony, you told me about the key, **Have Fun**."

"Greg, those are good answers. I don't doubt your sincerity or commitment. Time for Pam means time for you. That will be good. The 'all work and no play makes Jack a dull boy' cliché has merit. Come to think of it, those around Jack may become pretty miserable, too," said Anthony with a chuckle.

Chapter Eight
The New Phase

Greg began to view life differently. He no longer saw himself as moving from one fear to the next. Because his scheduling kept him ahead with a comfortable margin of safety, his daily *To Do List* demands felt less like *Got To Do's* and more like *Good To Do's*. This reduced pressure seemed to put a little more in his tank. He slept better. He wasted little time worrying. He came to value some tasks he used to think were just time killers: planning his day each morning and spending a few seconds of quality time with his brother and parents. Getting up at 6:06 a.m. also seemed to agree with him. He could get up and change into his jogging clothes, put on his headphones, and run. He could follow this up with sprints, pull-ups, sit-ups, power cleans, benches, and bridging.

He listened to his four-minute **Personal Commercial** nearly four times during his two-mile warm-up run. *The recording made him feel both safe and in control.* Sometimes he couldn't even remember hearing it, but the **Personal Commercial** always helped him keep his goals and daily actions in his mind and heart. He knew the **Personal Commercial** and the **Jingle** were working. *As easy as 1-2-3. Push, pull, turn. 1-2-3.* When a tasty food morsel presented itself, Greg often heard *1-2-3*. This reminded him of his goals, his weight target of 123 pounds, and that it was as easy to achieve as *1-2-3*. This usually made a *Twinkie* unappealing; however, an occasional indulgence kept him sane and able to avoid a binge.

Take Control of Your Life

At practice Greg took a break. While drinking from the white porcelain water faucet he thought of Pam. He would see her tomorrow. She gave him something to think about that felt light, warm, and breezy. Since the Anthony-inspired rapprochement generated a great relationship with Allen and his family, he'd been positioned to forge an agreement with his brother and his parents to take a low profile during Pam's visit tomorrow. He was a senior and while he had hung out with girls before, including a few movies and even a brief summer crush, he really felt like this was his first date. *Wow, I hope it goes well*, he thought. *I really want to kiss her,* he thought, surprising himself. He only remembered one time he had choreographed a date. It had worked according to plan but made him miserable. She was sweet, cute, smart, and friendly. She was, in fact, everything he had hoped for. But when they finally messed around, she cried afterward and he felt terrible. Even together they had felt lonely. They both were expecting so much, but the experience left them empty. They realized how incidental to each other they were. She saw it in his eyes. His fantasy didn't account for the aftermath: the confusion that quickly turned into disappointment. *I should have been better prepared*, Greg thought.

So why was this a first date? It wasn't her, he thought. Well, maybe a little. It was him. His comfort in his own skin would comfort her now, as it comforts him. Not that he thought *those* thoughts about Pam. Well, at least they weren't in his plans. But *a kiss was*, he thought. One kiss – one where I lean in close. Reach up and put my hands gently on her cheeks. I could ask her about her glasses. I like how they make her look more mature than her years. I'll tell her how good the glasses look. Then I will ask her if I can try them to see what it is like to look through them. Then I will use my hands to gently return the glasses to their sweet resting place on her olive-skinned face. I will lean in and, if she notices my lean and gives me any sign at all, I will kiss her. A *kiss* that I hope neither of us can forget. I will pull her toward me and hold her like she's never been held before. Not crushingly, but firm, controlled, and warm. She will feel more secure in those ten seconds than she will have ever remembered. But that was for Saturday.

He caught himself in this reverie and asked himself if she would seriously use the time to study. He knew she would and that made it all-the-better. His goals and hers could not be far apart. Studying will make us feel good about ourselves and kissing will make it even better. The kiss represents the icing, not the cake. Without the kiss, the study would have less meaning. Both are important, but together they represent a true connection of souls.

What if she hates anyone touching her glasses? Some people could be that way. *Good,* he thought. Take an otherwise uncomfortable action and then her favorable reaction will be my cue. If she is so sensitive as to not be open to my harmless ploy, I will know. *Good. A plan,* he thought. Would Anthony be disappointed or pleased I used visualization to plan a kiss with Pam? He couldn't remember Anthony disapproving or failing to condone anything that he had felt good about. But the date would wait.

Practice that week went quickly as did school until Friday.

Friday. The pressure began to pile back up. *Why?* He wondered. In practice a less skilled opponent surprised him with a straight-ahead double-leg and pick-up. He was embarrassed. It had been a while since a wrestler had picked him up into the air. It's a humbling experience, he thought. It has a great psychological impact on a wrestler. Two or three of those type drops could easily demoralize the defender even as it uses a fair amount of strength and energy by the rider. *I will train to have this excess energy and strength.* After the wrestler dropped him to the mat and they got up, Greg looked around. He wasn't the only one surprised by the move. His opponent had just gained some respect from the team.

Take responsibility, thought Greg. Yes, I erred but he did make a great move. I need to focus. It was a good move for him and I did learn from it. Expect the unexpected. That's what Anthony would say, Greg thought. Too bad there weren't points in Folkstyle like Freestyle, where just exposing shoulders to the mat gained points. The double-leg and pick-up move could score back points in both styles then. Why were high school and college (Folkstyle) rules so different from Freestyle and Greco-Roman (Olympic) wrestling rules? High schools and colleges must be pretty stubborn. The Olympics were plenty exciting. Mat wrestling had a certain appeal, but can be boring compared to big throws like the historic suplay of Chris Taylor in the Olympics. Dietrich, a 270-pound guy, hoisted the massive 450-pound Taylor over his head and dumped him for a pin. Now that's entertainment!

So why the nerves?

Tomorrow's date? Well, it must be but it shouldn't be. Pam seems to be taking it lightly. He had spoken a couple of times with her, and she seemed very sweet but not very interested in him. She clearly prefers Western Civ to me, he thought. No, it couldn't be her. Greg had already begun to discount the date, especially the kiss. Maybe he wouldn't even try it. No, it had to be the studying. The SAT was getting close and he had to concentrate on his grades. The colleges would see this semester's grades. Okay, so I haven't been working my classes or the SAT as much as I would have liked, although vocabulary study has become routine, thanks to Mom and Dad. I still need to work on algebra.

Maybe I need to redo my planning and cut something out. Maybe the study of Western Civ tomorrow? *No way*! he mentally corrected. This has been planned and booked and I still need to study Western Civ sometime, he rationalized. I'll cut something, he thought. I'll bet Mulino's study time affords him more workout time than mine. I'm just going to have to make each minute and each second count more. I need to use my brain to study smarter, not harder or longer. Maybe I can start with Pam. If she works on an outline of half the course, and I do the other half, we can both save time. She'll like that idea, he thought.

Greg then proceeded to pick up the same wrestler, who minutes earlier had embarrassed him. In a display of bravado, he held the wrestler up in the air for just a moment longer than necessary. As he brought him to the mat he saw many of the same wrestlers watching. He realized then he looked more like a showboat than a stud. Hubris, I still have plenty of it, he thought. I should let the points speak for themselves. Anthony had said that many times.

"Hey Greg! Go lift Dore like that," yelled Gallo, effectively chastising him much as he had already chastised himself. So why did he do it?

"Just practice, Coach," he yelled back after they stood up. Gallo furrowed his brow in disagreement. Greg knew he didn't buy it and the wrestler didn't either. He was angry and charging!

"Sorry," Greg said after his opponent had just pushed him hard off the mat. "You hit an excellent double. Sorry I was so unsportsmanlike about it. My fault. Keep them coming!"

Greg knew practice centered on friendly contact, even when going all out. That's why we have few injuries in practice. We wrestle hard but always fair. We respect everyone. I've breached our unspoken pact. As a senior and a new informal leader, I let everyone down. Move on, Greg thought. *One move, one time, forgive yourself.* I won't get surprised and if surprised, I won't retaliate except with points! Let your wrestling talk. Maybe I should put this into my **Personal Commercial**? He considered. No, I've learned this lesson.

Chapter Nine
The Study Date

Great run! Greg thought as he finished his breakfast. Why do the Saturday morning runs seem to go better? An easy warm-up run listening to my **Personal Commercial**, ten sprints of 300 yards, starting at the halfway point at the Fyfe and Drum, followed by cleans, bridging, pull-ups, and sit-ups. Maybe I just get a better start at 7:07? That extra sleep must be it. Three eggs over well with a generous helping of Swiss cheese on top, one slice of cracked wheat toast, and half a grapefruit served as breakfast. On a starvation diet and I still eat three times what my mom eats.

"Effluvium!" said his mom.

"Toxic or homemade gaseous waste?" Greg joked. "Wait, I've one for you. Actually two four letter words — *whit and whet*. How do you spell them and what do they mean?"

"I don't give a whit, w-h-i-t, and those two words barely whet, w-h-e-t, my vocabulary appetite," spelled Mom.

"Gee, Mom. That's good. I stumped two teachers on those. They ignored me or changed the subject but somehow seemed to give me the right answer the next day. I think I've got the whole school on the cusp of logomania. It gives me a frisson."

"Okay, now you stumped me. What's logomania and how does one get a frisson?"

"A frisson's a thrill, Mom, and if my vision is correct, Pam is walking up our drive. Mom, she has legs. She gives me frissons!"

"That sounds crude, Greg."

Take Control of Your Life [65]

"Mom, a frisson is a moment of intense excitement, a shudder. It can be a thrill or a cold chill, but not crude. Logomania is going 'word crazy.' But as I said, here comes Pam. Thanks for breakfast, Mom. Remind me when it's my turn to cook."

"Greg, was that your idea of levity?"

"Hi, Pam. Welcome to our humble columbary. I'll take your coat."

"Greg, how positively morbid! Isn't a columbarium a place for the ashes of the dead?"

"Oops, I think my grandiloquent thesaurus failed me on that one. Sorry, Pam."

"*Abode* is an acceptable reference to home or house, Greg. You may borrow it." Pam smiled as she lithely moved forward. She had the cheerleader smile but actually performed in the modern dance ensemble. It showed.

If I could move like that my wrestling would be untouchable, Greg thought.

"You brought notes, too?" Greg said as he noticed a more than ample stack of papers under Pam's arm. "Here let me help you with those."

"Yes, Greg. I outline all of my subjects. I summarize each day's notes at night, recap them weekly, and then monthly put together an outline. Sometimes I do it by chapter, depending upon the subject. For Western Civ, I have it based upon key figures or periods. St. Thomas Aquinas and Roger Bacon merit their own sections."

"Oh really? I avoid bacon; calories and cholesterol you know."

"Speaking of ignorance, what were Bacon's four causes of ignorance?"

"Ah, you got me," said Greg.

"A3C," said Pam.

"What?"

"Authority, custom, crowd, cover up. 'A' for appeals to unsuited Authority, 'C' undue influence of Custom, 'C' opinions of the unlearned Crowd, and 'C' displays of wisdom that Cover up ignorance. Greg, your ignorance seems to fall predominantly into the fourth category. Don't you think?"

"Oh, you do flatter me so," retorted Greg.

"Acronyms and mnemonics. My life revolves around recaps, acronyms, and mnemonics — things to help me remember. Thank goodness for my two D's."

"What?"

"Dance and my dog, Daffodil."

"Daffodil?"

"Yes, she's really cute. I saw daffodils outside the pound where I rescued her with my dad. She's a big, nearly daffodil yellow, golden retriever. But if she jumped on you, you might not see how the daffodil moniker fits. In fact, she'll be in your weight class if you keep losing. Do you ever eat? She's about 110, I think. That's about 18 less than me."

"This is cool. I learn your dog's name, your weight, and a lesson on bacon you can't eat, and you've been here what? Two minutes?"

"Greg, play nice. I have something you really want. You know — good notes in Western Civ."

"Sorry, Pam. I just didn't expect for you to tell me your weight. Most women guard that with their lives."

"You hadn't noticed I wasn't other women? How unfortunate."

"Pam, please. I think 128 is *great*. How tall are you?"

"But you wrestle 123. I know I saw the wrestle offs. You do wrestle 123, don't you?"

"Yes, but I weigh 128-130 most days. I just take about a day of light food, reduced fluids, and jogging in sweats to get to 123. Plenty cut more. I can't. I feel too weak and I hate the bigger cuts. One wrestler from Herrinsburg cuts 10-12, easy, before bouts."

"So, how tall are you?"

"I'm about your height. I'm 5′ 7 ½″."

"I'm 5′ 9″ even."

"No, you're not. Let's measure."

"Stand up," insisted Pam in an authoritative voice that struck both as funny.

"Okay, there's a mirror in the hall closet. We can use the opposing wall and mirror to see. Follow me."

"I'm not following you into any closet, Greg Gurist."

"Just *to* the closet, oh ye of little faith."

Greg proceeded from the study into the hall and opened the hall door.

"Stand against the wall, Pam."

"You first," insisted Pam. "I'll measure you. I'll make a small mark with my red highlighter. The mark will be just a speck, not much more than a microdot."

Greg backed into the wall as he saw Pam in the mirror of the open closet door. Pam stood inches away, lifting her arm up in front of him and putting the pen over his head. She touched his shoulder with one hand as she held the other straight over his head marking the wall. Greg enjoyed the tension of her closeness.

"Your turn," said Greg. He took her marker and put it over her head. As he went to place a mark, he noticed she moved. Looking back at the mirror, he saw her on her toes. That explained why she was about the same height.

"Amazing. We are the same height," exclaimed Greg. "Let's stand side by side, I was sure I was taller."

They both stood side by side and looked at each other's reflection. Pam looked good. Her eyes were a mesmerizing, bright blue-gray. Her thick and silky golden hair came just past her shoulders. Greg suddenly realized he had never seen her hair down. She usually had it up or pulled back, he thought. The glasses, he thought.

"Where are they?" Greg asked.

"What? Where are what?"

"Your glasses. Where are they?"

"I have contacts. I wear them when I dance or when I'm out."

"So you're dancing?"

"Funny. But yes, I do dance."

"Can I see a few moves?"

"Will you show me a few wrestling moves?"

Greg's dad walks in.

"Hi, you must be Dee?"

"No, Dad. It's Pam. Actually her last name is *Dega*."

"Oh, sorry. Glad to meet you, Pam. So how's the studying coming? You *are* planning to study?"

"Yes, Dad. Thanks. We are. I was just hanging up Pam's coat."

Pam and Greg headed back to the study. Now his dad knew they weren't studying and he knew his glasses strategy was seriously flawed.

"Contacts? You have contacts? Yes, you do look different — more approachable, less librarian. Can I see them?"

"You want me to take my contact lens out?" asked Pam.

"No. I just couldn't see them. Let me see."

Greg moved in close to her. He gazed into her radiant blue-gray eyes. She looked back but clearly felt uncomfortable. Greg backed away as he saw a faint rose hue envelope her cheeks and neck.

"Did I make you blush?"

"What? I don't think so. My cheeks are always rosy."

"No, they're not. In fact, your olive complexion is usually translucent but now it has turned opaque with your blush."

"Who anointed you the expert on complexions? You could use some Clearasil yourself."

"Ouch," said Greg.

She didn't act like she wanted to kiss me, he thought. Maybe I should have tried anyway. Greg glanced at his watch and Pam caught him.

"Are you late for something?"

"No, I'm sorry. It's just that I've been keeping us from studying."

"No, that's okay, Greg. It's good to get to know you a bit anyway, before I quiz you much further. You have read about Bacon and Aquinas? Aquinas is one of my heroes. Okay, yes, a balding Dominican Priest, but he successfully used reason within the constraints of the church without suffering the fate of my favorite 4-foot, 11-inch hero."

"How many 4-foot, 11-inch heroes do you have?"

"Greg, are you asking, 'who is Joan of Arc?' And don't even think about wrestling me, Greg. I'd probably win anyway."

"You would definitely beat me."

"You'd let me win, huh? Well, let's get some work done so your dad can stop smiling at me like something else is going on."

"Everyone smiles at beautiful women," Greg said brazenly.

"Thanks, Greg. You didn't say anything when I came in."

"I was thinking it, Pam. You look great."

Greg and Pam spent the next several hours studying and reviewing. Greg read her notes for an hour, and they discussed them for two hours. Pam reread another subject's notes as he read.

She wasn't just smart. She was even smart about getting smart. She had a system for everything, Greg thought. Plus she's very candid. Maybe I should just ask for a kiss? No, that's not very romantic. He did remember that his dad said that after first semester torts in law school most students realized that an unwanted kiss or attempt was either assault or battery or both. Greg didn't just need a cue. He needed a segue. Say, maybe she wants to kiss me? She's planned her whole life. I bet I play some part in it. I might as well wait and see.

Three and a half hours later, they were done.

"I've got to go," Pam said, announcing her departure as brusquely as she had arrived.

"Let me get your coat. Say, I joked about your notes before, but they are really good. I wish you were in all my classes."

"Oh really? Didn't you say you wanted to go to college?"

"What?"

"I meant it wouldn't be easy studying with you."

"Why not? I thought we did well…"

"Actually, we did do okay. I guess I was really talking about the hallway and my contacts thing."

As he finished putting her jacket on, she spun gracefully. Almost like a Russian single, Greg thought. *Wow, I wish I could be so fluid*! Like a Romanian gymnast crossed with a female yogi.

Her face moved in close to his and she asked softly, "Kissing me goodbye?" Greg saw a sparkle in her eye that seemed a dare as much as a request. She did make the first move, he thought. Just when I thought it wouldn't happen.

"Okay, but I hope you're ready."

"Try me," she said, as she closed her eyes and leaned in even closer.

She wouldn't forget it soon, he hoped. Fortunately his brother, after getting home, had headed out to the garage to shoot hoops. His mom had been in the kitchen. No one saw. Good, he thought. *Just ours to remember.* She had hugged him as firmly as he hugged her. It wasn't just a kiss. She meant it, he thought. He meant it too.

"You wrestle on Wednesday, don't you?"

"Yes."

"Is he any good? You know, the guy from Canyon Creek."

Greg paused for a time, thinking of his opponent. "He is real good. He'll be my first real test."

"No. You just had your first *real* test."

"How did I do?" Greg asked as she sashayed through the door. No, *glide,* he thought. *That's what she does.*

"Call me. I'll give you your grades."

Chapter Ten

Wrestling and the Doctor

Monday in school.

As Greg entered the school, he decided to swing by the hallway in front of the Dean's office to see the honor roll lists. There were about fifteen to twenty names per class. He looked under the juniors. Pam's name wasn't there. Surprising, he thought, very surprising. As he looked further he saw his own name under the seniors. Then he saw another list with just four names per class, *Highest Honors: Pam Dega*. Her name was first. Either the list was alphabetical, or she was *first* in her class. He didn't need to know whether she was first or fourth. He was impressed.

Top of her class and I had the nerve, no, Baconian type four ignorance, to criticize her habit of summarizing her notes each day, week, and month. What a good idea, he reflected. He wondered how long it took. He would ask her in class. It would be a compliment to break the ice plus he really wanted to know.

"So what's your secret?" asked Greg.

"Which one? Careful, it might cost you."

"How do you have time to review your notes every day? You did say every day."

"Greg. I'm not very smart. I don't know how people are able to take exams and do well without good notes."

"Yes," said Greg, "Good notes are important."

"You can read a textbook, but you really can't study from it. It's a 'wheat versus chaff' thing. The typical text has more dross than sauce. So I *boil and refine, then it's mine.* That's one of the mottos I learned that help me improve my grades."

"But Pam, tell me how this helps?"

"Easy, at the end of each semester I find I need only do a complete read of my notes. Then I just work on the mnemonics, acronyms, and associations and memorize the important things. I don't have to relearn, just remember. The few questions I do get wrong are usually ones of interpretation. Rarely do I miss something a teacher considers important. Even then, probably because of my solid performance on the objective portion, teachers appear predisposed to give me a good grade on the subjective part."

"Pam, this leads me to the SAT. How do you plan to prepare for it?"

"I know the verbal section revolves around vocabulary. I understand about 99% of the test comes from a list of about 2,500 words. At 50 a day that's 50 days, or really about 10: one probably already knows 80% of those words. But Greg, you asked how long recapping my notes took. My answer is that when I first began doing it — after my unsuccessful first year in high school — it doubled my study time. Now, I don't think it takes me any longer."

"What? You summarize your notes after every class, then weekly, then monthly, and then each semester. How do you find the time?"

"Greg, it just replaces other wasted study motions such as attempting to recall a class discussion."

"That's why you're at the top of your class?"

"Top of my class? I didn't tell you that."

"I was looking at the honor roll this morning."

"Oh, you wanted to know how I did?"

"Well..."

"Were you surprised?"

"Well, at first I thought you weren't on the honor roll because I didn't see your name. Then as I looked at the seniors and just beyond that was the *highest* honors list. I will say that I was less surprised to see you with highest honors than I was that you weren't on the honors list. And by the way, your name is first. Does it mean?"

Pam nodded. "I'm really embarrassed about it. The cute guys are all intimidated. Not that you aren't cute."

"Good save, Pam, but that's okay. I do get my share of compliments. But the fact that most of them come from friends and family tells me there might be cuter guys. But I never wanted to be cute anyway. Besides, I'd rather be ruggedly handsome in an athletic-intelligent sort of way."

"Ruggedly handsome? Whose dream are you in?" giggled Pam.

"I hope yours. Did I just say that?" asked Greg.

"You're not in mine yet, I'm still busy grading. You understand there are five categories: warmth, passion, love, devotion, and courage? Good thing you didn't call me yesterday. I had some old files to review. There are still a few kisses from grade school needed for benchmarking."

"Grade school? You are comparing me to some guy you kissed in grade school?"

"Guy? You inferred but one guy? And the grade school thing — you did want a good grade, didn't you? Of course, I could grade on a curve. Would that help?"

"Ouch! Where did you learn to talk like that? Aren't you an only child? You didn't have brothers, did you?"

"You hadn't yet asked about my family. While I don't have siblings to harass me, I have the next best thing. I have several cousins who are practically brothers. When my dad's brother died they were raised in part by my parents. In fact, one of my cousins is the second best wrestler on the team. You do know Steve?"

"Dore? Steve Dore's your cousin?"

"Yes, I thought you were afraid to kiss me because he was my cousin and a lot bigger, stronger, and I hope meaner than you."

"I wasn't afraid to kiss you, and please keep your voice down. We are getting a bunch of stares. It's not like a school hallway can give us much privacy."

"Yes, in fact, my only conundrum about grading the kiss was the threshold issue."

"What threshold issue?"

"Should I deduct points because you didn't initiate the kiss?"

"No, on the contrary. By allowing *you* to ask, I earned points in the warmth and devotion categories. Didn't I?"

"Nice, Greg."

"Say, who's the best wrestler on the team?"

"You know more about wrestling than I do, Greg. You mean it's not you? I *am* disappointed."

"Oh, I didn't mean to put me into the equation."

"So Greg, it's not all about you? How refreshing."

"Where did you learn to talk like that? Did I already ask?"

"Steve is my cousin. Are you listening? He has a mouth as minatory as his muscled biceps."

"I like Steve," said Greg only somewhat convincingly. He *was* cordial with Steve. At an all-muscle 225, he was a lot to handle on the mat, and so Greg dreaded drills where he was his partner. Picking him up was a workout all by itself. Fortunately, he can't keep up with me on the track or the rope climb, thought Greg. Unfortunately, he's a real monster on the mat. Some even heavier guys, overweight non-wrestlers mostly, he could handle, like our sophomore heavyweight who's 250, Carl. But Carl can't wrestle. I just spin behind him, drop to an ankle, pull on it, and trip him. He usually goes down before the trip and then he's mine. It's even more amusing to watch, I'm told. But Steve Dore was big, strong, and fast, a legitimate heavyweight. He had football scholarship offers from several colleges that see him as an instant starter at linebacker. That says something. *Cousin*, he thought. That's not so good.

"See you in class," Greg shouted over the long buzzer that signaled the start of the next class. He had made Pam late for her class. He could not remember her ever being late for class; not that he would know. He was often late. No big deal. He walked into science honors class. He knew he was late but Mr. Vlasco usually looked the other way. Besides, Mr. Vlasco would often make him feel good about something he'd recently submitted or proposed. Greg was working on a 96 or better in the class, a real achievement. Not even Pam got many of those, he thought.

"Greg, can I see you after class?" asked Mr. Vlasco.

"Sure," responded Greg, more surprised at the teacher's tone than his message.

"You wanted to see me?" he asked after class.

"Greg. I like you. I think you have great potential."

Greg knew he was in trouble. Anytime someone said you had great potential they really meant you had really messed up something and had no excuse. How easy is that to take? It's like cutting off any potential escape avenue before a fight begins. Greg smelled trouble.

"Greg, I don't know the best way to say this, but several teachers and I have spoken and we are very concerned about you."

"Why?" inquired Greg.

"You look pale and your face seems emaciated. You often look tired. And you are regularly late for class."

"My face?"

"That's not all of it. We need to talk to the wrestling coach and recommend you stop reducing weight."

"No, no, please don't do that. Don't talk to the coach. I have already cut most of the weight I need to cut."

"Greg, you look horrible. You look drawn and your face looks gaunt and perhaps a little jaundiced. You're only 17."

"Actually, well yes, Mr. Vlasco. I am sorry for being late, but I'm fine. I'm healthy. I am a little tired, but I get up at 6. And I am doing well in school."

"That's actually our point, Greg. You are doing well in school. We just think you will do even better without wrestling."

"Please, Mr. Vlasco, I know the coach doesn't want any trouble. He'll probably cut me from the team. And my parents will probably make me quit if you tell them what you are telling me."

"Greg, we actually think you should withdraw from wrestling."

"What? Mr. Vlasco, you don't understand. I can't give up wrestling. My life is an ecosystem."

"An ecosystem?"

"I don't know how else to put it. I love wrestling. It can't be replaced. Wrestling helps complete my life so as to make school interesting. My science project, some of the data on success, and positive thinking comes from wrestling."

"Greg, from what we see, wrestling can ruin your health and your life. Sometimes you come in with a black eye or taped fingers. None of that could be healthy. You couldn't possibly get anything out of it."

"Mr. Vlasco, I really respect you and your opinion. Can I please ask you to give me two weeks? I will not be cutting any more weight and I won't be late for class. I'm sure the color will return to my face."

"Greg, I like you. Since I'm the one chosen to speak to the coach, I can delay it a few days. I don't like to do this but we hate to see you do this to yourself. Since the Genevieve scandal…"

"Genevieve weighed 80 pounds and looked like a skeleton and couldn't pick up a pencil. I have a 205-pound bench press," Greg said, quickly tripping over his own words. "Just a little time, Coach, I mean Mr. Vlasco. Give me just a little time. Please. You won't be sorry."

Greg left once he had a *stand-still agreement* in place, borrowing his dad's words for a legal agreement to prevent something, usually a sale. Mr. Vlasco agreed to one week. Greg was elated for about one second. His face wouldn't change in one week. His complexion wouldn't change. His weight wouldn't go up, he still had a little more weight to cut. His timeliness could improve. Tired? Why did he tell Mr. Vlasco he was tired? He wasn't really tired. Why? Do I look tired? He looked at himself in the mirror as if for the first time.

He called Anthony.

"Can we meet?"

"Anthony, how can they do this to me?"

"Do what?"

"They don't think I should wrestle."

"Who doesn't?"

"Mr. Vlasco, my science teacher doesn't."

"Okay, Greg. Please, from the beginning."

Greg proceeded to give Anthony a brief overview of the situation.

"Anthony, what should I do?"

"Greg, what do you want to do?"

"Don't ask me, Anthony."

"Greg, I mean, what would you like to happen?"

"Anthony, you know I want to wrestle. Wrestling defines me, just as school and Pam do."

"Then what can you do to be sure that you stay on the team?"

"That's what I need your help for, Anthony."

"Okay, Greg, I'll help. Please list Mr. Vlasco's concerns."

Greg listed them.

"So Greg, you look pale, you look tired, and you are late for class. Is that all?"

"Yes, I think so, except they are worried about my health. We had Genevieve, a bulimic, scare the school. She almost died. Now everyone notices a gaunt face. He also noticed a few of my injuries. But really they have been no big deal; a few black eyes, taped fingers."

"Anything else?"

"Yes, Mr. Vlasco threatened — or actually plans — to go to the coach and maybe my parents."

"Greg, how can you allay Mr. Vlasco's concerns?"

"Okay, I can always get a little sun and I certainly can get to class on time, although no one ever complained before. I have always been late. The teachers always just let it go. They probably like me. Now they are reacting just because one teacher noticed my cheeks getting thin. Who wants puffy cheeks anyway?"

"What else could you do, Greg?"

"Well, they also said I didn't look healthy. At the beginning of the season I skipped the required medical exam. I was supposed to take it but I missed that day of school. They never asked again and I never volunteered. I could go to a doctor and get a clean bill of heath."

"Now you're thinking, Greg. I knew you didn't need me for this one. But have you left anything out?"

"I don't think so."

"Greg, how about your parents, don't they support you?"

"Well, yes, I think," he answered unconvincingly.

"Why not do as you say? First, get to class on time. I would also spend some time considering why you have been late. I suspect you will learn something. Second, get out in the sun if you can. That's good advice for us all. Third, be careful to get enough rest. You are still growing and working very hard. Get what you need, seven hours should be the minimum. Fourth, do as you said and go to a doctor who can substantiate your health. You should test as healthy and very fit. And fifth and finally, enlist the support of your parents. If your studies are going well, you're not late to class, and the doctor and your parents support you, I doubt the teachers or coach will object."

"Now I know what to do, Anthony. Thanks."

"Greg, you're welcome, but remember, I just reminded you about your parents; you did the rest."

"Then you must bring out my best. Thanks again."

Greg wondered. There were many lessons here. He always took wrestling for granted. That would stop. He had usually been late. That would stop. He wasn't getting much sun. That, too, should stop, he thought. I love the Jersey Shore. Even in winter it is beautiful. Why don't I take Pam there on a date? My parents love it so they could drive. Even Allen could have a good time. The beach and the ocean offered plenty.

What else? I have never really sought my parents' support for wrestling. They know and probably understand, but I have never confided my burning desire to wrestle. They deserve to know. It defines me. The discipline of the training regime, the rhythm, the moves, the power, the speed, and the control, winning and being at your physical best – *that is wrestling*. They all come into play. They all made you a better person. They made you feel alive, real, and worthwhile. One on one competition and yet still a team sport. Much like real warfare. Much like reality. But it's all about having fun, too. Hard work isn't hard when it's fun. But hard work does feel impossible when it isn't fun. **Work Hard** and **Have Fun**, two of Anthony's keys, thought Greg.

Greg thought more deeply. I didn't talk to my parents. What was I thinking? Aren't they important? Don't I care about them? Why was I keeping this to myself? I know I need and want their support. They always just *let* me wrestle as long as my studies don't suffer. They should know the truth. I need wrestling. It makes me. It defines who I am and who I want to be.

That evening Greg had a long talk with his parents. They got it. They took him to the family doctor to satisfy their own concerns about his health. The doctor conducted a physical examination. Greg's resting pulse and blood pressure were low but not dangerously so. The doctor passed upon Greg's health but left Greg with an admonition related to responsible weight loss.

The next day Mr. Gurist spoke with Mr. Vlasco. He showed him the results of Greg's physical examination. Greg had weighed 126, just three pounds from his wrestling weight, and the doctor had found no evidence of ill health. Quite the contrary, his resting pulse was 52 and his blood pressure equally low. Greg's father made it very clear to Mr. Vlasco that Greg was healthy and would wrestle at 123. While Mr. Gurist didn't play the legal card, Mr. Vlasco saw that Mr. Gurist was not to be taken lightly. Greg had been given a clean bill of health and he had strong parental support. Among the faculty and staff there was never again discussion of Greg's weight.

Chapter Eleven
Canyon Creek High – The First Big Test

"No, no. I didn't mean it! I didn't mean to hurt you. I didn't think it would rip. Firestone, I'm really sorry!" Greg awakened in a sweat. He almost never had nightmares. This dream was different. This was real. It was about a real event. It happened last summer during wrestling camp. His name was Glenn Firestone.

You were wrestling. You were heavier and stronger. He threw in the legs and you were insulted. Why? Why? Well, no one usually had the opportunity to throw legs. You stood up too fast. You were too strong. You were incensed. He threw in the boots and reached for your arm like in the famous Greek statue, "The Wrestlers," for a cross-body ride. You countered.

You grabbed his arm and nearly ripped it free at the elbow. Technically, it was a legal move; you pulled his arm. But before you started you knew it would hurt. You didn't think about injury; you just pulled hard and fast. You felt a tear, a rip. He screamed. You let go. Did you apologize? You don't remember. You can hear his scream now. That's what woke you! His scream.

Firestone is in the line-up for the Canyon Creek match on Thursday, at your weight. Yes. That's why you had the dream. You will face Firestone in two days. But the injury was in the past. Firestone was then 140, maybe 145, and you were 165. Now you would both be 123. This match would be different. Greg wasn't looking forward to it. There could be no victory.

Later, Tuesday after practice:

"I can beat him. Anthony, but I don't want to wrestle him."

"Sorry, Greg, but unless one of you forfeits you will have to wrestle. Those are the rules."

Greg looked at Anthony and saw his usual smiling face. This time the smile seemed wiser.

"So tell me Greg, why don't you want to wrestle him?" Greg proceeded to explain what happened last summer. "Did you really think you would injure him when you pulled on his arm?"

"I am not sure if I thought I would hurt him. I didn't stop to think. I wanted to teach him not to throw legs in on me. It's demeaning."

"If you had it to do over again, would you do it?"

"In a match I could be forced to."

"What?"

"When a wrestler throws legs in, both wrestlers are exposed to lots of forces and some pretty ugly situations. The top guy pretty much tries to rip your body in half. He needs to in order to turn you over. He can throw a half nelson or do what Firestone tried; reach back for your arm and pull it around, then turn you to your back. It can hurt. I don't have the flexibility of many guys so it hurts me even more, which is why I don't like it. This is why I fight it. If he controls *my* arm, he could put me on my back and pin me."

"And?"

"The only way I can stop him once he has the leg in a cross-body ride is to control his arm and to use all the force I can. I really can't control if he gets hurt."

"So Greg, it sounds like you would do in a match what you did last summer. Would it usually injure the guy?"

"No, Anthony, I don't think so but I can't be sure. But I would use it again."

"Greg, if that's true, what bothers you about last summer?"

"Good question." Greg maintained a fairly prolonged silence in thought and concentrated as Anthony patiently awaited the results of his soul-searching.

"I felt possessed by an aggressive, almost evil, intent. Then, what I wanted to do, happened in a flash; it really happened. I wasn't doing it to get out. I was doing it to stop him. In a match, it could have the same result but I wouldn't be hoping to hurt him or anyone."

"Greg, it seems your malicious intent combined with the painful result has created a reason for guilt. Was there another alternative?"

"That's it, Anthony. In a real match I might have to do it. But here, I could have just asked Glenn to stop. I may have felt a little wimpy but the incident would have been forgotten shortly thereafter."

"Well then, Greg, you should feel guilty. It was wrong. There was another way out for you both. This guilt may be compounded by the fact you didn't resolve the issue in your mind. Have you resolved not to do this again?"

"Yes I have, or at least now that you mention it, I do resolve not to do it again."

"Good. Now do you forgive yourself for doing it?"

"Forgive myself? That is *hard*, Anthony. I don't know. No. I guess I haven't yet or don't. Maybe I can't."

"Have you made peace with God over your injury to Glenn Firestone?"

"Yes. I have."

"Do you believe that God forgives you?"

"Yes, of course I do."

"Then why don't you forgive yourself?"

"I can't. At least I won't unless Firestone forgives me."

"Maybe he has."

"Maybe he *will!*" said Greg.

"Greg, he may forgive you. It is good that people forgive us. But Greg, forgiving yourself and God forgiving you is even more important than Glenn's forgiveness. I think his forgiveness is important, but not critical. While sometimes one is unable to obtain forgiveness from the injured party, God forgives you without it, and you can forgive yourself without it. Additionally, forgiveness is something that can help the forgiver."

"How is that?" Asked Greg.

"Harboring anger creates a burden that can be relieved through forgiveness. Forgiveness is one of the keys, **Forgive and Repent**.

God forgives you as soon as you sincerely ask. Once you have resolved not to repeat a transgression and have sought God's forgiveness, it should be a natural step to forgive yourself and move on. Reminding yourself of something bad you've done has little productive value after you have resolved not to repeat it. Forgiveness helps you move on."

"I understand. I agree. I know what I have to do."

"What's that?"

"I need to see Glenn before the bout. I need to see him now."

"Greg, it's 7:22 p.m."

"Well, actually tomorrow then. May I please importune or better yet impose upon you for a ride? I'll try to get there before their practice. I don't think anyone but Glenn will recognize me. I need to get there before their practice starts and hopefully back before mine starts. I can get out of school a little early. Mr. Vlasco is my last teacher. He has been super since my dad had that *friendly* chat."

The next day:

"Glenn, good to see you. I just came by to say hi and to make sure there were no hard feelings about last summer?"

"Hi, Greg. What do you mean, 'hard feelings last summer?' "

"We were wrestling and I remember injuring your arm and…"

"What? Oh, I remember now. I threw a cross-body ride and reached for your arm and I…or you…well…somehow I hurt my elbow. Yes, I remember. No big deal. It was sore for a little while. I didn't have a cow or anything. Stuff happens. Why do you mention it? Say, aren't you wrestling Thursday? At 123?"

"Actually, yes. You are wrestling at 123 too, right?"

"Then we meet again," chimed Glenn. "I have other moves. So why are you here, Greg? I mean you are pretty much the enemy."

"That's why I am here, Glenn. I felt bad about hurting your arm and I wanted to say I was sorry."

"You're kidding me?"

"No, I really mean it. I am sorry for hurting your arm. I just wanted there to be no hard feelings. Wrestling is hard enough without having other thoughts in your head."

"So you are doing this to psyche me out? It won't help. You better be a lot better or you better be saying your prayers."

"That's what I wanted to hear. No hard feelings then?" asked Greg.

"Not 'til match time," said Glenn, smiling broadly. "Now get out before someone recognizes you as the *enemy*. I think we tarred and feathered the last Flemington Central guy that came down here."

"Good luck," retorted Greg.

"Hey, you, too, Greg...But be prepared, we're going to kill you guys."

After wrestling practice, with Anthony:

"Anthony, I feel better."

"Great," replied Anthony. "But why?"

"Glenn forgave me and now I can forgive myself."

"That is great news, now you can wrestle with Glenn and not with the distraction."

"Yes, I can. Surprisingly, Glenn seemed to barely remember. It was definitely bigger to me than him. Evidently, his injury wasn't as bad as I had supposed. I believe he certainly felt it a normal consequence of wrestling and I told him I was sorry. While I don't really know him that well, I certainly think we are on good terms, at least until Thursday when he will come at me hard. But I bet he won't throw legs much less give up his arm." Greg spoke with sincerity because despite being forgiven, he knew he'd had an improper motive when he'd wrenched Glenn's arm in that match. It still troubled him.

Anthony noticed Greg's somber tone and said, "Forgiving yourself is hard but resolving not to repeat your transgression should help you forgive yourself just as much as receiving forgiveness does."

"Precisely," said Greg as he finally began taking an upbeat tone.

Thursday's match came swiftly. Flemington Central had split four bouts with Canyon Creek and the score was tied at six apiece. Greg and Glenn's bout started. Flemington Central's fans were psyched and it showed. The wrestlers were fairly evenly matched. Glenn was 5' 7" and a little faster; Greg was 5' 9" and fairly strong. Glenn's several years of wrestling showed. Greg, in a less orthodox style, mostly countered and his pancake to double was starting to work.

Glenn came out fired up and after just a few seconds of locking up executed a smooth snap down and spin move to get behind Greg, but Greg sat out quickly to try to avoid the takedown. The referee scored both moves. Suddenly it was 2-1 Firestone.

"Your move Greg, your move!" shouted Coach Gallo as Glenn continued to shoot on Greg who seemed content to sprawl enough to avoid any further takedowns in the period. Period two, Glenn chose bottom. He then jumped to his feet and Greg dropped down on a leg as Glenn turned into him. Greg hung on until a stalemate was called. The partisan crowd cheered as the process continued for the full period with Greg cither lifting his opponent and returning him to the mat or dropping to a leg and performing a smeltsly.

At the end of the two-minute period, Greg had 1:59 seconds riding time, reflecting one second for the quick takedown and escape of the first period and the full two minutes of riding in Greg's favor for the second period. An escape in the first 59 seconds would give Greg a 3-2 win.

Third period and Greg immediately attempted a stand-up, but Glenn drove hard with a tight waist and ankle, keeping Greg on the mat. 10 seconds, 20 seconds, 30 seconds passed. Glenn was maintaining a ride as Greg's stand-up continued to fail. With just five seconds to neutralize the riding time, Greg sprinted off the mat kicking like a mule. He turned in just soon enough to be awarded the timely escape. Glenn again began an aggressive attack, shooting singles and snap downs with Greg moving backwards and off the mat.

With 30 seconds left, the inevitable happened. Greg was warned for stalling. The openly partisan crowd booed but the call was a good one. Greg hadn't made an aggressive move the whole match. Nothing changed for the next 20 seconds. The match was in the hands of the referee and he made the decision. The second warning came with just five seconds left and Glenn was awarded one point.

The bout ended disappointingly in a tie at 3-3.

The team score, now tied again at 8-8, gave Canyon Creek just enough so that they went on to win. After the match, several fans and wrestlers told Greg he was robbed, that he should have won. Greg knew better. He just didn't have it in him. He didn't want to lose but he didn't really want to win. Greg hadn't planned a tie. It just happened. He just couldn't muster the mental edge to be aggressive against Glenn.

"What happened?" Greg asked Anthony the next day.

"We tied."

"How did your Visualization go before the match?"

"It didn't. I never finished it," said Greg.

"Oh," mused Anthony in a concerned tone.

"Anthony, forgiveness isn't binary. You can't flip a switch and presto you forgive and are forgiven. I felt I owed Glenn something and gave it back to him with the tie. But now I feel I cheated my team. No one blames me because they either saw that Glenn was really good, which he was, or that the referee shouldn't have made the call with just five seconds on the clock, only 25 seconds after the first call. You can hang on the smeltsly all day and never get a stalling call. But I didn't really try. Now I let my team down while I was trying to make up for a past transgression. Fairness is hard," sighed Greg. "Did I do the right thing?"

"Greg, I can't answer that for you. But I'm proud that you went to Glenn and attempted to make things right between you. That took courage. As far as the match, only you and God know what was best," offered Anthony. "But Greg, it is very hard when we try to make up for our mistakes. Sometimes things have a way of compounding. What do you think Glenn thought?"

"I didn't think about Glenn."

"Greg, I thought you said you were trying to make it up to Glenn?"

"Well, yes."

"But you didn't think about Glenn's reaction? Do you think he wanted your pity? Do you think he wanted you to throw him a bone in the form of a tie because of what you did?"

"I think he would be truly pissed if he thought I gave him anything. He would have thought of me as self-righteous or something," admitted Greg.

"I agree. Glenn would have been insulted that you were patronizing him. I don't think he's the type that would want your pity. Few do. Most of us want to make it on our own. Your lesson with Glenn started with forgiveness and you did well. Making reparations is also a good thing and is the repent part of **Forgive and Repent**. But reparations for many things are probably best left to God. Once you have apologized, felt true remorse, and committed to not repeat your error, you should move on. If you merely owed someone money, by all means pay it back. But short of that, please exercise extreme caution when attempting any reparation. You should not interfere where you are not welcome."

"This is how the fourth key, **Forgive and Repent,** is meant to work. But Greg, I certainly understand that you weren't excited about being aggressive with Glenn. It was a normal reaction after the injury. Much like the injury itself, I would now take inventory of what has happened. Learn from it. Then move on. This is **The Seven Steps** of the **Personal Growth Cycle** and the **Ten Keys** in action. Please use them. As you go through a forgiveness process of asking and receiving, I recommend you do so alone in prayer."

"Thanks, Anthony. Life is complex, isn't it?"

"Precisely."

Chapter Twelve
The First Real Date

That weekend Greg sees Pam.

They have a study date followed by a real date. A big Saturday. Greg continues to fantasize about Pam. He knows he wants to hold her and kiss her and he's pretty sure she plans on it as well. But the rest of his fantasy intrigues him even more. Since she has been the aggressor, he plans to be patient but tuned into her subtle lead. While she wants to lead she also must want romance and chivalry. *Wow! How am I supposed to know this stuff?* At the same time he relaxed, knowing that not knowing was equally okay. He doubted Pam wanted Don Juan. That is, he hoped she didn't.

When Pam walked in, Greg was already in the study, having just finished a great morning routine: Up at 7:07 a.m., a good round of sprints by 7:47, followed by two hours of study, then bridges, sit-ups, power cleans, benches, and chin-ups until 10:55, a very productive hour of exercise with about a half hour of warm-up and cooldown time. His 300-yard sprints, followed by 30-second rest intervals for 10 to 12 repetitions, with a two-mile run warm-up and a five-minute cooldown, had given him the energy to finish takedowns in the third period.

After sprints he worked out with weights: power cleans and bench presses; sets of eight, five, then three, building to 165 for cleans and 185 for bench. Chin-ups included sets of 30, 25, and then 20-25 and were followed by wrestlers' sit-ups of 100-plus and aggressive bridging. Greg did this routine every Saturday and

Wednesday, except the sprints. He sprinted every Tuesday, Thursday, and Saturday. A hot steamy shower after each session seemed to make him feel he could do anything. At first, his mom complained that he wasted water, but after he explained the critical need for recuperation and cooldown she acquiesced.

Now he felt great. There was something sweet about being cut. As good as a tight physique made him feel, the knowledge that few if any of his competitors were using wind sprints or Zatopek intervals gave him a physical and mental edge. He knew that fewer still were doing power cleans, which combined with chin-ups and benches gave him the raw power to wrestle strong. When you train by picking up 165 for reps in nearly a double-leg motion with power cleans, a 123-128 pound guy could feel pretty light. But it was probably the cathartic value of the hard work and sweat followed by the long, hot shower that truly revitalized and refreshed. He could pop out of the shower and actually feel like doing his whole routine again. That feeling gave him a sense of strength and entitlement. He had earned victory before ever setting foot on the mat.

He rose and walked toward Pam in a relaxed fashion, flashing a very natural and engaging warm smile. His smile unbridled her enthusiasm but her cautious nature held her in check. Sure they had known each other but a few weeks, but it felt like much longer. Greg sensed the same dynamic tension and warm feelings. *Endorphins Corral Frissons*, thought Greg, revealing a part of one of his affirmations within his **Personal Commercial** Anthony had helped construct. The words stuck in his head now. Whenever he would feel even the slightest bit edgy or at the first tinge of nerves, he would say aloud "*Endorphins Corral Frissons.*" He would visualize the endorphins chasing the frissons like a cowboy herding cattle. That thought combined with the near clinical action of the two natural bodily fluids working together had a powerful effect on him. He used it now.

As he watched Pam, he moved straight to his *Endorphins Corral Frissons* affirmation, using the endorphins and very pleasant feelings that came with gazing upon her. The affirmation herded the noradrenalin created frissons. This should be a very special moment. He realized that seeing and moving towards Pam had caused the same potentially crippling feelings that a big match could produce. That's when he jumped quickly to his affirmation and visualized about the endorphins and frissons, or noradrenalin rushes, as Anthony accurately called them. Greg liked the word frisson; the pronunciation of which sounded like the shuddering feeling itself and actually derived from the French word for cold. Anthony helped him use that word in his **Personal Commercial**.

Turning frissons into energy and action allowed Greg's performance to excel. The more feverish the pitch of battle, the better he could now perform; something Bill Russell had that Wilt Chamberlain didn't. Chamberlain always played well but never optimized in the crunch like Russell or Mr. Clutch himself, Jerry West, the guy posing for the NBA logo. Athletes that had it, like Michael Jordan, said the bigger the challenge, the better his game. Exceptional performers were those who could turn excitement, stage fright, fear, or a challenge into dynamic energy that allowed them to perform in their zone. Greg now had it or at least a piece of it and he regularly thanked Anthony for helping him get it.

He used to fear fear. Fear had been the enemy. Now he knew fear was his friend. What helped the caveman escape from wild animals? The frisson did. That shot of noradrenalin gave people energy for *fight or flight*, but when used improperly made one a deer in the headlights, a meal for the predator. Greg now welcomed fear as the trigger to release the body's natural drug that enhanced performance. In fact, both the word frisson and the feeling of a frisson had started to become Pavlovian signals to Greg, provoking the energizing response after just a few weeks of using the **Personal Commercial**. The response was so powerful he began to look forward to frissons.

"Greg, where are you?" Pam asked as he stood in front of her in reverie.

"So much for staying in the moment," blurted Greg.

"Okay, then where did you go?" continued Pam.

"Oh, yes. Well. Do you really want to know?"

"Amuse me," exhorted Pam.

"I was just telling my mom about frissons and endorphins."

"Oh? Endorphins are the good juices that create runners' high? Does this raise or lower the price of tea in China?" asked Pam impatiently.

"That's it, Pam. I was using one of my positive affirmations to help me constructively focus my excitement."

"I excited you? That's good. I *should* excite you but what were you telling your mom?"

"That's not important, but do you want to hear about frissons or not?"

"You're on."

"Well, Anthony, the guy working with me on the mental aspect of wrestling, has given me a powerful tool to deal with fear and excitement. Anthony explained the tool in simple terms. Still with me?"

"I'm all yours."

"*Cool.*"

"It's a figure of speech, Greg. Don't flatter yourself."

"Okay, well, Anthony said endorphins and noradrenalin are natural bodily secretions. Endorphins are the pleasant substances that allow runners to run pain-free for hours. Just as you said Pam — runners' high."

"Yes, I run a little myself. I could be running soon."

"Say, you could do stand-up."

"Carry on, Dr. Gurist."

"Okay, noradrenalin helps one perform at one's peak and in the zone. Staying in the moment and staying calm allows your endorphins to come into play as needed. Staying positive and happy guarantees endorphins will be in good supply. Properly and timely recognizing the need for noradrenalin can only occur in a relaxed state where endorphins and your normal body state are in control, allowing the secretion to come at the precise moment of need."

"So Greg, what happens when one is nervous, like you?"

"Pam, when we, not just me, sense danger, noradrenalin flows. The problem is that often at the moment of fright there is nothing to do with the noradrenalin. So it may just sit in your system until you use it. At first it is perceived as a frisson. If there is no physical action, fight or flight, the noradrenalin just stays. If this is a false alarm (in the form of an unjustified fear) the fright that caused the frisson continues to send the noradrenalin into your system only to run around uncontrolled and cause your muscles to tense up. They use energy and you become nervous, then irritated and then when they are fully consumed, you naturally tire."

"So what happens next?"

"Once you know you have this great ally coming to your defense it behooves you to take control. You want that ally to show up on time but not too early. Therefore — and this is the best part of Anthony's tool — why not take those very healthy endorphins and put them in control. Stay positive and at the peak of alertness. Make a deal with the noradrenalin and promise to tell it when it is necessary. The endorphins help. The endorphins corral the frissons so that you are ready to go at a moment's notice. Stay happy, positive, and in the moment so that you can keep your promise to the frissons and tell them when they are needed."

"I like that, Greg. Does it work?"

"Absolutely. All performers, whether they are public speakers or athletes, have a way of relaxing so that when they need the boost, it is there. Much like the jockey saves the whip for the last crucial sprint, one can control his noradrenalin the same way. The magic starts with that same message. At the very first warning of noradrenalin or frisson, I would begin my visualization of corralling those wild stallion frissons with my cowboy endorphins."

"How about an example? How do you use it?"

"Well, I begin by staying very positive, in the moment and perfectly focused. When I feel even a twinge of a frisson, I visualize the endorphins corralling the frissons. My regular wrestling warm-up, which is now a ritual of sorts, keeps me in a comfortable controlled state. Then as external stimuli come, I corral the frissons with the endorphins. This maximizes my performance."

"So Greg, we're wrestling now?"

"No, but when I'm not in a wrestling mode it works much the same. At the first hint of a frisson I importune the endorphins to corral and team up with the frissons to optimize my performance."

"So what frissons hit you when I walked in? I make you nervous? I'm touched."

"Pam, when you walked in, I immediately felt them. You exhilarated me but didn't incapacitate me because my frissons were nearly immediately corralled by my endorphins. I felt good."

"I wish I had that effect on everybody. I like this frisson corralling tool thing."

"Thanks, I think."

"Greg, you are unpredictable. I like that."

"Pam, your beauty created the frissons."

"I don't usually wear this outfit."

Pam's golden hair, rich and full, fell softly onto her shoulders. Her walk and her sleeveless tank top showed off her beautiful olive colored skin. She looked healthy with the strong yet soft muscles of a young gymnast. Greg was struck with her natural beauty. Her complexion had a pleasingly warm glow. Greg stopped walking towards her as she glided towards him. This marked the second time she had stuck him in his tracks. The frisson made him stop. He inhaled the moment, marveling at her fluid motion. He reacted to the total picture of Pam dressed mostly in black with tights that emphasized her dancer's legs and callipygian fitness.

"I hope you don't mind. I came straight from my dance class. I dried my hair quickly. It will probably frizz a little soon."

"Frizz, no *frisson*", thought Greg. "That's what I'm feeling. No. Warm fuzzies, not frissons."

"What are you thinking, Greg? You're just staring at me, still enraptured by the frissons? I thought they were corralled by now. Don't you like my Danskins?"

"Yes, I like it, them. I said I did. I said you were too beautiful."

"Whatever do you mean, Rhett?"

"Frankly, my dear, I do give a darn."

"Cute. I thought I might catch you with that one. A+."

"What?"

"You've just passed the 'ever read a romance novel?' test."

"Movies count?"

"Of course."

"Neat. Now if I can just ace my SAT."

"Let's see: rent, bifurcate, sew, split; which doesn't fit?"

"That was *sew* easy."

"I think you're on your way. Say, I brought the Western Civ notes, but I'm okay with working vocab. I'm sure glad I got your tongue untied. I thought it might require major surgery. And whatever would I have done with no nitrous oxide and only dull blades? Now tell me, what's this about me being too beautiful? It sounds like a line to me. And by the way, I like it."

"I just couldn't stop thinking about kissing you as you walked in."

"Please decide soon. About Western Civ or vocab, I mean. Are we alone now, Greg?"

"Sort of, my parents are in the living room and my brother should be honoring the detente decree. This should at least assure his spying follows Geneva Convention guidelines."

"Greg, I want to study but I can see a kiss or maybe two wouldn't hurt to start. It took you so long to start on our first date, our *study* date."

"I heard that."

Their kiss started slowly but heated up rapidly. Greg hadn't really done much kissing but her lead made it easy and comfortable. He held her gently at first and then their mutual embrace progressed. The excitement level continued to intensify until a voice, just feet away, broke the passionate silence.

"Yuck! You are *kissing* her! Yuck!"

Greg relaxed his arms but continued to hold Pam, prolonging the wonderful moment. "Allen, we had a deal," Greg said, without leaving Pam's loving visage.

"I know, I just had to get some batteries!" he blurted.

"They're in the kitchen closet next to the pantry...on the top shelf...just where they've been for centuries."

Greg smiled at Pam.

"Centuries?" Pam whispered to Greg. They were both sure Allen already knew where the batteries were.

Ignoring Allen's head-over-shoulder leer, Greg and Pam maintained eye contact as he departed.

As Pam let her arms fall naturally to her side, Greg cupped his hands on her cheeks, cradling her face as he kissed her again passionately. Not a beat was skipped as Allen moved just out of sight.

"Shall we?" Pam asked, as Greg moved to the desk and Pam assumed her supine study mode in the makeshift study area, a.k.a. frontisteria.

Later, they took a stroll and saw *Oliver* at the Flemington Village theatre. They made a pizza from a mix at Greg's house before Pam's dad picked her up. The movie was sad but they both were delighted to know they were equally inspired by the aspirations of an urchin. They kissed again in the movie, which helped to assuage some of the more lugubrious moments and stanch some of the inevitable tears.

That night changed Greg's life. Pam became an influence on him that strengthened his resolve to do his best. He now thought of her when he reached any precipitous moment. He often wondered how she would react to his decisions and actions.

He later described these feelings to Anthony:

"Anthony, I'm 17 years old. Pam's soon 16. Can I be in love?"

"Wasn't Bill Shakespeare's Juliet 15?"

"Don't worry, Anthony, I don't think anyone is going to die here."

"Seriously, Greg, any relationship *you* think is serious *is* serious. How could it be otherwise? You become your own litmus test. I can only say, enjoy and be thankful for all you have and remember life is for keeps. The wins, the losses, the loves won, the loves lost; they all count. They all affect who we are. Your experiences are as real now as they will ever be. Sometimes you may look back and see what you thought was love as merely lust or just the result of a captivating smile that seemed much more."

"Are you saying that Pam and I may just be a flirtation or…worse, simple lust?"

"I think you know."

"I do, Anthony. She is all of my dreams rolled into one. You were right about dating. I would have gladly suffered a thousand rejections knowing Pam would come along. It's almost like you knew she would come."

"Greg, you said it yourself — your pursuit of vocabulary brought her into your life."

"Anthony, Pam is more than I ever thought I could win or deserve. Her beauty humbles me, her intelligence motivates me, and her work ethic makes me a better wrestler."

"I think you just told me, Greg. If you see these things in her, then you have indeed found a wonderful person. However, time makes for a great barometer of relationships and you and Pam are very new to each other. That's not bad. I just recommend you wait before you start choosing a best man."

"Wait Anthony! I've already chosen you as best man!"

"Now, I can affirmatively say you should back off."

"Anthony, come on. I'm kidding. I don't want to marry Pam. Not yet. I'm still a senior. High school students don't get married," Greg said this with a wry smile. It was obvious that Greg was joking about marriage but perhaps serious about Anthony being the

[102]   Steve G. Vogel

best man. He had felt the need to acknowledge the strong bond between them.

Chapter Thirteen
The SAT and The College Decision

The SAT was suddenly upon Greg. With just a week to go he sat down with Anthony to discuss his strategy.

"Did you study vocabulary?"

"I memorized the 2,500 word list Pam gave me. I already knew all but 400 of them. Then I studied two other SAT words lists, one from school and one from my parents. I learned about 10 words per day. It wasn't really hard, that's actually less than one per waking hour. I can't say I know them all but I would guess I know over 98% of them and can probably guess right at another 1%. I'm ready."

"Did you work on grammar and reading comprehension?"

"Just a little on grammar. Like you predicted, my reading comprehension went way up once I improved my vocabulary. How did you know it would work?"

"That's exactly what happened to me."

"You took the SAT?"

"Not exactly," said Anthony. "How about math?"

"I didn't have to do too much math. I love it and I have always been pretty good with numbers. I have worked numerous problems, memorized the important ratios and formulas, and improved my speed under pressure, but I am still nervous."

"Greg, have you used your exercise for nervousness, your frissons tool?"

"That's exactly it. The SAT seems different. The exercise doesn't seem to work very well. The fear is so shapeless or amorphous and I find it hard to grasp. So much that I don't know how to redirect the frissons with my endorphins. I don't know when they are coming and I'm not real clear what to do with them when I discover them."

"True Greg, the unseen enemy is the most feared. Since your affirmation isn't working you must stop and find this protean beast you fear. Fundamental to fear is the unknown. Most fears fade once viewed in the light of day. Then based upon your faith in yourself, God, and the Universe, fears lose their mystery and their power. So tell me, what is it, exactly, that bothers you?"

"I do know I need to do very well and the competition is intense to get into the top schools. I know I have but one chance to take the SAT and if I don't improve on my average score I won't get into an Ivy League school. If that happens, all my other hopes and dreams may disappear. There is no net here, Anthony, and I'm only 17. It doesn't seem fair. I don't have a way out. That's it! That's why the frissons won't go. There is no way out — *huit clos*."

"Good, Greg, so if you were to find a way out and could get some comfort as to fairness, you could corral the frissons with the endorphins?"

"I'm sure of it," Greg hurriedly replied, knowing Anthony had an answer that couldn't come too soon.

"What if you don't get into an Ivy League school? There are excellent schools outside the Ancient Eight. Second, if you make great grades, transferring becomes an option. Third, excellent grades from a solid university will get you into a top tier graduate school. What is most important to you?"

"What I really want is a great education from an East Coast school that can help make me a national champ."

"So tell me, Greg, how well do academics and wrestling combine?"

"That's the problem. Staying on the East Coast eliminates the perennial wrestling powers of Iowa, Iowa State, Oklahoma, and Oklahoma State. Of the Ivies, Penn, Harvard, and Cornell do well in wrestling. But the schools I like most, where both academics and wrestling seem to blend well, are Michigan and Lehigh. Michigan isn't close to the East Coast, thus Lehigh, Penn, and Cornell are my only real choices."

"So with your current SAT and GPA, which schools might you get into?"

"Based upon my guidance counselor's assessment, if I finish at my current top 5% class rank, I should get into Michigan and Lehigh but perhaps not the Ivy League schools. I need to do much better on the SAT."

"Greg, are you interested in the Ivy League?"

"That's my problem Anthony. I've studied hard for the SAT and I would love to get into the Ivy League, but I'm not sure I really want to get in. I mean *go*."

"Why?"

"Anthony, I feel compelled to go to the best school, an Ivy League school. I should place academics first and go. There may be NCAA champs from Columbia, Harvard, Princeton, Penn, and Cornell, albeit precious few."

"I see your conflict, but wouldn't you rather put yourself in a position to make the decision rather than allow the SAT folks make it for you? Until you get into one of those schools, you can't turn them down."

"That's just it. I wouldn't be able to. That's why I am so conflicted."

"Greg, your problem is tortuous. I don't have an answer..."

"Wow, Anthony! This is a first," Greg interrupted.

"But," Anthony said, "I think *you* can find an answer. Be sure to sit down and make a list of any and all reasons this process may bother you. After your review, prayer and meditation may help you resolve this cognitive dissonance, your unsettled feeling. Be sure to work hard on your list first, remember the adage 'the Lord helps those who help themselves?' The Lord only helps those who truly need and deserve His help."

"I get it. I'll work it through. You'll help too?"

"Precisely. I'm here. By the way, Greg, after your conflict is resolved, be sure to use the same controlled warm-up for the SAT that you use for wrestling. That way you can turn on the 'Endorphins Corral Frissons' visualization."

Greg did the exercises Anthony had suggested. He went through lists of why he feared the SAT. While some made sense, some didn't and he couldn't be certain which were most responsible for his fear. After a painstaking effort Greg was certain that he had worked through most of his fears. He had found a solution to each. He was prepared for and expected success and his back-up plans were so solid that failure wouldn't be feared. He had a totally positive attitude, like Mr. Clutch who always wanted to take the last shot. He wanted the ball.

One such fear he originally discounted, but Anthony told him to pursue nonetheless, turned out to be the most real: his parents. He loved his parents and their praise, but it seemed with each incremental success their requests of him continued to mount. They had already set the bar so high that the best he could ever do was meet their expectations. He could never exceed them. With that, he felt doomed to fail. He just didn't know when.

Anthony encouraged Greg to share this with his parents. Greg waited until Saturday just after dinner, just before Pam came over.

"Mom, Dad, it's never easy for me to start a very serious conversation with you guys so I'm just going to start. You know I love you both very much. Don't you?"

"Son, what's wrong?"

"Well Mom, it's about college."

"I have been doing my best to understand your study time. What, hasn't your brother been good about it?"

"No, Mom. Allen has been fine."

"What then?"

"It's me — no; it's you two."

"Greg, you are usually more articulate than this."

"Think loquacious, son, not laconic," chimed Mr. Gurist.

"Greg, what's the problem? Has Mr. Vlasco said something?" asked his mom.

"Dad, I feel I am living my life for you, not me. It seems whatever I do it's not good enough. I am not even sure which college I want to go to because you guys are always telling me what I should want."

"Son, we are only trying to help," they both said in near unison.

"Look, the weight of the expectations you placed on me feels like an albatross around my neck. I don't feel free to move, to be myself."

"Greg, we have supported your wrestling. We like Pam. We do support you."

"Yes, but the approval feels conditioned upon my next performance. You have no idea how much these expectations have placed a burden on me. They stifle me. They confuse me. I only recently realized why I was having so much trouble with the SAT."

"Why, Son?" said his dad.

"It was that I wanted to choose the college I would go to and if I did really well on the SAT, then you would choose my college."

"That's ridiculous, Son. We support you. Can I ask where you want to go to school?"

"I don't know but I may choose Michigan or Lehigh over Harvard, Princeton, or Yale."

"Why, Greg?" asked his mom.

"First, I think the academics at Lehigh and Michigan are very comparable to the Ivies. Did you know that the percentage of undergrads that go to professional schools is very sizable for all of these schools?"

"Second," Greg continued, "wrestling is a very real factor. I know wrestling will make me a better person. It already has. The discipline I use to study, I developed through the discipline of hard training for wrestling. This same discipline has improved my grades. Did you notice my grades improved last year as I switched from basketball to wrestling? Wrestling has helped me deal better with Allen. It even helped me find Anthony."

"Son, we will try to stop setting off the fusillade of expectations you deride. We are proud of you now. We do want you to continue to improve, but we don't want it to be a burden on you, certainly we don't want to be an albatross! We do accept you for who you are. We would still love for you to go to Harvard or Yale," said his dad.

"Or Penn, like your father," interjected Mrs. Gurist.

"Yes, Dad, but you went as a graduate student and I could do the same."

"Please let me finish," continued Mr. Gurist. "Greg, you can absolutely choose your school. I believe that you will do well, wherever you go. And we will always have our sights set sky high for you. Don't take that away from us. But please know that we fully respect your decisions and who you are. Personally, I am glad you have come to us with this. You *are* ready to be more independent. I support it."

"Me, too," said Mrs. Gurist. "I'm your mom and I will always be your mom and I will always want the best for you. I'm still going to tell you things you don't want to hear but you should feel it's okay to have it your way. I also support your decisions. You can choose your college. Is that what you wanted to hear?"

"Well, yes!" said Greg. "Yes, I want to pick the school and still feel I have your 100% support and approval."

"Son, would you like this in writing?"

"Only if you think I need it in writing. So Dad, do I?"

Greg enabled his parents to see the seriousness of his dilemma and why he was so conflicted. He had high enough expectations of himself. With the albatross of his parents ever-rising expectations he had often felt crippled. When his parents fully understood, they supported him. He found later that they were truly mortified that their praise and expectations had become such a big obstacle in his path. The big confrontation helped. Greg felt emancipated. Sure, he relied economically upon his parents, but it seemed like his decisions, short of being self-destructive, would have their full support.

Greg now thought, as he walked into the SAT, that his fear had been the best thing that could have happened. It had gotten his parents to preemptively bless his college decision. How else could he truly make the decision himself?

Greg entered the large examination room. It was game day and he was relaxed and playful. He followed the same routine as when he prepared for wrestling. *He was not going to let his attitude happen by chance.* The frissons queued to help with the heavy lifting of the exam. They would help when needed. His Endorphins

[110] Steve G. Vogel

had Corralled his Frissons. His Visualization worked. They made it fun.

Chapter Fourteen
Pam Meets with Greg's Parents

Pam greeted Greg as he exited the examination room:

"How was it?" she asked.

"That's it? How was it? I expected, 'well, did you give a whit about using your wit?' "

"Gee, Greg, now I am worried. You're using the weakest of puns. What do I ever see in you?" She laughed. "How about pizza? Oops. Hey! I'll eat all the crust. The cheese and the sauce won't kill you."

"Okay. You're right. That sounds good. I can have a pizza treat and still stay close to my eating schedule. Wash it down with iced lemon water and I'll be mighty fine."

"Great. Let's go."

"Hey, I still can't. I didn't get in my Saturday workout this morning because I didn't want to lose the edge going into the exam. I am way too mellow after sprints and a shower. I also have some iron to pull. Can we have pizza at my house in say two hours?"

"Can you make it an hour and a half?"

"Sure, if you don't mind me stinky."

"How about I get there a little early and you rush things a little for me. There's a documentary about the war I need to watch for Western Civ. I mean *we* need to watch for Western Civ. It starts at six. Please tell your parents I'm coming."

"Sweet. See you, Pam."

"See you. Hey, how did you do?"

Greg turned back. "I was beginning to think you didn't care. There were two words I didn't know, aperçu, for one, and a couple whose meaning I wasn't 100% certain of, but on the whole, I felt good. I got through the reading comprehension without a real rush. That gives me great confidence. Heh, I might set the bar so high you won't be able to beat me."

"So you think you got a perfect score?"

"I didn't say that."

"Oh, I think you did. You don't think I could get a perfect score? Some do. More than a few who get into the Ivies do. On the other hand, it appears the Ivies take pride in refusing a few perfect SAT scorers each year. MIT's really the smart school; they let all perfect SAT scorers in."

"Pam. Let's talk later." Greg kissed her on the cheek and headed towards home.

"It means, sudden insight, Greg."

"What?"

"Aperçu means a sudden insight. Cool word."

Greg was mentally wasted and Pam could be exhausting. *Trouble in paradise?* No, even at their worst they felt more right than anything else in his life. Even wrestling, he thought. *Wow! Even wrestling.*

Greg headed home at breakneck speed. He mentally worked on what he could cut. Sprints, power cleans, benches, and chins were the cornerstones. He could do chins later, during the date, he thought. I wonder if Pam could do one. "Two birds," he said, an excuse to see Pam do a chin-up and a way to save time. After the SAT talk, Pam wouldn't shirk from any challenge. He would do chins, bridges, and sit-ups with her, after the pizza. He could challenge her to all of them. I should call and warn her to wear her tights; nothing to lose there. He called her and left a message with her mother just saying, "Dress to exercise." He was pretty sure telling her mom she should wear her slinky Danskins was risky at best. Regardless, Mrs. Dega always sounded so happy and today was no exception. Greg was sure she approved.

Greg's sprints went well. He logged the times of each doing 300-yard dashes down his street, mid Fyfe and Drum, where he had marked them off. 49, 49, 48, 48, 48.5, 48, 48, 48, 47.5, 47 = 48+1, he thought, or a 48.1. Now he was sure he did well on the SAT, at least the math part. With just a 30-second interval between sprints he still felt good. Still, he was a long way from his 45-second target but solid nonetheless. The gasping felt good. He used to dread wind sprints at school on the mats; now he looked forward to them. What was once a gasping pain became a friendly feeling to Greg. Like the frissons converted to healthy fluids Greg knew these pains were but symptoms of fully taxing his aerobic capacity. Without that unpleasant sensation how could he know if he had pressed hard enough to challenge his heart, lungs, and legs to do more? He felt the same when he worked with the heavier guys and he did sets of squats with them on his back in a fireman's carry position. Back and forth, each carrying the other until the lungs and quads burned and the back ached. Like heavy power cleans, it definitely helped his wrestling.

Warming up for cleans and benches and cooling down from the sprints, Greg moved his arms and did some duck walks on his way back to his house. Seeing these antics used to cause a few of the neighbors to look askance but now they just wave and sometimes ask how the season is going. However, the sprints could still cause a minor trauma for the elder neighbors with poor vision or hearing. The road was well traveled and Greg's sprint path led straight down the newly paved street. He walked the sidewalk now and kept warm and loose. He grew excited about lifting.

Getting stronger during the season usually happened only to wrestlers who never worked out in the off-season. Guys lifting year round saw only modest gains. With Greg's serious weight cutting his lifts dipped more than he wanted them to but they were respectable. He still felt ripe for a recent best. He wouldn't go for a single max, but he would see if he could get a max weight for four. In the bench, a 185 for four was his short-term goal. After a 135 for eight reps and a 165 for five reps he moved to 185. With two quick ones the third one was a struggle and the last a real struggle, but he got it. No wonder my workout partners seem lighter this year. I am stronger.

Cleans were next. A power clean represented a work of art much like a kip-up on the high bar. To perform it properly requires that you pull the bar smoothly from the floor and pop it as it moves past your hips and catch it with a dip onto your shoulders. The rhythmic movement and the solid thud of the bar against his chest and shoulders made Greg feel alive and powerful. His 155 by five felt great. His third with 170 felt even better.

It seemed seconds later and he was feeling the brisk streams flowing from the showerhead onto his arms, shoulders, back, and thighs. The hot water pounded his flesh while he gently flexed, soaped, and rubbed his muscles. It felt good not just in the shower but later that day. He knew he recovered faster. Like drinking water during practice, it helped recovery time. He used to skip drinking water to toughen up but he found the water helped him work harder, recover faster, and generally produced better results. He now felt warm, relaxed, and oops, maybe late.

He jumped out of the shower just in time to hear his mother yell, "Pam's here, come on down…or should I send her up?"

Wow, his mom's progressiveness would have been enthusiastically welcomed had it been better timed.

"I'll be down in a second," retorted Greg. Launching a full-scale attack on his dresser he retrieved underwear, pants, socks, and his favorite red Lacoste shirt. Almost jumping into his clothes he managed to reach the living room just seconds later. He looked in and saw Pam in a red top with a long black skirt. Coincidentally, the two of them matched. Greg has chosen black cords with his red polo.

"Darling, you do know how to tango, don't you?" said Pam. Then Greg's parents broke the silence in laughter.

"Yes, I do," stated Greg emphatically. "Quite well in fact…Scarlett," he added. "Care to dance in celebration of my SAT?"

"But you don't know how you did. You can't really," said Pam.

"Who said we were celebrating my high score? I thought we were celebrating the release of the three-month grip they've had over me! Haven't you all said I have been a bit edgy lately?"

"A *little*?" challenged his mom.

"Mom, please, we have company," said Greg with a mile-wide-smile. "Okay. I'm back. But please expect the edginess to return in time for Regions."

"I thought you were aiming for States, Greg? I'm a little disappointed. I wanted a State Champ boyfriend to take me to the spring formal. Too bad that Easton guy hasn't called me back…yet," Pam said with a wink.

"Pam, I was a little worried based upon your reputation for scholarship that you might have you hands full with a guy like Greg," joked Mom.

"Oh contraire, ma mere," quipped Greg. "Pam is about five or ten jousts up on me with intellectual witticisms, sarcasm, and puns. After I threw down the gauntlet, she picked it up and slapped my face with it."

"Ouch," said Pam. "Brand new and yet so familial this all seems."

"See, Mom? She's safe enough for now, at least until I take her to the Christmas Dance."

"But, Greg? Oh what shall I ever wear?"

"Don't ask me now, but if they let you dress for modern dancing, you can come as you are. See, Mom, a perfectly matched pair we are. Don't worry about us."

The evening turned into a *meeting with the parents* date. Greg hadn't told his parents to stay out of sight. He had rushed through his workout and the thought hadn't occurred to him. Fortunately his brother was out at a basketball game with friends. Pam seemed to rise to the occasion. Parents may intimidate some, but Pam seemed as comfortable in Greg's living room as anyone else there.

His parents were equal parts fascinated and impressed. Pam presented an intelligent, confident, and demure young lady. Although she clearly showed her feminine side, her well-grounded demeanor and humility made her appear exceptionally mature. In fact, her outfit was proof. A tight leotard-like top could look seductive or little girlish. The fact that his parents didn't even seem to notice her outfit proved to Greg they thought her very sophisticated.

After the family sharing of pizza, salad, and dessert, Greg excused himself and Pam to his room where he said they would play darts. Greg's statement went uncontested and the two quickly disappeared, leaving Greg's mom and dad to revisit the evening. Their approval of Pam was clear. When they saw their mutual respect and high regard, they were no longer suspicious of Greg's deep and sudden attachment to Pam. She was the real McCoy.

Greg took Pam straight to his closet where he had his chin-up bar. He playfully demanded to see if she could do a chin-up. While flipping off her shoes, Pam slipped off her skirt and Greg's eyes almost popped out. They might have hadn't he quickly realized that she was merely removing the wraparound skirt covering her Danskins.

"Hey, warn a guy or something," Greg said. Pam meanwhile progressed from one to two to three and even squeaked out a fourth chin-up.

"I know, not bad for a girl."

"Heck, not bad for anybody. I'm impressed."

"Okay smarty, now you. How about a googol? You know, ten to the hundredth? Show me what you've got," Pam said as she rewrapped her skirt, stopping Greg in his tracks literally, again.

"Well?" she said.

"Well, give me a second here. You have unfairly distracted me."

"Oh, you want this back off?" She said coyly.

Now they both knew she had his number and could play it on cue.

"I don't normally do my chin-ups with my eyes closed but I may have to now."

"Oh really? Still afraid of me? Are the endorphins having trouble with the frissons, Greg Gurist?"

Greg ignored the question and proceeded to knock off 32 chin-ups.

"Well?"

"Okay, not bad, shy of a googol but not bad. Now let me feel those biceps, Greg."

Steve G. Vogel

"No way!" Greg blurted. "I mean why?"

"You felt my biceps when I first came to your house. Remember? I didn't put up such a fuss. Did I?"

"Er...okay, sure. I mean no, you didn't. Of course you can," said Greg as he shyly rolled up his sleeve.

Pam moved or rather glided forward, continuing to amaze him. "Both arms," she said as she grabbed both biceps. Then in one natural motion she pulled his arms toward her and wrapped them around her waist.

"Here," she said. "Stop the fuss. I'm with you now. Can I feel your abs? Steve says his abs make him feel fit, like his biceps make him feel strong," Pam commented as she slid her hand innocently under his shirt. "I do feel safe here," she said suddenly as she affectionately touched his hard stomach. Pam then began to hug Greg, showing an especially vulnerable and loving side that would have been unimaginable just seconds before in front of his parents.

Wow! Greg thought. She made me feel better than any spoken words ever had. Without thinking, he picked her up and carried her to his bed, not considering his next step. She didn't object. He laid her down gently and contemplated lying beside her but felt a bit compromised. His brother could walk in at any minute and his parents could knock at the door just to say goodnight, or to ask when Pam's parents were due. He knelt beside her and began to kiss her. This time he was leading and not following. He let his heart guide him, much as he had let her guide him during their last embrace.

"I want you," she said.

Greg didn't say a word. He was thinking: *I want you, too.* He then said it, "I want you, too. But Pam we can't. I can't."

"Not here, not now, silly. I'm not talking about lovemaking, Greg. I'm talking for keeps. I want you. I want to be with you. I hope I'm not scaring you."

"No, Pam, as long as you don't have a pair of scissors in your hands, you won't scare me," Greg said in an unsuccessful attempt to lighten the conversation. Then he decided to take a chance and tell Pam how he really felt.

"Pam, you are scaring me, but I confess I like it. When I see you, when I see you move, anytime, anywhere, all I can think about is how much I want you to be a part of my life. I've told Anthony about you. He asked me if I was going too fast too soon and I said yes, but that nothing had happened between us."

"Greg, this is not about sex. This is much more important. Sex can make people feel closer, but truthfully I can't imagine it. I can't imagine feeling any closer. But I want to."

"You want to what?" asked Greg.

"I want to feel even closer to you. Sex or not, I don't even think it matters that much."

"Oh, it matters a lot. I think about it all the time."

"Really? With me? With others?"

"Pam, let me finish. From the first moment I saw you in class when you sat down right in front of me, I have been uncomfortable in Western Civ."

"What?"

"Yes, Pam. I have been thinking about you all year, and long before you suggested we study together. Thank goodness I nearly stumped Thomas on those words. I feel we make a great match, no, a perfect match. I want us to be close, always."

Ring, Ring. The phone's unmistakable high-pitched tintinnabulation signaled Pam's dad would appear in minutes. But the spell was not broken. Short of professing love or perhaps beyond expressing love, Pam and Greg took a huge step that would connect their hearts and souls. They knew it and their parents suspected it and realized there was little that could or should be done. These were two young adults who appeared to understand life as few teens could.

They were close after that night. The banter was always spirited and Pam would tease Greg incessantly, especially at school, so that few ever suspected their mutual respect, increasing devotion, and blossoming love. This dissembling kept life interesting. It also kept the school from discussing them as the intense hopelessly-in-love couple that they most certainly were. Only their parents knew. Few suspected that it was much deeper than a kinship of dueling wits, personifying a relationship befitting the troubled youth of the era.

That night also marked a night of calm resolve for Greg. He knew what he wanted and he knew it wouldn't be easy to achieve. Few high school romances made it, certainly not the college bound. Greg and Pam knew they both would grow. They each had, unbeknownst to the other, vowed to find a way to go to school and not get caught up in the whole lurid college scene.

The relationship helped improve Greg's wrestling. He worked every bit as hard – maybe harder – but he never got lost in it. He made it a priority to have fun. He used the two keys in unison, **Work Hard, Have Fun**. When the pressure came, he rarely felt it.

Chapter Fifteen
Christmas Break

Anticipating the Christmas holidays, Pam's parents scheduled a trip to Boston to be with her family. They invited Greg to come, showing how much they respected and trusted him. But Greg had a holiday wrestling tournament and, to further complicate matters, Pam's 16th birthday fell during the break. Everyone struggled to make suitable plans. No one felt fully satisfied with any of the alternatives.

Coming to the rescue, Greg's parents offered Pam the option to stay with them and sleep on a reasonably comfortable foldout bed in the study. Pam's parents did not object to Pam staying over but really wanted to be with her on her birthday. Finally one compromise proposed seemed to appeal to all. Pam would go to Boston and stay for Christmas and her birthday but would come back in time to see Greg wrestle in the Scotts Valley tournament.

Greg and Pam then planned the night of the tournament for a personal celebration of Pam's birthday, Christmas, and their reunion. His parents would be traveling most of that day but would return late that night. Greg and Pam would likely have from about eight until midnight alone. Assuming his wrestling went well, Greg would be in Finals until seven and home by eight. So, when Pam arrived that day she was to come either late to the tournament or meet him at home at eight after securing a key from trusted neighbors.

One scheduled train could put her in town by five and as she hoped to get to the tournament at least in time for Finals, Greg and Pam both knew that it could be tough. She could be later than planned and surely would be tired from the trip. Whether she made it or not, Gallo had promised the wrestlers making Finals, and their significant others, safe passage home, even if it took a bus, he had said jokingly.

Soon the holidays were upon them.

The Scotts Valley tournament, an all-day Saturday tournament, attracted nearly 200 wrestlers from New Jersey/Pennsylvania and New York, with the bulk of the wrestlers from the New Jersey/Pennsylvania border, from both public and private schools. The entry fee was minimal and students usually paid their own fees. The event was held at the high school in Scotts Valley. The draw was random. The weight classes were usually similar or close to regulation high school weights, although a large or small contingent of entries in any weight class would cause changes. This made it somewhat risky to attempt to cut weight as you could end up cutting only to end up giving up as much as five to seven pounds. This actually made it easier for most participants as the tournament fell just after Christmas when most wrestlers were a little heavier than in season.

Greg reasoned that 125, which had been a popular weight at the tournament, would be a good weight for him to enter. Greg weighed in at just under 125 to find shortly thereafter that the weight classes were 105, 112, 119, 126, 133, etc. He felt good that he would not be giving up but a pound to some lucky guy weighing in at 126.

His weight class had 24 entries, which gave one third of the wrestlers byes, meaning they didn't have to wrestle the first round. Thus two thirds of the athletes had to wrestle five bouts to win.

The tournament had no wrestle backs, so that it was sudden death up to Semi-Finals. The losers of the Semi-Finals would wrestle for third place. With no wrestle backs, if you were so unfortunate as to run into a State Champ early, you were done early. No one seemed to mind. The bouts took place on four mats and the brackets were posted behind the stands. Some wrestlers were eliminated when they failed to show up for their bouts simply because, despite loudspeaker announcements, they mistook the mat number or color.

Greg saw his chart and only recognized one name other than his own. Don Tasker. He wrestled for Grover High School. He was an Eastern Pennsylvania Regional Champ at 123. He displayed an imposing physique of a chiseled 5' 7" with an especially thick upper body. Greg's jaw dropped as he saw the bracket. Meeting Tasker in the Finals was one thing but he had him the second match, which was Tasker's first. Well, Greg said to himself, this is great news. Either I get home early and meet Pam's train or I beat Tasker and win my first tournament. I don't know anyone else here who could beat me. Greg was sure that Tasker had no idea who he was, but he knew that he would be watching him wrestle his first bout. Greg then worked on strategy.

Greg considered one strategy. To conserve energy he could go for a quick fall, assuming his first opponent cooperated. But that would put Tasker on notice. He decided he would just do very little. Just tie up the first period and not let much happen. Then wait until the third period to get a reversal or takedown to win. His strategy would be to wrestle defensively and coast. He wanted to keep it all in the bank for Tasker. This was important but could become critical as bouts while planned to be an hour apart could end up just 25 minutes apart. One couldn't accurately predict.

The match began with Greg's opponent driving hard and fast on a single leg. The guy seemed pretty quick and reasonably strong but not very smooth. Greg fortunately saw it coming but was a little late in reaction. He threw his right arm and elbow into the driving shoulders of his opponent and sprawled hard, exerting a lot more energy than planned. The move worked and the challenger was flat but had gotten in deep on Greg's leg. Greg reached over, grabbed his opponent's leg over the top, and locked him up. As both wrestlers continued to work the ref let the action continue. Greg found himself in control with just a few seconds left on the clock. *I need to hang on to hold the two*, Greg thought. An escape would make it 2-1. Greg held with just a tight waist and far leg, cautious not to tip Tasker on the leg holding smeltsly.

Second period Greg had choice and took down. He relaxed, hoping to be ridden out the period with little or no action. His opponent had other ideas and moved hard on a crossface and near leg and had Greg on his side close to points. Before Greg could counter, he ended up rolling through and giving up two back points. Doing nothing was harder than I thought, Greg told himself. He then began working to control the arm of his opponent, getting a hold of the wrist. He turned in for a switch, but the guy stepped over and nearly caught Greg again for back points. Greg felt a frisson move through his system. Doesn't this guy know I'm saving my energy for Tasker? Greg grimaced with a smile and pulled himself up.

Okay, stand up, Greg, he thought. The score was 2-2 and by now his opponent had a point for riding time built up. If the match stopped now he would lose. Greg stood up, broke away, and turned in quickly just off the mat and the wrestlers were brought back to center. He had escaped but wasn't awarded the point because they were off the mat, or so called the ref. Greg did the same move again but broke free while still on the mat. Now he had a not-so-comfortable margin with riding time working against him.

In the third period, Greg knew he had to either ride him out the whole time or go for back points. Just riding him out seemed too risky. Greg needed back points. He looked for a cradle when his opponent sat out in an escape attempt. Maybe he could catch him. Greg kept the tight waist near elbow pressure on and soon his opponent sat-out. Greg released him but before he could turn in for an escape or reversal, he chinned him back and held him for two back points. But he slipped out of Greg's grasp and escaped. There, Tasker wouldn't fear a chin-back. The score was now 5-3 in favor of Greg with less than one minute on the clock. Greg now coasted like he had hoped he could the whole match. Afterwards Greg talked to the coach.

"Say Coach, it's harder to try to slide by than to win."

"That's right. Volume control's always difficult. Wrestling works more like a light switch than a dimmer switch. Greg, I see it all the time, at all levels. Once an athlete loses the strong desire to succeed, his wrestling takes a real tumble. Didn't you want to win that one? It looked like you didn't."

"Actually, Coach, I attempted to lay low, knowing I have Tasker in the next round."

"Oh yeah? Tasker. I see his name."

"I hoped he might be at a higher weight class. He's pretty big for 126. Did you see him?"

"Actually, I'm not sure I would recognize him. But don't worry you didn't impress him with that match. I bet he thinks you're just another fish on his path to a trophy. I think he won this last year."

"Well, he won't win it this year!" said Greg emphatically.

"Then you'll have to do a lot better than that, Greg."

"Hey, Coach, I told you I was laying low."

"Yes, really low. He put you on your back. I haven't seen you on your back since Dore picked you up and dropped you. I even think that was just in fun."

"If Tasker catches you letting up, you won't need the ride home, you'll have time to walk."

"Don't worry, Coach."

Fifty-five minutes later Greg heard his name over the loudspeaker as he completed his Visualization. He had never really cooled down so he still felt good to go. He still had the lingering taste of battle. Greg knew the taste as the one that football players try to get out of the way early. Sometimes through helmet butting or locker butting they would attempt to mirror that first contact to take the edge off. In wrestling, a player may slap his own face or his headgear; everything works a little, nothing replaces a few seconds of actual battle. Greg felt *frissons* — his new best friend. That and the crossface to his back had awakened him. He didn't underestimate anyone, certainly not Tasker.

The buzzer went off. Tasker tied up quickly and went to work on gaining an underhook for a throw. Greg didn't feel comfortable giving the underhook even though it might give him an opening if he moved first, quick and hard. Tasker felt strong, real strong — too strong. Greg knew he had a fairly strong upper body, maybe as strong as any he had faced before Tasker. It was Tasker who moved first and locked his arms and moved in for a bear hug and Greg turned in and gave up the takedown while avoiding back points. "Two, red," called the ref. After they moved off the mat, Greg got a fresh start in the down position. He knew he had to move quickly. Tasker was strong. Instead of a stand-up, Greg race crawled forward and Tasker lunged forward trying to grab hold of his feet. "One point escape, green!" yelled the ref.

Greg had had enough of tying up with Tasker. Greg kept backing up and backing up until they went off the mat. Once more, twice more, Greg continued to back away. Just as Tasker grew impatient with the pursuit and less cautious in his forward motion, Greg dropped low on Tasker's legs and tied them both up tight for a very controlled double leg. He almost lifted them high enough for back points as he put Tasker down and turned him towards his back. Tasker twisted hard, regained his base, stood up, and was out in a few seconds. Greg had his takedown and had found Tasker's Achilles heel, he had almost no sprawling ability! Was it weak legs or back? Regardless, Greg felt that once he went under him and got in on the legs the takedown was his. With the score tied at three apiece Greg went to work.

He again faked a tie-up, backed off then shot. This time it worked even better than the first. But now after the takedown he hung onto Tasker's legs and rode him low until the end of the period. Leading 5-3 after one, Greg worked hard and had Tasker beat. Soon, the ref blew the whistle and raised Greg's arm. Tasker looked dumbfounded.

Gallo appeared no less shocked and in attempting to cover up his surprise made it all the more visible to Greg. "Did you see his arms?" said Gallo.

"Nice match, Gurist. Nice match. Beautiful double, but you hung on his leg for nearly two minutes — smeltsly you call it? Eventually they'll call you for stalling on that."

"Maybe in States, Coach. We can worry about it then."

Greg won his next two bouts with less fanfare, although each presented its own challenges. He'd learned from Tasker that while his own moves were important, he also had to take into account his opponent's strengths and weaknesses. This had come to him in his visualization. After he saw how Tasker was built, he had trouble visualizing using a pancake on him or even working many upper body moves. He also found that in his visualization his natural tendency was to work his high-percentage moves on the lower body. He visualized the use of what worked, even if it included some *junk* moves in order to ride guys or control the match, like the smeltsly and backing away. Sure they weren't pretty, they would never make the highlight reels but did increase riding time, help set up takedowns, and they work. Backing away seemed to be incredibly effective on the impatient aggressive type. Greg now remembered they used to work on him. Sure, he would like to pin everyone like Mulino or Gable.

The Finals would start in minutes and Pam still wasn't there. I guess I'll see her at home, he thought. He asked Gallo one more time if he had seen her and to look out for her. Greg stepped out for the Finals bout against another very solid wrestler from Pennsylvania who had placed in Regions at a lower weight. Greg thanked himself for not indulging at Christmas. Pam's absence had made his dieting a little easier. Although she was very considerate in what she ate in front of him, she couldn't resist a little chocolate. This didn't always help Greg who had his own challenges with chocolate. But he yearned for syrupy French toast.

Greg used backing away, circling, and locking up the leg to control the tempo and his opponent. He controlled and won a close bout using all the tools he knew to work. He looked more workmanlike than flashy but nonetheless had Flemington Central fans standing and cheering widely. Pam must be at home, he thought as he searched for her face in the crowd even as his hand was raised in victory. Coach Gallo cheered, stood up proud, and talked to other coaches about his strong team.

Gallo, often given to hyperbole, helped lift Greg and said, "We'll have a classroom named after you for this." The team laughed and the bus ride home went by rapidly. Greg felt very high from his win but he realized how much more fun it would have been had Pam been there. For a brief moment he felt his heart stop and he got a sick, hollow feeling, maybe he should have gone with her to Boston. The Scotts Valley tournament win felt great, but what did it prove? Well, it did yield a cool trophy but it wouldn't guarantee me a wrestling scholarship, thought Greg. The State tournament presented *the* ticket for most wrestling scholarships. No State title, no scholarship. There were few exceptions.

"This did build my confidence," Greg thought. "I'll wrestle differently now. I will consider my opponent first. I will take advantage of junk when necessary and I will let the match come to me instead of force it. Oh yes, and I won't try to coast!"

Chapter Sixteen
Pam's Return to New Jersey

    Greg fiddled with the keys in the door, desperately hoping to find Pam inside or to see her coming to open it. He put his trophy down on the coffee table in the living room, excited to show Pam but not finding her. He called the neighbor to see if she had stopped by. No, they hadn't seen her. Greg had been fairly sure she would make it to the tournament. When she didn't come he figured she might have been tired and wished to rest for their big evening. But no sign at all seemed strange. He wondered if her parents had changed their minds. Perhaps they had become nervous about her only partially chaperoned visit.

    Greg searched for the number Pam had given him for her aunt in Boston. He soon found it and called. In a few seconds Pam's mother answered. "Hi, Greg, how are you? How did the tournament go?"

"Oh great, Mrs. Dega. I won."

"Good to hear, Greg. How did Pam like the train? Can you put her on?"

"Well, no ma'am. She's not here yet."

"Not there? Greg, we put her on the 8:08 train from South Station. *She should have been to your house or the tournament by 4 or maybe 5 at the latest.* We actually expected her to call but assumed a call from the tournament…it might be difficult. So we thought you two would call when you got back to your house. Greg, have the neighbors heard from her?"

"No, I called them first. I looked for her at the tournament and the coach looked for her, too, and he didn't see her. She's not here."

"Okay, Greg, we'll call you when we hear. Please call us, too," said Mr. Dega who had taken the phone from Mrs. Dega after she screamed for him. He hung up quickly.

Because Pam had always been so responsible, everyone feared the worst. She had always stayed in constant communication. Her parents knew her whereabouts 24 hours per day. Although occasionally a joker, she wasn't much of a prankster. Her parents called the South Station and found out that all the outbound trains had run that day without incident. They called the local police and then State Police in New Jersey. After being put on hold by the New Jersey State Police for what seemed an eternity, and after Mr. Dega painfully verified his identity as Pam Dega's father, they were told. Pam was at Flemington Central Hospital. Her condition was critical. She was unconscious. That was all the information the New Jersey State Police had. Any other news would have to come from the hospital in Flemington.

Upon this news, Pam's parents departed posthaste without calling Greg. Greg meanwhile had continued to search for Pam. In talking to a neighbor who was fond of tuning into the police frequency on his bear scanner, Greg learned that an automobile accident had occurred just outside Flemington on Route 202. An ambulance had rushed an unidentified female to a local hospital while the driver of the vehicle had been pronounced DOA. Greg quickly found out more details including the location of the nearest hospital, which was just minutes away in Flemington. Greg ran the two miles to Flemington Central Hospital.

Bursting into the emergency room area, Greg unceremoniously cut to the front of the line to ask about Pam.

"My girlfriend was rushed in a few hours ago. Where is she?"

"I'm sorry, son," said a matronly nurse. "May I help you?"

"Yes, ma'am, please. My girlfriend, Pam Dega, was traveling from Boston to Flemington and took a cab, I guess, from the train station to Flemington. We couldn't find her and I heard there was an auto accident just a few miles away on Route 202, she was coming to see me."

"And who are you, son?"

"I'm Greg. Greg Gurist. I'm her boyfriend."

"Well, I am sorry, son, but we can't give out information to anyone but close relatives. I am sure you understand."

"No, ma'am, I don't," said Greg as he desperately pleaded for information. "Look, she was coming from Boston to be with me. I think that means something."

The nurse gave Greg a serious look and then consulted her records.

"I'm sorry but we aren't releasing any information at this time."

Greg looked incredulously at the nurse.

"I don't get it. Pam, my girlfriend, is here in your hospital in critical, maybe worse condition, and you won't even acknowledge that she is here and you aren't going to let me see her? Is that about it?"

"I am sorry. Rules are rules."

"Well, who's in charge? Let me talk to him or her."

"I am and I am sorry. We can't help you. You can wait. As soon as we have authorization I will come get you. Is that fair?"

Greg all but screamed, "Ma'am, *that is not fair!* I want to see her. She needs me now!"

Greg had no rights whatsoever. He couldn't see her. They wouldn't tell him her status.

"My honesty got the best of me. I should have said 'brother' or something," Greg told his dad when he called home from the hospital.

"What do I do, Dad?" he asked.

"Greg, when Pam's parents arrive, they can give you the required permission to enter her room. I am sure they will."

Greg hung up the phone and saw Anthony walking towards him.

"Come with me, Greg. We have very little time."

Greg, further surprised by seeing Anthony and wondering who told him, followed him with requisite celerity. Anthony ushered Greg down several hallways and turned into the Trauma Unit to an intensive care room where Pam lay near lifeless, engulfed in a morass of tubes and wires connected to machines and monitors.

Greg glanced at Anthony as they approached Pam. He saw her face was red from the trauma with splotches of yellow, black, and blue. He could barely recognize her. Her critical condition was obvious. Realizing her fragile state, Greg's face went pale and his eyes began to tear.

"Greg, she has been waiting for you. She needs you."

Greg just looked back at Anthony in horror and shock.

"Waiting for me?" Greg finally said in broken speech and through tears.

"Yes. You don't have much time. Talk to her, Greg, but don't cry. She needs you. She needs your strength and your reassurance."

"Of what? What should I be saying?"

"Greg, she's dying. You must be positive and summon your courage and be with her now. You must be strong; much as she has always been."

"Pam, can you hear me?" Greg looked back at Anthony who nodded assuringly saying, "She can, Greg. She *can* hear you."

Greg didn't know how or why Anthony knew. Perhaps the doctors had said. He started talking to Pam with the huge burden of knowing their time was limited. Greg grabbed Pam's hand and gently squeezed as he spoke: "I love you, Pam. I am sorry to have waited to tell you. But you are so smart, I am sure you have known. I wanted to tell you. I hope you'll forgive me. I know you love me, too. I am here for you. I am thinking wonderful, peaceful thoughts. You make me so very happy. Remember now and forever you have me and I will never, I can never, lose you."

Greg continued to talk to Pam, to hold her hand, to profess his undying love and devotion. He spoke with a warm loving tone suddenly devoid of the panic and tears of minutes earlier. He went into a state of meditation and visualization. Holding Pam's hand and talking to her about pleasant experiences. He told Pam of his dreams of them together. He told her how proud of her and impressed by her he was. He then prayed to God for only the very best to happen to her. He hoped she could live.

After some time — Greg couldn't know how long — Anthony discreetly tapped on Greg's shoulder and began.

"She told me to tell you three things. She had hoped to be able to tell you herself, but it appears she cannot." Anthony turned to Pam as if to ask her something, and changed his mind and turned back to Greg. "First, she is honored to love you. She says she has loved you for a very long time."

"Yes?"

"She wants you to tell her now that you know. That you know she loves you. She wants to hear you say it. Greg, if you can, please tell her."

Greg leaned over Pam again and whispered sweetly that he loves her and that he knows she loves him, too.

"Second, she said your grades were incomplete."

"I don't understand?"

"Greg, she said you would remember not receiving your grades and that you would want them but as of yet you could only receive an incomplete. She said you would know what she meant. You would know what to do."

"Anthony, she can only be talking about my…kiss? She wants my kiss? I can't kiss her. I can't even reach her lips." Greg looked at Anthony who gave him a look that Pam might have given. He almost heard Pam say, *What? Now you're afraid to kiss me? Too much equipment in your way?*

Greg moved closer, navigating obstructions as best he could. He climbed up and arched over the equipment and bed and saw her lips from just inches. Amazingly, they were mostly untouched by the lethal accident. He kissed her lips gently but warmly. He held her hand a little tighter as he whispered in her ear, "I love you, Pam. I'm not afraid. I don't want to lose you. Please don't be afraid. You are strong. Our love is strong. I love you and I want you, too. I am yours now and forever."

Greg felt her squeeze his hand and heard her let out a breath of air. It was her last.

After a moment of silence Anthony said, "Greg, she's gone. Now we must leave."

Greg's face further etiolated. His eyes began to tear as Anthony grabbed his arm and led him out of the room towards the waiting area. A buzzer went off. It eerily reminded Greg of the end of something…class…a period in wrestling? Doctors and nurses hurriedly brushed by them as they exited.

"The third thing, Anthony, you said three things. What was the third thing?"

"Greg, she said the categories were for warmth, passion, love, courage, and devotion. She needed your last kiss, should you be brave enough to reach her side and deliver it under the extreme conditions."

"What for?"

"She said that you had already earned highest honors for warmth and passion. By your courageous move to find her and kiss her you passed her final test. You then received highest honors in all five categories."

"But Anthony, I don't understand. Pam talked to you? Who told you Pam was here?"

"Greg, you know we weren't supposed to be in there, so I recommend you not mention our visit to anyone. And please remember, I was never to be here."

"But Anthony, several staff members saw us."

"Greg, I wasn't to be here," Anthony insisted as he disappeared around the corner.

Just after midnight, Pam's parents arrived at the hospital. Dr. Hegira explained to them that Pam had died at 11:38 of a severe blow to the head from an auto accident.

Mrs. Dega's face, already swollen from tears, was now frozen in disbelief. Greg waited until Mr. and Mrs. Dega came from the discussion with Dr. Hegira. As they exited they saw him and embraced him saying, "She's gone. She's gone."

Chapter Seventeen
The Funeral

Flemington Central High School students attended the services honoring one of their top students. Hundreds attended the funeral. There were flowers throughout St. Joseph's Church where Pam had been a regular attendee. Her grief-stricken parents were inconsolable. Greg seemed stoic, almost catatonic.

Greg saw Anthony at the funeral. He stood conspicuously during the eulogies, which comforted Greg as he spoke.

Greg spoke passionately, maintaining his poise but ending with a tear. He said he loved Pam dearly. He spoke of her grace and charm. He said he spoke to her and hoped she could hear him. He said he was amazed by her intelligence, sincerity, wit, poise, and warmth. "She's an angel now. She was an angel even while here on the earth… Few people were as loved as she was."

Everyone seemed surprised at what Greg said. Perhaps their public bickering prevented many from seeing their true relationship. As the fellow students listened and reflected they realized the two must have been close to be able to verbally spar with such emotion. But they were surprised at how well Greg took it all. Many doubted his sincerity as he spoke in celebration of her life more than in mourning her death even as a tear rolled down his cheek.

Greg met with Anthony shortly thereafter.

"Anthony, some people have asked if I had meant what I said at Pam's funeral. They are calling me callous. Some have said I'm in denial. Others have said I couldn't possibly love her and not grieve a lot more. But I cried for 24 hours straight. I prayed that she would come back to me. I prayed that it was all just a bad dream and that I would wake up and find Pam with me. I prayed that I would see Pam in my dreams and that she'd be safe. I prayed that I would find someone to replace her. I prayed I would never find someone to replace her, that I would get over her, and I prayed I would never get over her."

"Then in the middle of one prayer, I realized that my prayers were all about me. I began to wonder what had happened to her. No, I don't mean about the accident. I know what happened. There were witnesses. Just a bad accident, there was really no one to blame. What I mean is: where is she now? Can she hear me? Did she still care? Did she go to heaven? Does heaven exist? Did she love me? Does she still love me? What does it all mean? I prayed for answers. I didn't get any."

"Prayers aren't always answered on cue."

"So how long do I need to wait?"

"To heal?"

"No, for the answers to my questions."

"Greg, you have asked the questions of a lifetime. Some questions have only transitory not permanent answers. Some answers you may have already gleaned. Still others will take both time and healing."

"Thanks, Anthony. I think you have told me. I'm not even ready to ask these questions, am I?"

Chapter Eighteen
Wrestling with Weight

Greg remembered walking as a pallbearer and vowed he'd never do it again. Knowing that her body laid lifeless just inches away made him sick to his stomach. It didn't go away. As he lay in his bed thinking, his alarm, set on weekend and Christmas holiday time at 7:07, went off. Maybe he couldn't control his eating but he would still do his workout. It would ease the pain and transition into the day. Facing a long day without a workout seemed unconscionable. Sweating inside a windbreaker under a sweat suit still gave him a good feeling. Greg went back to sleep.

"Greg, are you sick?"

"What, Mom?"

"Are you sick? I don't think I've seen you in bed at 8:30. Aren't you working out?"

"Yes, Mom, I'm just getting a late start."

"Skipping a workout? You could always use a break. You run too much anyway and you know you can hurt yourself lifting weights."

"Mom, how many times have I hurt myself weightlifting?"

"I said you *could* hurt yourself. You should be careful."

"Mom, I won't hurt myself."

"Mom, I couldn't sleep last night so I got up and ate. I ate and ate and it felt good. Didn't you notice?"

"What?"

"The clean refrigerator. I finished the pizza, a box of Cheerios, and all the Oreos. It felt good. Now, I just want to sleep. I certainly didn't feel like running so when the alarm went off, I went back to sleep."

"Greg, don't you think you ought to get up, anyway?"

Greg got up and worked out. Surprisingly it offered little solace. Greg felt slow and lethargic, almost robotic. He didn't bother to weigh himself, knowing he was well over his target, all of it having to do with his recent binging. One could put ten pounds of water and food in your stomach one day and three days later be back to weight without doing much more than going back to a controlled eating and drinking program.

He sat down for lunch with his mom.

"I know you eat chicken, don't you, Greg?"

"Yes, Mom, I eat chicken, especially your chicken."

"How about my special roasted potatoes? I don't think you've had any since September."

"Probably not since June. Remember I started cutting weight then?"

Greg continued to eat.

Several days passed.

Then Greg finally did it. He weighed himself — 143 — 20 pounds over. This was the same weight that he had cut down to from 165 over the summer. He had spent late September to early December getting from 143 to 123. His next match was in two weeks and he needed to cut 20 pounds. He began that day. He watched his weight that evening. He ate a reasonable meal, heavy on protein and vegetables and light on starches with just fruit for dessert. He got up the next day and weighed himself, 141. Then again the next evening, he weighed 143 again.

Several days passed, school resumed and the cycle continued. Greg seemed to eat reasonably but he wasn't losing weight. In fact, he had added a pound so now he was 144 in the evening and 142 in the morning. He maintained his workouts but still ate more than normal and his good eating habits had become a combination of good food plus any food he wanted. After a week of school where he had yet to smile he decided he needed help.

Greg went to Coach Gallo.

"Coach, I'm over and can't make next week's match with Scotts Valley."

"How much over are you?"

"Enough. I can't make it."

"How much?"

"After yesterday's practice I weighed 139."

"You mean 129?"

"No, Coach, 139."

"But you were 125 just three weeks ago at the tournament."

"Coach, I haven't been myself. I just keep eating. But I know I can fix it but I can't cut 20 pounds in ten days."

"I can't tell you to cut the weight, Greg, but I need you at 123. A pin could be the difference with Scotts Valley."

"Coach, I've been thinking the same thing but cutting so much, so fast. I think it would hurt my chances at States."

"States? States? Greg, I think gaining 20 pounds over the holidays killed your chances at States. I had high hopes for you. 139? How did you get there?"

"Coach, I'll try to get down by next week. But don't count on me. I'm not going to starve myself and risk losing muscle only to wrestle weak and lose. That won't help the team or me."

"Greg, make it. Please."

"I'll work it."

Greg met with Anthony soon after.

"I can't do it. It's too hard."

"What do you mean, Greg? What is too hard? Why can't you do it?"

"I just don't feel like it."

"Greg, you miss Pam?"

"Of course I do. I just don't feel it. I don't feel good about anything. I really just want to lie down and wake up and have it all go away. I want Pam back. If she were here, I wouldn't have trouble getting back on a sound eating schedule. I could face two weeks of perfect dieting."

"Remember our first session where we reviewed your goals. You were having some modest difficulties with dieting then. You then recalled your successful dieting from this summer."

"I had a plan then and I used several diets. I used the egg and grapefruit diet and then the low-fat cottage cheese and Fritos diet, then the Special K breakfast diet. Then I would mix in some protein powder and V-8 juice for dinner. I was running several miles a day and digging out basements. Weight loss was easy. I reduced three pounds a week when I was dieting and over the summer reduced from 165 to just under 145."

"So what diet are you on now?"

"My mom calls it a Twinkie diet but a better appellation would be the Twinkie and seefood diet."

"How does that work?"

"Easy, I eat Twinkies and all the food I see."

"This sounds like the grade school version of Greg Gurist talking."

"Sorry, Anthony. I couldn't resist, just like my eating: I can't resist. I eat when I'm hungry or sad or angry or lonely. The problem is I am always one of these and often more than one of these."

"Okay, let's start from the beginning. List your goals and let's work through them."

Greg proceeds to recount his goals: long-term, short-term, and planned actions. Anthony reviews the lists and they make some additional adjustments.

"Anthony, my **Personal Commercial** no longer sounds right. Somehow with Pam dead, it can't be the same. It shouldn't be the same. I need to reflect her absence."

"That makes sense."

"And I have to start all over with dieting. My **Personal Commercial** should focus on diet now."

"That, too, makes sense. Begin by setting your goals and action plans and reviewing all the things you need to do to succeed."

"Well, you probably thought I was kidding but I stop at the Wawa every day after practice and buy Twinkies, Oreos, Devil Dogs, and chocolate ice cream."

"How do I stop this habit?"

"Remember the 21 Points for Health and Weight Control?"

"Sure I do. I can't recite them but they include planning meals, eating fresh natural foods, indulging on occasion. This one I remember well. I'm at your indulging point."

"You are incorrigible...but funny. They are:

21 Points for Health and Weight Control

1. Eat fresh, healthy, natural, whole foods: Lean meats, fish, poultry, whole grains, milk, eggs, fresh vegetables, and fresh fruits should predominate.
2. Visualize yourself at your ideal weight; use a real or fabricated picture. When the thought of food comes to mind, don't fight it; replace it with the Visualization of your perfect lean self.
3. Plan your meals.
4. The first three days of the diet are the most difficult.
5. Record your eating and exercise results daily. Weigh yourself weekly or more often.
6. Know why you want to lose weight. Know why you haven't yet lost weight. Know why you have failed in the past.
7. Find and do exercises you like and fit them into your lifestyle.
8. Walk, exercise six days per week (Aerobic, Flexibility, and Muscles).
9. Make healthy foods and only healthy foods readily available.
10. If you break or falter don't panic; get back on track immediately.
11. Occasionally indulge but indulge modestly; it prevents binges and pain.
12. Never eat out of habit, boredom, anger, misery, or when very tired or in front of the TV.
13. Eat well and enjoy your food; modest portions of healthy full color spectrum gourmet food will satisfy all the senses, allowing you to stay on a diet for life.
14. Eat reasonable portions at consistent hours. Don't miss breakfast and eat within an hour of each workout.
15. Bad diet habits never die but they can be replaced by good ones. Create good diet and exercise habits.
16. If you must snack, snack healthy: fresh carrots, health food bars.
17. Consume salt, caffeine, and alcohol sparingly. Avoid artificial and processed foods, especially altered oils and sugars. They wreak havoc with the metabolic system, e.g., diet sodas may encourage your body to store fat.
18. Drink water and take natural vitamin and mineral supplements.
19. Get adequate rest each night; 7-8 hours or as necessary.
20. Many diets can work; find what works for you, one you can stick with.
21. Don't give up. Weight Control is a lifelong exercise."

"This helps me. I need to get rid of the Twinkies and add carrot sticks. I need to suck it up and get past the hunger pains of the first three days. I need to remind myself why I am doing this. I need to get some resolution about Pam. I need to find a path home that doesn't pass the Wawa."

"If getting past the Wawa presents your biggest obstacle, I am sure you will do well in getting back to 123."

"So help me then. I feel powerless over food. I just can't stop eating."

"Are you hungry now?"

"Yes, I am."

"What will you do when you leave the library?"

"I'll go home and hopefully not stop at the Wawa. I'll see what's in the refrigerator. My mom will probably intercept me and volunteer to warm up some of what she cooked Dad and Allen for dinner. It may just be leftovers but my mom's a great cook and the dinner will be good. If I'm good that will be my eating day; if not, I'll eat double portions at dinner. I'll then go to my room. Do homework. Then I'll go back to the kitchen later or to my cache of Twinkies and eat again before getting to sleep at eleven."

"Greg, you've got to ask yourself if you really want to get back in shape and pursue your goal of States."

"It's not just me. I feel I'll be letting down my team, my family, my scholarship opportunities, and my future. I don't want to quit. I've come too far. But I need help."

"What do you need?"

"First, tell me about Pam."

"What do you want to know?"

"You were at the hospital before me."

"Yes, I was visiting a friend at the hospital when they brought her in."

"How did you know it was Pam?"

"I saw her, Greg. Then I called you. Your line was busy and I called your neighbor at the number you gave me. He did tell you?"

"No, he told me he heard it over the police scanner."

"How come Pam talked with you?"

"I know the hospital, Greg. I learned of her condition."

"Did you have anything to do with her death?"

"What?"

"Did you let her die?"

"Greg?"

"You could have helped her."

"I did the right thing. I wanted to be sure that you two communicated. Even though she was too weak to talk, she heard you. Pam did communicate with you. Didn't she?"

"Yes, but you knew."

"I learned that Pam had been operated on. The doctors had concluded that there was little to be done. The severe damage to the skull had only warranted reducing the edema-related pressure on the brain, stanching the flow of blood and removal of some bone fragments threatening incremental hematoma. They stabilized her and put her on life support systems awaiting her parents. Dr. Hegira described her as *noncognitive comatose having suffered a subdural hematoma severe enough to curtail life*. I went to her when she came out of surgery. She told me to get you and what to do if you didn't get there. I did what I could."

"But she was in a coma? How could you talk to her? Why didn't you try to save her?"

"Greg, I'm not a doctor."

"You're right. I didn't mean to accuse you. It all came out wrong."

"Don't whitewash it, Greg. I just hope you don't truly feel I in any way caused Pam's death. If you even suspect it, we probably should no longer be associated."

"I'm sorry. I *am* sorry. Forgive me. I am simply distraught."

"I accept that and I forgive you."

"I get it."

"You get what?"

"I am eating to punish myself for Pam's death."

"But it wasn't your fault."

"Yes, but someone should be punished. The driver's dead. The doctors did all they could. You weren't culpable. I must blame myself. I am punishing me. I'm not sure I should stop punishing me. That's why I am eating."

Greg began to cry and Anthony put his hand on Greg's shoulder. He reminded Greg that he's not to blame.

"Pam is a good person."

"Then why did she die?"

"Just because you are good doesn't mean you won't die. Greg, you are good but you will still die. It is part of life. Remember **Accept Death and Face Fear**? This critical key may help you confront your fear and accept your body's mortality. You know and believe this. Now you must accept it. Sometimes acceptance requires more than logic and even more than emotion. It requires faith. Greg, Pam has been a great test of faith for you. You *know* what happens when you die. You *know* her soul lives on. You believe she lives and thrives in her next existence. You know it and feel it. You believe it. Now accept it. Take the leap of faith. The step for you may actually be quite small."

"I need to walk my mind through this. I need to think, pray, and meditate. I want to. I need to. See you, Anthony."

Chapter Nineteen
Facing Faith

Greg went home and went to his mom and told her he loved her and that he needed her help. He wanted to get into shape and he needed her understanding and her help. For the next four weeks she shouldn't ask him if he wanted anything to eat. She would help him by getting the junk food out of the house. If Allen wanted some he could stash it in his room. She should tolerate Greg's solitudinarian existence as he worked to get his mind back on track. He told her about Pam.

"Mom, I have been eating to punish myself for Pam's death."

"That's horrible, Greg. Actually, moribund — you do still want me to flex your vocabulary?"

"Yes, Mom, re-enter the fray."

"Why are you punishing yourself?"

"Well, Mom, she came down from Boston by train for me and if I hadn't wrestled, I would have picked her up. So she wouldn't have died. Right?"

"Wrong, Greg. Aren't you the one saying the Universe is fair? Didn't you say God is all-powerful and all-just, that *good things happen to good people who do good things?* Didn't you say nothing bad can happen to good people?"

"Yes, I did but now I realize I may have been quoting Anthony, and I'm not so sure I believe it."

"Well, I believe that God and His Universe work quite well. Pam died for a reason. Just because we don't know that reason doesn't make her death your fault. Greg, a stranger at the grocery store recently gave me a poem by Alice Cary. At first I thought he was a beggar, but after handing it to me, he walked away before I could reach into my purse. The poem is over a hundred years old. It's not about death but life. It's titled Nobility, it speaks of justice:

True worth is in being, not seeming,
In doing, each day that goes by,
Some little good, not in dreaming
Of great things to do by and by…
We get back our mete as we measure,
We cannot do wrong and feel right,
Nor can we give pain and gain pleasure,
For justice avenges each slight…

We cannot make bargains for blisses,
Nor catch them like fishes in nets,
And sometimes the thing our life misses
Helps more than the thing which it gets.

For good lieth not in pursuing,
Nor gaining of great nor of small,
But just in the doing, and doing
As we would be done by, is all.

Through envy, thru malice, thru hating
Against the world, early and late,
No jot or our courage abating,
Our part is to work and to wait.
And slight is the sting of his trouble
Whose winnings are less than his worth;
For he who is honest is noble,
Whatever his fortunes or birth.

"It's a nice poem, but I don't get it."

"It embraces all you have spoken about: justice, hard work, goodness, truth, kindness, loyalty, love, and nobility. Don't lose sight of all of the things you have come to believe, trust, and love, including me, your dad, and Pam. You can still love her. You can forgive yourself. You can do what she would have wanted you to do."

"What?"

"Go to States, get into a great school, and have a great career and meaningful life and..."

"What else?"

"Get back to *1,2,3*. Pam always liked your cut abs. Now I bet she couldn't find them."

"*Mom!*"

"Let's just say a little birdie told me. Forgive my indiscretion. Levity took over."

"Wait until I see Allen."

"Now, Greg, you shouldn't do that. I caught him snooping — more accurately, reconnoitering. Fortunately, I sent him back to his room. You should thank us both."

"Thanks for the poem, Mom."

Chapter Twenty

Gurist the Coach

Greg struggled through the next week. The Wawa temptation was abated as his mother assisted and picked him up from wrestling practice. Her encouraging words during their brief rides home kept his mind off Twinkies. One day she began the ride by telling him how succulent the fat stripped white meat chicken is. The next day she described in great detail the garlic and basil prepared swordfish and how his dad had wrestled Allen for the best portion, but that she had saved it for him. He only broke once.

Late Tuesday evening of the second day of his diet, he had a huge bowl of Special K with skim milk. The calories consumed while substantial didn't hurt as much as the failure to shrink his stomach, putting him back by nearly the two full days.

Nine days later Greg got to 128 after a water-deprived practice the day before the match with Scotts Valley. He had estimated he could reduce five pounds per week of real weight, calculating a 4,000 per day caloric burn and a 1,500 per day intake of hard boiled eggs, chicken, fish, spinach, broccoli, and salads. He knew his 22 pounds over comprised about 10 pounds of water and food weight and 12 pounds of real body weight. Since he had lost about eight pounds of real weight, then he had lost eight pounds of food and water weight. He felt he could safely lose the rest of the food and water plus another pound of real weight overnight. That would bring him to 125. He weighed in before the end of practice and walked off the scales.

Coach Gallo approached him. "Where are you?"

"128, Coach."

"How are you feeling?"

"I'm a little more winded than I want to be."

"We're having a pretty good practice in preparation for Scotts Valley."

"You can pull the five?"

"Coach, I can routinely pull five, even six, the day before but not after cutting this much. I think I'm probably three pounds away. I need to eat dinner, I'm already feeling weak, and I won't be able to swallow my dinner if I don't drink a little."

"So you can cut it?"

"Coach, I can cut it, yes, but I won't be able to go six minutes."

"That's not an answer, Greg."

"Coach, Sean has as much chance of winning against Scotts Valley as I do if I cut another five. I've already cut most of the food and water weight. My stomach's empty."

"My self-confidence has been strong all season long, especially after winning Scotts Valley. Cutting and then getting my butt kicked might be more than I can handle. Coach, I tried. I can't go."

Gallo looked at Gurist with disdain. "Get Sean. And Greg?"

"What, Coach?"

"Sean better win."

Greg's heart leaped high as he realized he would escape the pain of a 24-hour fast with nothing but a carrot stick or two and a few cherished ice cubes. Then ambivalence struck. The pain of responsibility for Sean's win hung over him like the sword of Damocles. Greg began his visualization of coaching Sean to victory.

Greg found Sean and told him the good news. Sean was 124 and eager to wrestle.

"How do I win, Greg? Can you help me win?"

"I don't know, Sean, but you have the tools. You're aggressive, strong, and quick. The Scotts Valley guy didn't wrestle last year so we don't know anything about him. We need to concentrate on you, Sean. Let's spend some time on the mat. Somehow I have a second wind, knowing I can eat tonight."

Greg always shot in straight on Sean for a quick single. It had become automatic, and Sean thought it happened because of Greg's skill but Sean simply failed to anticipate the shot or had a very weak sprawl.

"Why do you expose your legs and not fight me off when I get under you?"

"Greg, you're just too good."

"Thanks, Sean, but I think you need to just get a little lower. Try it."

Sean bent down a little farther and prepared to use his hands and arms to counter the shot. Greg then recommended a simultaneous sprawl and elbow arm thrust to counter the takedown.

"Sean, don't you play football on the JV team?"

"I start at Safety."

"When I shoot into you, you need to drive your forearm into me as you sprawl so that you stop my drive or flatten me. Just like a football block, you've got to hit me hard and get your legs back. If you push me down or to one side, you can power back into me for a takedown or spin on me if I'm flat."

Sean and Greg worked just that one counter for 30 minutes until practice ended, even escaping the dreaded wind sprints. Gallo left Sean and Greg alone hoping Greg's knowledge and self-confidence might rub off. Sean's powerful build and quickness helped him improve in less than 20 minutes. He successfully defended four out of five of Greg's attempts. One he turned into a takedown of his own. Greg then worked on Sean's attitude.

"Great, Sean, I'm tired. Let's call it a day. You did well."

"You weren't going easy on me at the end?"

"No, I wasn't. Sean, when you anticipate, sprawl, and drive your forearm into me, you defend well. The only shots I scored on occurred when I kept circling and got you when you weren't in position to counter. Overall, you did very well. You even scored on me. Are you excited to wrestle?"

"Yes."

"Nervous?"

"A little."

"Why?"

"It's my first varsity match."

"That's right, Sean. It's your first varsity match. No one expects you to win. In fact, they expect you will lose."

"Thanks, Greg."

"Seriously, they may expect it, but Sean, I wrestle 123, too; you are stronger than most, quicker than most, and as tough as anybody. You just need to anticipate a little more and then push hard. I just don't know if you want to win."

"I want to win. I really want to win."

"Wrestle takedowns as hard as you did with me and you'll beat the guy."

"Really?"

"Really."

Greg had considered walking Sean through a visualization process. There just wasn't enough time to get him to use it and have it help. Greg decided he could do the next best thing. Greg became Sean's personal coach from the pre-match weigh-ins through the match and even got Gallo's permission to stay close mat side for the match. Gallo at first resisted the idea but agreed after he acknowledged he had made Greg responsible for Sean's match.

Greg warmed up with Sean and talked to him the whole time, filling Sean's head with the same words he would hear in a visualization. He had Sean go through his stand-up escape and his arm-bar pinning combination. All the while Greg offered strongly supportive affirmations of Sean's strength, speed, and toughness. For Sean, it all seemed like a dream and suddenly he was face to face with his adversary in battle. He had fun with it as Greg had encouraged him to do.

Sean kept his strong defensive posture so well that his opponent kept seeking a good angle that never came. Finally the Scotts Valley guy shot hard and Sean countered even harder, driving him straight down. Sean spinned and, being so fired up, he drove an arm bar. He couldn't get deep enough, quickly enough, to pin but it didn't matter. Sean won handily and became the hero of the match.

Greg, relieved he hadn't let his coach or team down, went back to Anthony hoping for a rapprochement. Greg knew he had been biting the hand that feeds him and needed to forgive himself so that he could act more reasonably with Anthony.

Chapter Twenty-One
Accept Death and Face Fear

"I did it, Anthony. Thanks, you helped a lot."

"You made 123?"

"I came close, and I'll be ready for the next match. I actually helped my team and fellow teammate Sean to victory. It felt good. I now understand a little how you feel. In a way helping someone else win feels almost as good as being the winner."

"Or even better."

"I also figured some things out."

"Pray tell, what?"

"I've never heard you say that, Anthony. It sounds cynical."

"It isn't good. I think I was bracing myself. Our last discussion has caused me to question the effectiveness of my work."

"Anthony, I am sorry, but you helped me and my mom helped me see it. When I said I would pray and meditate, I did. When the answer didn't come, I then decided I must already know the answer. You taught me that, Anthony."

"What do you mean, Greg?"

"You taught me that God would answer my prayers if I had exhausted my own resources. Well, I realized I hadn't seriously considered Pam and her existence based upon my belief in God and the afterlife."

"Did you decide to accept her death?"

"That's exactly it, Anthony. I didn't decide. I just know or I believe so strongly it is much the same. My mom reminded me what I have told her many times and I believe it. She gave me this poem. She got it from a stranger."

"What is it, Greg?"

"I know Pam loves me. I feel it. She loves me as I love her. She's present. She has told me I have much to do in my lifetime; that I had better do well — that she will be watching. That she will see me again. I should feel happy for her, not sad. That's the part I took really hard, but believe now. I know she's fine and happy. That's when I decided to stop mourning her death because I was only feeling sorry for me, not her. She's an angel and that's nothing to be sorry about. Anthony, am I crazy?"

"Greg, from what I know, Pam is one very fine soul. I believe she's doing well. I know it just as you do. So why would you think yourself crazy?"

"I just thought through my belief system as you would. I began with, is God all-powerful? Is He all-just? If so, then whatever happens in His Universe must be fair. If everything that happens is fair, then everything happens for a reason. If one is good, then only good things or fair things can happen to you. Therefore, there are no accidents. Then a good person, doing only good things, could only have good things happen to them. Anthony, as you say, *good things happen to good people who do good things*."

"Pam was a good person. I believe that our soul lives, so she certainly lives on. I see no reason why she would love me just days ago and that her soul would stop loving me because she was dead. I know she loves me. I know she is safe. I believe she is happy and wants me to be happy and to enjoy my life and to work hard. This is what I told the people at the church."

"Greg, I think your talk comforted many people in the church. Few religions ever discuss death. Fewer still talk about heaven. It is much as you say. The soul continues. We continue to love and care and hopefully grow. I believe Pam loves you today as she did. I hope more people take the view of faith as you have. The world would be better for it."

Greg still loved Pam. He worked out harder and studied harder. If Pam watched him she saw a fine young man working hard to learn, grow, and do good works. He had the greatest difficulty with his attitude. He felt guilty having fun. "Survivor syndrome," doctors called it, a malady causing guilt, absenteeism, and reduced motivation. Greg wondered: why Pam and not me?

Greg began a conscious program for increasing his enthusiasm, motivation, and happiness. Working with Anthony they again reworked his **Personal Commercial**. They added some upbeat background music. Anthony amplified the already upbeat inflection in his voice. Greg worked on understanding all of the reasons for his sorrow: guilt of surviving, the loss of her companionship, regrets of never having been intimate, knowing her irreplaceability, the guilt of wanting to replace her, and guilt about having fun. The list grew long and required him to confront many fears.

He confronted death in a way few men under 40 ever did. Anthony had said confronting death presented one of the greatest challenges and therefore had one of the biggest paybacks in terms of attitude improvement. **Accept Death and Face Fear** was one of the keys. He brought into his consciousness all reasons for his grief and fear. He put in his **Personal Commercial** more reminders of these solutions and other accomplishments and reasons to be happy. Most importantly, he resolved and had Anthony say in his **Personal Commercial** that he would be happy and had a right to be happy.

Pam's mom continued to be inconsolable. She believed that something she had done had caused God to take Pam away from her just as Pam's life had turned around. As no one she talked to knew her innermost feelings, no one could console her. Greg began to spend an occasional Sunday afternoon visiting her mom. He expressed much of his view of life with her and spoke of Pam openly, even though it had often led to tears.

Eventually, one day before Mrs. Dega's tears could begin, Greg asked her if she believed in God. He asked if she thought God was fair. He continued the dialog that he had had regularly with Anthony. The words seemed to be little comfort to her. Then Greg took a bold move. He told her of some of last year's conversations with Pam. He explained that she truly trusted and believed in God. He told her that Pam believed she had done what God had asked of her and that he knew that she was satisfied with her life.

Greg then looked Pam's mother in the eye and said, "Pam thinks she did very well here on earth. She knows that God has and will treat her well. I believe she is right. Don't you?"

The tears didn't come and she didn't answer. Greg left soon thereafter. Pam's mom began to think that she had been self-centered about her death. She had believed that God had taken Pam away because she wasn't a good enough mother. Soon after Greg's plea she would begin the process of accepting that whatever had happened to Pam it was for a good reason. Pam had deserved no less.

Chapter Twenty-Two
Getting Back on Track

Greg's next few matches were lackluster. He won all but one of them on strength and strategy, but lost a close one because he hadn't watched the clock carefully and let up before the buzzer, giving up deciding points. Confronting death gave him a calm resolve. Later it grew into a comfort and an acceptance of all things good and bad. In fact, good and bad took on new meaning. He realized he wasn't alone. Most people like him had things going on that no one else could see and fewer still could understand. It was not just the grief. What gripped him harder was the reality of life. Like the posters said, "Life is not a dress rehearsal." He now took things more seriously and more lightly at the same time.

He had come nearly full circle. He would do his best. He would optimize every second because he knew his time could be up at any minute. This didn't set him into a panic mode, because he now felt he belonged in the world and the Universe. This gave him a long-term view. He would be content not to get everything he wanted right now. School seemed to be going well, his SAT scores were outstanding, and he'd achieved a 99th percentile quantitative score and a 96th qualitative score. Good enough to get into nearly any school.

Two months later, before Districts.

"Facing death has a powerful effect on you," Greg said to Anthony. "It reminds me of the feeling that would allow dauntless

Joe Namath to predict an upset of the Colts and go out and calmly do it. I'm no Joe Namath, but I've got that. Like my **Personal Commercial** says, I am dauntless, intrepid, fearless. Nothing bad can happen to a good person with good intentions and good actions whose soul lives forever."

Greg's routine seemed like a daily feat of Jobian proportions. Now that he had God, the Universe, and a life strategy behind him he left nothing to chance. He knew that students of Pam's caliber were smarter. He knew that athletes like Joe Namath or wrestlers like Dan Hodge or Dan Gable had more talent. So he didn't attempt to deny the truth. He simply trained harder and smarter.

When he could, he watched the best compete. Film was scarce but he got what he could. Greg knew he had a few strengths. He always out conditioned his opponent. He had very balanced strength. From grip to hip, he had it. He worked it. He did sprints and lifted up to a week before Districts. His style, once labeled hard and straight-ahead, was now cautious, controlled, and smart. It could be called bait: the strategy was smeltsly and capitalize on mistakes. The ultimate thinking defensive wrestler, Greg could control the flow of the action by the smeltsly, the whizzer, and backing and circling. He found these simple moves allowed him to slow the progress of a match and tire a strong and well-conditioned athlete.

He was also very patient. The huge majority of great high school wrestlers could be baited into a desperation shot easily countered when the score was tied at 2-2 in the third. If the score went into overtime Greg's conditioning gave him an edge. He had never lost an overtime bout. Greg knew that Mulino represented one of the fastest, smoothest, and toughest wrestlers ever. He knew he could go with him. He wouldn't let Mulino get physically close. Mulino worked well on his feet. He had won so many matches by fall in the first period no one knew how good he was on the mat or how much endurance he had. Greg had a plan. No tie-up. He would stay low so that Mulino couldn't gain upper body control. No one had tried this technique so at the very least Mulino would see something new.

Greg knew that if he was low and got in on Mulino's legs that he could lock up a leg and force a stalemate. If Greg made it to the second period he knew that Mulino would feel out of sync and perhaps lose confidence. He hadn't been tested in at least two years.

In training, Greg practiced with both heavier and stronger wrestlers and lighter and faster ones, gaining some assurance that he could stay out of Mulino's path for a full six minutes. In the third period, if Mulino became reckless he would capitalize and take him down. If not, he would plan for overtime.

Greg knew that in States stalling might be called more frequently. The smeltsly was almost never called as stalling when used in defense of a takedown. It should, however, be called stalling as a riding technique. It was called when obvious but rarely in dual meets. There were few clearly defined rules other than for blatantly backing away.

Greg knew he needed to shoot and circle. He then began allowing his practice opponents to back him up and then move in a circle so that he was just in front of his opponent with his opponent's back to the edge of the mat. An aggressive double could surprise a rival who felt he could get out of bounds. Greg knew a double could also give Mulino a chance to throw his patented pancake or lateral drop. But if Mulino was driving forward, they would surely go off the mat.

Greg practiced this circle and shoot technique to perfection. He had begun perfecting it since the Scotts Valley tournament.

Beating Tasker had given Greg enough confidence to know he could go with Mulino.

Chapter Twenty-Three
Districts and Regions

Flemington Central did well at Districts. Fortunately, Greg had good solid competition but no serious threats. His conservative style usually kept the score close. It was usually not until halfway into the third period when, after applying the conservative style, he could break loose. A guy could appear to be going even with Greg and then get pinned late in the third period. This occurred in Greg's first match.

For the District Finals, Greg faced a fast and rubbery Gumby-type. Moving in on a double leg Greg put him down to the mat but he still hung on, preventing a takedown. Wrapping himself around Greg and reaching over for an ankle he hung tight and Greg couldn't move up. The ref soon called a stalemate. As Greg had enough strength to lift his opponent and drop him to the mat, he decided to do exactly that to convert his next double. A high lift and drop to the mat shook this Gumby-type off and Greg scored.

Region Finals were another story. With the defending regional champ, David Garris, Greg kept the score close and expected it to go into overtime but with one minute left the ref called Greg for stalling, for backing away. Then 35 seconds later with just 25 seconds left to go in the bout he called Greg again for backing out, although the coach and Greg pointed out he had circled to keep on the mat and in bounds. This put Garris on top 2-1. Greg needed a late takedown to win. With his opponent now beginning to back away, Greg took several very good shots. He got in deep on a single, countered quickly with a whizzer. Greg loose-armed the hold and came behind for two points at the buzzer. Or so he thought. The judges said time had expired. The ref raised the opponent's arm. Despite protestations by Coach Gallo, the ruling stuck. Greg lost.

I'll get Garris in States, Greg thought as the ref held his arm but raised his opponent's.

Chapter Twenty-Four
Planning for States:
The Seven Steps and the Ten Keys

States! On to States went Greg. He was only the second wrestler from Flemington Central High School in the past three years to get there. Each of eight regions sent three wrestlers. States lasted two days. Greg's high school, friends, and family were all very impressed. While few gave him much of a chance, as regional runners-up had rarely won States, Greg had a goal. Get to the Finals and use his strategy on Mulino.

Mulino, unlike Greg, had cruised through to States. At Districts and Regions he pinned all but two guys and those he outscored by more than 10 points. He had given up but one takedown and he decked that guy 45 seconds later. He wrestled in a high-speed cruise control (or maybe bruise control) like Gable who pinned over 92% of his opponents his last two college years. Mulino dominated high school wrestling contemporaneously with Gable's college dominance.

After Regions Greg told Anthony how he was doing. Greg wanted a check-up with Anthony so that he was prepared before he moved ahead.

"Can you review the **Personal Growth Cycle** and the **Ten Keys** with me so I can be sure I am applying them the best way I possibly can? I know we've covered most of this ground before, but it may build my confidence and help me know that I have done all I could, so that I am free to pray. I pray every day but I mean a very specific prayer focused upon me doing my absolute best at States. Win or lose, Anthony, I want to be sure that I go as far as I can."

"Greg, I'm happy to walk you through the **Personal Growth Cycle** and the **Ten Keys**, but you are the only one who can determine if you are following them."

"Great. Let's start!" said Greg with strong enthusiasm.

"To start, please keep in mind that all the steps and keys work best, and sometimes only when all of them are firmly in place. Recapping, the Cycle begins with the first step, which is to **Think Positive**."

"Greg, it must be turned on at all times. Without a Positive Attitude you are wasting your time. You must believe in yourself. This means to always see the good and to always think constructive thoughts. It means be worry-free; as if life were a Disney movie. Be positive, think positive thoughts and do positive things."

"This shouldn't be confused with ignoring reality. It also shouldn't keep you from preventing calamities when you can. You don't ignore a hole in the roof because you are optimistic that it will never rain. This isn't true optimism. *True optimism is well grounded in reality.* You are prepared for every possibility and you use preventative measures even as you focus on the positive. Once you have done all you can, you should be and deserve to be optimistic. Remember looking for the good and thinking about the good will bring good. Greg, how well are you applying the first key?"

"This key comes easy to me. I am a positive person. If I find pony poop, I look for the pony. My faith also helps me believe and know that God's Universe works perfectly. I know it does, and I think that only good will happen to me, but then, things do happen. I can be blinded by events such as having Vlasco attempt to wreck my wrestling career. Pam's death still haunts me even though I know she lives on and is well."

"These events occasionally put negative thoughts in my head. But then I take the two-step approach you recommended. I realize that every thought that enters my head offers me the opportunity to accept it or reject it and let it pass through. I let the negative one pass through quickly and replace it with a positive one. For Pam, I replace the negative thought of missing her with the pleasant recall of our first kiss; a magic moment that still keeps me sane. I know it isn't a long-term fix, but it really seems to help now. As far as wrestling goes, the only negative thought that crosses my mind involves Mulino. I fix it by quickly seeing all of his energy flowing into me. This energy of his allows me to duck under him and move behind for a takedown. I know I am good here."

"So you will beat Mulino?"

"I can beat Johnnie. I'm not worried whether I do or don't. I know that he has more skill, but he has never faced me. I won't allow him to use his best moves. He will have to beat me using only the moves I leave him with. And calling him Johnnie — and I have no idea what anyone calls him — has definitely taken the fear level down a notch. I don't think he's stronger than I am and I doubt he's as well conditioned. What do you think, Anthony?"

"I am sure he will have his hands full with you!"

"Is that a pun, Anthony?"

"The second step in the **Personal Growth Cycle** is **Accept Fate**."

"This acceptance requires you to have a solid grasp of reality; to know who you are. It truly helps to view the Universe as being fair. This logic says God is fair and good. Know this. There are no real accidents. Accidents, too, happen for a reason. To know these things allows – it requires – you to accept your lot in life. If you were born with an infirmity, it is for a good purpose. Accept what you have. If you have lemons, make lemonade. Don't pine or claim your situation deplorable."

"Many people have struggled through infirmities that helped them become exceptional human beings. Some war prisoners suffering the horrors of the death camps still found a purpose in life and achieved spiritual growth. Surely we can do the same."

"Anthony, this key feels right. *My faith gives me complete confidence in my fate.* Sure, Pam's death hasn't been easy but the brief time I spent with her was a wonderful gift. As opposed to pining, I can revel in the fact that I received so much from her in such a short period of time. In so many ways I am so blessed by health, family, and friends that acceptance should rightfully be easier for me than most."

"Precisely. We all have some personal tragedies. What a great view, Greg. It also tells me that you have made progress on the first key, **Learn Who You Are.** To **Accept Fate** and in order to change, you need to accept who you really are."

"Socrates talked about the importance of knowing yourself. It is part of a balanced and examined life. Certainly, without knowing where you are, it is hard for you to decide where to go. It is even harder to get there. The goal setting exercises you did when we first put together your **Personal Commercial** required an inventory and personal assessment of who you were, where you'd been, and where you were going. In fact, your Personal Journal allows you to record, measure, and discover who you are. What do you think, Greg?"

"I learn about myself each day. I keep up my Personal Journal each day. I have built a unique style around my wrestling strengths. I am very strong but only reasonably fast. I don't have a huge arsenal of moves. I do have several very powerful defensive techniques. I use what I have, to do the very best that I can. I don't mourn the fact I can't always make the most exciting throws. I do listen to criticism. I don't believe all of it but I consider it all. My opinion of me doesn't normally sway far from the constructive feedback of friends and strangers alike."

Greg continued. "I know the third step is **Set Goals**."

"I continue to review my strengths, weaknesses, accomplishments and analyze my goals to be sure they fit me. I walk through all the action steps and test my commitment and resolve. I make my goals measurable and realistic. I work through each of the actions necessary to achieve my ultimate goal. My **Personal Commercial**, especially with my **Jingle**, keeps me in tuned with my goals at all times. I even think my conservative wrestling style grew out of my specific goal of winning. Rather than just going for the cool move or the pin, I have the goal of winning. This came to me unconsciously and as a result I now wrestle to win, not to look good. Anthony, the process you put me through to first test my goals and then to be sure they were in my heart has probably helped me more than anything else we've done. However, I do wonder if I focus on this step too much. I set goals for almost everything and I record results in my Personal Journal."

"What do you mean?"

"I set goals for how long it takes me to fix my breakfast. I record almost every weight I lift each day. I keep track of my takedowns for each match. I'm averaging just over two takedowns a match, and I average two back points per match as well. I record my pulse and weight each morning. I log my grades and homework in my Personal Journal. I record how well I follow the steps and keys. I attempt to have at least two good and positive interactions with people each day. I have short-term goals and long-term goals and action plans as required for my **Personal Commercial**. I also try to follow a *To Do List* each day. This also helps me with the first key of learning who I am. I know I drink way too much diet soda. It is one of my vices. I began recording that as well. I have slowed to less than one per day."

"Greg, you appear to apply this key well but don't miss the underlying objective of goal setting. Goal setting is to help you progress to your highest purpose in life. Goals and your analysis and pursuit of them can help you find what your personal self-actualized self can be and should be. It can help lead you to purposive living, this means living each day with intention and purpose. Find your purpose, Greg, and live it."

"Anthony, I conceptually agree but right now I know the best I can do is to study hard, make myself useful to my family and friends, and wrestle my heart out. To try to figure out my special purpose seems a lot to ask of me now. But I do think about it and I do pray to find my way. I am seeking to know. Am I there?"

"Yes, Greg, I know you should feel good about your goal setting. We don't all know what we were best meant to do but you already have many hints. Your goals themselves speak much about you. Your personal inventory and self-assessments have taught you much. You appear on the path to discovering your true purpose."

"After setting proper goals you must **Visualize Success**."

"You do this very well. Each day you visualize your success in your **Personal Commercial**. You see yourself winning. When you hear me talk about you reflecting upon your success and seeing and imagining the enjoyment of your successes, you do this. You do this when you mentally prepare for each and every important bout, when you create your own personal movie scripting and perform each move down to the color of your anklet. You visualize the match clear through to success when your hand is raised and when you see your coach, teammates, and parents cheer. You feel the satisfaction of winning long before you win. Your visualization also prepares you for contingencies. It helps you plan and set the framework for your plans, goals, and actions."

"I love this step, Anthony. I want to thank you again for helping me visualize. Asking me to look up into the stands as I was visualizing my hand being raised in victory helped me make my visualization real."

"Tell me about **Work Hard,** Anthony? That is the fifth step in the **Personal Growth Cycle**. I don't seem to do any hard work."

"What, Greg? You don't work hard?"

"Most of what I do is such a privilege. Think about it. I study. This isn't hard or at least it isn't often hard. Sure, sometimes I don't want to do sprints when I awake at 6:06. But, I've yet to decide not to run once I've gotten dressed. Sure, I'll fish out on a sprint or two, but I usually end up doing a make-up that same workout. Even then my dogging it is usually just listening to my body, which I do because I should."

"Greg, you've already said it. **Work Hard** doesn't have to mean hard work. Sometimes, **Work Hard** is just what we need to do to get out of bed or through the sticky points in life. You have made the most important point. *The more your life is focused on doing the right thing, right now, for your existence, then you are more likely to see hard work as having fun.* **Work Hard** doesn't and shouldn't prevent **Have Fun**. Greg, I'm like you; my life is fun over 90% of the time. Only rarely is it drudgery. Even when it is drudgery I then feel good because I know I am meeting this key. But then the strangest thing happens and it goes away. Once I recognize my work is drudgery and I recognize I am meeting the **Work Hard** key I feel much better about my work."

"Can I now say it, Anthony?"

"What?"

"Precisely. That's why I don't think I do much hard work."

"Greg, you are even further along the path than I knew.

[174]   Steve G. Vogel

"Thanks. Okay then, where were we?"
"**Measure Results**."

"Thanks. We spoke of this when I told you of my goal setting and the results and my Personal Journal. What am I missing?"

"**Measure Results** has a magical quality, Greg. Even scientists agree. The Hawthorne studies prove that almost anything measured will improve. Perhaps one of the hardest things to do, you already do quite well."

"Really? I'm available for any compliments, accidental or not."

"Greg, your Personal Journal shows the very effective job you do to **Measure Results**. You remember the **Personal Growth Cycle**. You have a very positive attitude. You accept your fate, set goals, visualize your success, work hard, and now measure results. You do exactly that. You record many details and you read and reflect upon them. Thus you discover when the action plans you make don't further your goals. Your new winning wrestling style reflects the constant monitoring of your results. Measuring, seeing what works and what doesn't work. Measuring combined with Visualization helped you develop your new wrestling style. Your measures are there to help you know yourself. Remember your first **Personal Commercial**?"

"Yes, it inspired me to action. It reminded me of my goals. It made my goals and activities second nature. I started doing all the right things. It turned out I started to do really important things in furtherance of my goals that weren't even in my action plan. This prompted me to change my action plans and to reformulate how to achieve them. In wrestling I couldn't win by adopting someone else's style. I needed to understand my own strengths and capitalize on them. Remember the reason I started making my 6:06?"

"Are you referring to the fact that you needed a windbreaker for running in the rain and cold?"

"Yes."

"Anthony, once we used the Whys Approach, the idea of getting up at 6:06 to do my sprints was so hard, we found out. I looked at my Personal Journal and noticed I often got up when the weather was nice but didn't when it was very cold or rainy. This explains how the keys work together. Without the **Personal Commercial**'s *failure* you wouldn't have looked harder to find out why you weren't able to get up at 6:06. Failure can be a great teacher. And only through the measurement of results were you able to spot the problem."

"Anthony, the final step in the Cycle is **Analyze Results**."

"I pretty much do this as I measure and as I reset my goals or analyze my goals. Why is this a separate step?"

"You are properly synthesizing the steps. It is important to take a few moments each day to review your Personal Journal. If you had a great day it is important to understand why, so that you may replicate the success. Likewise a bad day may also teach you something. While measuring has benefits, the full benefits come with analysis, just like in your science class."

"Got it."

"So tell me about the **Ten Keys**. Are they less important than the **Personal Growth Cycle**?"

"Ranking importance of steps and keys is like ranking body parts or wrestling skills, you can do it but you still need them all to succeed."

"For instance, **Learn Who You Are**? Doesn't goal setting, measurement, and analysis help you do this?"

"Yes, Greg, they are the primary ways you learn about yourself. But the reason this key stands alone is to recognize its importance and to be sure that some of your time is spent specifically on getting to know yourself. The **Accept Fate** step is critical to allowing yourself the clarity of thought to accurately see yourself. You will never see your own flaws if you don't accept yourself, as one must when you accept your fate. So Greg, how much have you learned about yourself in our six months working the **Personal Growth Cycle**?"

"I think I see myself quite accurately because my measures are so detailed and objective. Scales don't lie. Weights don't lie. They go up or they don't. My power clean lift is very measurable. My sprints are measurable. My wins and losses are measurable. My grades and SAT scores are measurable. I measure my approval ratings with Allen, Mom, and Dad. I give myself check marks for their good comments and bad. I can't hide from myself and I don't. My goals and their pursuit test my mettle and provide great feedback as well. I often log quality of sleep in my Personal Journal. This I see as a current and future indicator."

"Sounds good. Good work. I do believe you are getting to know yourself quite well."

"Anthony, **Tune In to a Higher Power**, the second key, can really help me now. I know that this key for me is the cement that puts all of the keys together. I also see, as you once said, that prayer is best done after one has tried his best and failed. I still thank the Lord for all I have and seek His guidance, but I only ask for really important things and then I only ask after I have done all that I could do to deserve His help."

"That's the key to **Tune In to a Higher Power**. God hears all prayers but how can He take anyone's prayer seriously if they haven't done all they can do?"

"Anthony, I am still a little confused."

"At the risk of appearing to beg the question, the next key, **Pray and Meditate,** is perhaps the best technique to **Tune In to a**

Higher Power. For you as a Christian, the higher power is of course Christ. People have many different views, but the God of all major religions is truly very similar and one and the same, I believe. For those who have not come to believe in Christ many still believe in the Universe or the Universal Unconscious. They still know that there is a collective power or something bigger that they can and perhaps have already tuned into for help."

"Tuning in is a *decision to listen.* One doesn't need formal prayer or meditation to tune in. When you decide to listen to God, you will hear Him (or the Universe). Once we make **The Seven Steps** and the **Ten Keys** a part of our lives we can be tuned in. Once we are *living purposively* and staying in the moment, living with mindfulness, we will find that every moment of our lives can become a prayer or a state of meditation. Just make a decision to listen and you will **Tune In to a Higher Power**."

"I should know how to pray. I have been praying my whole life."

"Greg, **Pray and Meditate** *is* simple. We thank God for all He has done and we ask Him for things we really need. We seek His guidance, help to do things, and understand things. A problem solving request may be the best prayer one can offer. If you have a legitimate need, ask the Lord for assistance in understanding how to get it. Meditation, much like prayer, is best done when your mind is quiet, when you can set aside distractions. The relaxation alone may help calm your nerves and free up misguided energy."

"More so than mere relaxation, meditation can help you hear the answer to your prayers. It can help you tap into the collective unconscious, or God. Just as listening is a decision, hearing is a similar decision. There are many good books on meditation but fewer on how to pray. Some simple thoughts may help. First you relax, calm your mind, and thank God for all he has done, then ask for those things you need and can't do alone, and listen very intently for answers. Sometimes this is like doing some deep thinking with God effectively holding your hand."

"It should happen when you listen to your **Personal Commercial** and pray and think. Answers will come to you, solutions to little things and big things that may have eluded you.

You may notice that many answers actually come to you when you are listening to your **Personal Commercial**."

"Thanks for saying that. I have often felt strange that while I was supposed to be listening to my **Personal Commercial,** I often found I was coming up with solutions to some problems I had been having. So this means my **Personal Commercial** is working?"

"Precisely. Even as you tune out your **Personal Commercial** it is still getting in. Just like the jingles on TV. It is often during a run or a walk, while listening to one's **Personal Commercial**, that ideas to otherwise unsolved problems pop into our minds."

"Greg, the fourth key, **Forgive and Repent**, has a powerful effect on anyone who carries the burden of guilt."

"A proper conscience helps us determine when we have wronged people. If we have morals, then we will feel guilt and remorse. Proper atonement requires that we make up for the impropriety. However, if you just punched someone, you can't very well retract the punch. But you can apologize, ask forgiveness of God and yourself, and resolve to control your anger in the future. If you can make amends, do so. The world is fair, what goes around comes around, so be sure to do good things so that good things will happen to you."

"Remember that forgiveness, both giving and receiving, has a powerful baggage-removing effect. If you dislike anyone and especially if you truly hate someone, the hatred you harbor will eat at you and do nothing but weaken you. When Christ said to forgive your enemies it wasn't necessarily something that you did solely for your enemies. It is something you also do for yourself. Hate is a cancer that grows inside. Forgive and free the cancer."

"Whether harboring hatred, anger, lust, envy, or other negative emotion causes cancer itself really doesn't matter. It does cause pain and illness. So *forgive and live*. Make peace with everyone. Even for soldiers on the battlefield, where killing may be critical to survival and preservation of country, having hatred won't help. You can choose not to hate even in the worst of times. None of this hatred and lack of forgiveness will help. It can only hurt."

"Anthony, I study Zen. My mom asked me why and I said because the Zen monks approach life from a refreshing view opposite that of western civilization. It isn't about technology and *To Do Lists*. It is about the moment. This taught me about meditation and helped me to be my best during the six minutes of a wrestling match where as soon as you break concentration you can lose the match."

"This provides a perfect introduction to the fifth key, **Live in the Present,** Greg."

"In wrestling, every second counts, just like in life. In wrestling, lose concentration, you lose the match. In life much the same happens. Life slips by somehow while you're busy planning something else. Don't miss out on life. Don't spend time worrying about things that are out of your control."

"The serenity prayer often attributed to Reinhold Niebuhr says it best:

> *God grant me the serenity*
> *to accept the things I cannot change;*
> *the courage to change the things I can,*
> *and the wisdom to know the difference.*"

"One can only truly live in the moment. Fretting about the past or the future is both unproductive and hazardous. Worst of all, you miss the best that life has to offer: the birds chirping, the warmth of the sun, and the beauty of nature. When your mind is cluttered they all pass unnoticed."

"Life is not a dress rehearsal. Greg, this is incredibly hard to teach. One devout mother told me recently, 'I would love to live in the moment but I find I am always worrying about my children. I worry about whether or not they eat, what I pack them for lunch. I worry whether other students are nice to them. I worry about tobacco and drugs that may tempt them.'"

"She then asked, 'What is wrong with this motherly worry?' She said her mother did the very same thing and everything worked out. I asked her if she believed in God. She said 'yes.' I asked her if God was all-powerful and all-just. She said 'yes.' Then I said, 'Don't you believe that after you have done all you could that the Lord would take over from there?' She honestly replied, 'I had never thought about it like that.'"

"I then asked her how worrying could possibly help? She only responded, 'Isn't it a mother's duty to worry?' I asked her, 'Does the Bible tell us to worry?' She couldn't think of where it did. I think she may even feel guilty about worrying."

Greg answered, "She feels guilty about worrying? It doesn't sound as if you solved her problem."

"I just try to help people who ask. I'm not always successful."

"Well, if you ever need a reference, you'd get a supernal one from me."

"You *are* working on diplomacy, Greg."

"Precisely."

"Back to the housewife: I do think she's worrying a little less and doing a little more about it. She started taking a little more initiative by getting involved in the grade school so that she could positively influence her children's environment. She worries less now because she has less time to worry. Worry is a *sign* you have too much *time*."

"Living in the Present is also the easiest way to live. Like the other keys, this one plays a part in the others. We need to forgive others and ourselves so that our minds aren't clogged with guilt and worry. Greg, you've just started to drive so you may not yet relate but a policeman in your rear view mirror is a good test of living in the moment."

"The first part of the test is failed if he sneaks up on you. You fail because you were not paying close attention to the road and traffic around you. But the next test is when you see that policeman in the rear view mirror. Do you smile or do frissons of paranoia envelop you? If you don't remember one of these reactions you may the next time it happens. Someone who obeys the law and is a careful driver has no fear when a policeman appears in the rear view mirror. Those with a guilty conscience, whether due to habitual speeding or more egregious activities, may experience frissons of fear. If your blood pressure rises, you are not Living in the Present, free of worry and guilt. You are not fully living."

"Anthony, this key is hard. I often daydream. Living in the Present for six minutes is extremely hard. It seems only because the result lies in the balance am I able to concentrate during a complete match. A whole day is unimaginable."

"**Live in the Present** requires practice, the right attitude, and may not even begin to appear until most of the keys have begun to take affect."

"What attitude?"

"The attitude that comes with the true knowledge that every second counts. So, live each second to the fullest. You don't have googols of them. You can still have time for reverie. But don't have it while you're driving or wrestling. When you act, act. Do it with intention. Live with intention. Take care in all you do. **Live in the Present** acknowledges that there really are no unimportant activities. Think how powerful that is. Have you read Salinger's *The Catcher in the Rye*?"

"Sure, we all did as sophomores."

"Greg, what was the book about? Who was the catcher and why was it important?"

"Is this a trick question about foul language? We certainly were entertained. Like a sugar-coated pill we all found amusement in Holden's candor and scurrility. But it was simply about growing up. Everyone wants to save people when they are young. We all start out wanting to be firemen."

"What happens, Greg?"

"Well, we find out that we can't all be or we can't always be the *Catcher* who saves people."

"And what does this mean?"

"Anthony, this means we should grow up and understand that to die nobly for a cause is something we can't usually do. So instead we should live humbly for one."

"Greg, what is living humbly for a cause?"

"Live in the Present?"

"Precisely. Live each second. Living in the Present is its own reward. We are each given opportunities to contribute to our own welfare and others. If we live in the present, then we can perform well regularly."

"Anthony, I know of death. I faced mine. I could have been in that taxi with Pam. I know not just intellectually but emotionally, I could die at any time. This knowledge helps me live in the present. You never know how much time you have. I have faced Pam's death and with it my own. And fears, I still have them and I seek them out and confront them as you have taught me."

"Precisely, Greg. I think you have done much to learn the sixth key: **Accept Death and Face Fear.**"

"Your ability to recognize the noradrenalin rush of fear and to use it to your advantage shows you truly understand fear. Fear represents a reaction to the unknown, a signal or warning. Listen to the warning and take the appropriate reaction. Don't hide from fear or the reaction. Use it that way and your life will be better for it."

"For many people, death represents the biggest fear. One may fear travel by plane or train. One may fear crossing the street. Accepting death as inexorable and combining this belief with the fairness of God and our acceptance of our fate causes death to lose much of its hold upon us. If you believe God will judge you fairly, then death no longer carries the magic power of rendering life futile. Life becomes more pleasant without the fear of death hanging over us."

"Anthony, when I accepted the fact that I could and ultimately would die it had a calming affect upon me. I felt a certain release. It made me more relaxed and helped me feel a sense of purpose, but I wasn't very happy about it. The knowledge of death didn't make me feel happy. Maybe, that's why I find the seventh key, **Have Fun,** so compelling."

"Greg, you seem to **Have Fun.** You often joke. You take life very seriously without taking yourself too seriously. Some people feel that play is wrong or undeserved. Play promotes the first step of having a positive attitude. It is critical to keeping up a good attitude and not burning yourself out. The person who works so hard as to ignore the rest of his life is merely a cliché. That person could have trouble finding heaven. Many people don't feel good about feeling good. It's that simple."

"Simple? That sounds like a riddle. Why is fun important? Accepting Death is important, but having fun doesn't have any obvious benefits."

"Greg, remember the endorphins — the great natural chemicals that flow in your body when you smile and when you laugh? Scientists can prove endorphins help us. We all know that smiling feels better than frowning. Fun helps us in many ways. We all need exercise but not many people want to do sprints at 6:06. However, many people have a favorite sport such as basketball, soccer, baseball, golf, or volleyball..."

"Or wrestling?" interjected Greg.

"Precisely. And as much as we can make fun *fun*, we should. Remember in *The Adventures of Huckleberry Finn* by Mark Twain? Huck made painting fun for Tom and Tom enjoyed helping Huck. Although Huck's motives were suspect, he surely made work fun. We can do this at home or at the office. It may be even more important when facing an unpleasant task."

"If one finds work a chronic drudge, then it is surely time to consider a new line of work. The closer you are to living a *purposive life*, the happier you will be when performing your daily tasks and work. Look at those around you. Most happy people are doing what they want to do. Greg, you said this yourself when we discussed hard work. You said that most of what you did from studying to working out to wrestling was fun. Make wrestling at States fun. Enjoy it. There is no next year for you. Enjoy it. Have fun. Wrestle loose and you will do your best."

"But I have to concentrate."

"Greg, this doesn't take away the fun. Games require concentration, too."

"I get it, Anthony. Thanks."

"**Love Everyone**, the eighth key, regrettably sounds banal. It has become cliché. The word love is used and abused but make no mistake, if there were but one key, Greg, **Love Everyone** would be it."

"How's that? How will my loving everyone, help me beat Mulino? I don't really think this key applies to me, right now."

"Greg, we talked about the power of fun and the endorphins, those wonderful chemicals your body makes to help you? Love can do this and even more powerful things. Love keeps families together. Love raises children and helps us have compassion. One often talks about the beauty of the bride. Love makes one shine. People get better."

"But Mulino won't care about my love."

"You will be better, stronger, and more alive with Love in your heart. You will be free to wrestle hard. Don't hate Mulino, love him, respect him, but don't fear him. If you love him, Greg, how can you fear him? It is hard."

"I won't fear him or give him power over me if I love him? That makes some sense."

"**Help Others**, the ninth key, seems to be something that you work on, Greg."

"How you interact with your parents, your brother, your teachers, and your classmates shows you care. You seek to help. The hardest part about helping, before you make a decision to be helpful, is to know when and how to help. Sure, those who desperately need our help are sometimes obvious and they shouldn't always need to ask. But with others, we need to be sure we are both wanted and necessary. Tying your brother's shoe when he is two years old is properly helping him. But as he gets older and more capable your help may become interference in his personal growth."

"Wait for people to ask for your help. Only then can you be sure that those requesting will be receptive. The words nosey, busybody, and know-it-all describe improper helpers. You may also feel more appreciated. You will receive more 'thank-you's.' "

"Anthony, don't we also honor our fellow man by helping as best we can where we are wanted and needed?"

"Precisely. But it takes much effort to know when one is truly needed. But it should be easy to tell when one is wanted."

"I continue to learn this, Anthony. My brother presented a good lesson for me. I always thought my brother wanted to know everything I know. While it may be true he certainly doesn't always or even often want to learn it from me. We get along so much better now that I don't interfere."

"Anthony, what about **Pursue Your Purpose**?"

"Ah yes, the tenth and final key. What would you like to know?"

"Am I pursuing my purpose by wrestling?"

"Greg, you are the expert on you. But since you know the answer let me ask you again, why do you wrestle?"

"I love it. I think the moves flow like a bird in flight. You use all of your muscles including your brain. Every match is unique like a chess match. You can participate as a team, but it is just you out there on the mat. You don't have to wait for someone to throw you the ball. We use no tools. It is just you with very little protection. You get to use many different techniques. You use speed and your brain. Flexibility, strength, and conditioning all play a role. It requires a very high degree of fitness and a very low body fat level. It is simple to understand. In most matches it is obvious who won. Your parents and friends can watch and they find it exciting. It is perhaps the world's oldest sport. It was an original Olympic event."

"As you said, Anthony, it is character building. I count on myself and only look for the moral support from the team. I balance exercise, weight control, strength and still use my mind to win. It takes planning, hard work, discipline, and perseverance; almost all the keys. Anthony, wrestling makes me a better person."

"So then, how does it fit in with pursuing your purpose?"

"Wrestling may not be my purpose in life, but it seems to play a huge part in helping me reach my goals and maybe I'll find my ultimate purpose by working hard."

"Precisely. So Greg, is this the discussion of the **Personal Growth Cycle** and **Ten Keys** you had in mind?"

"Yes! I am convinced I am on the right track, but I still have much more to do. I think I can take wrestling at States very seriously without missing out on the fun of the experience. I don't hate John."

"John?"

"Mulino. I don't hate him. I don't fear him. I can't yet get to the love thing, but I don't wish him or anyone else harm."

"Greg, let me ask you. Are you prepared for States physically? Have you done all you can and should do?"

"Yes, I think so. I am prepared. I have worked hard. My workout seems to me to be as good as anyone's. I make every practice count. I set goals for every practice, every workout. I record everything in my Personal Journal. I improve each day. My resting pulse continues to fall. My morning pulse has gone from 60 something to 47. My sprints have improved. My cleans and benches are up. I have devised a style that fits me. I follow my wrestling plan on match day even when it bores me. I study the opposition. I use a **Personal Commercial** *sui generis*, uniquely created for each pre-match warm-up. I get up for each match the same way and it almost always works. I can't remember when my endorphins didn't kick my frissons into high gear to help out. What have I left out?"

"Greg, I believe you always keep a positive attitude. And have you completed your visualization before each bout?"

"Yes."

"Did your visualization come with real details so that you could see your parents in the crowd?"

"Yes."

"Did the wrestler have a face? Perform realistic moves?"

"Not always a face, but yes as to moves."

"Did they wrestle much as you visualized?"

"Anthony, sometimes my visualization ended up being very far from the actual match. But surprisingly, each visualization helped me in some way. I was always less distracted and I usually worked through what I would do during the actual match. When my opponent gets a bloody nose, I am in the moment enough to drift towards my coach to hear good advice. I would say overall I am less flustered by things I didn't think of because I had quick answers ready for almost everything that happened."

"That is exactly what visualization should do. It would be nice if we could predict what a wrestler will do but mentally visualizing a match, especially for those wrestlers you know, can be very powerful. Your thoughts construct patterns that your body can follow. The technique helps you learn without the actual experience. It helps you prepare for everything."

"Sometimes when people pack for a vacation they can do a fast forward, assessing the myriad details of the entire trip. This way they rarely forget tickets, socks, ties, hotel reservations, or a map. Remember to keep the visualization positive and realistic. If you are going to an unknown location such as a rival gym, you may want to attend one of their matches in advance. The fewer surprises, the better and the more your Visualization is accurate, the more benefit the visualization can be. Greg, do you remember how I tested your visualization about a wrestling match?"

"Sure, you asked me to get into the visualization and when I did you asked me, 'Look up into the stands. Do you see your dad? How is he dressed?' I thought that was odd."

"But it worked. When you said, 'I don't know,' you often weren't really in the visualization mode. Visualization can be difficult but once mastered can be a powerful force for good."

"You're right. I love it. It shocks me how my conscious mind, once relaxed a little, can go off into a dream-like state. I use it more and more. It's a *Directed Daydream,* isn't it?"

"Precisely, Greg. Maybe we should call it, '3D.' You need a real visual. Some have never had a conscious daydream. For one, the experience may be difficult. But it gets easier with time. Some actually fear it. They may fear losing control and of course they can. But if they do they may merely stop the dream and start again."

Chapter Twenty-Five
States

Greg began his final week of preparation for States. He would wrestle and drill a little more for speed and agility. His strength work was done, and he would be careful and go lightly on sprints but still get in solid workouts. He was intent upon hitting his peak at States.

The Seven Steps and **Ten Keys** stayed in his mind and a new **Personal Commercial** was recorded. He choreographed the whole event. Before the event, he drove down to the host site with Coach Gallo. Atlantic City was not far. He saw where the mats would be set up. He added crowds and noise as he remembered from last year, when he was a spectator. He now remembered in his visualization to have fun. He saw the people, his coach, his parents; he even looked for Pam. He didn't know the 24 wrestlers in his weight class, only John Mulino and a few others, including the regional champ, who shouldn't have beaten him, David Garris.

Greg visualized for the better part of an hour, stopping and starting and repeating. He would visualize more in practice, doing so while wrestling so that the actual moves matched his thoughts. He would never make a move or take a shot that he wouldn't take in the real match. He would even call top and bottom. He saw his colored anklet identifying him as green or red. He would adjust his headgear. He became better and better at his visualizations, even surprising himself with the reality of the details.

Take Control of Your Life

While formal practice had stopped after Districts, his training continued smoothly. He had Sean and a few others agree to spar and go takedowns to keep his timing and moves in sync. Pulling back on his training even as slightly as he did was hard, but it helped. The Greg of last year would have burned out by over training. He wanted to stay hungry for the tournament. At States all wrestlers had solid technical skills, a fair amount of strength, and good endurance. Just a small increase in any of these could be the margin for victory. Greg always believed he had one more gear in him, and he felt it kicking in during this final week of preparation.

Friday morning, the weigh-in went smoothly, 122 7/8. No wasted cutting. No severe dehydration. No cramps and no need for much more than water, apple juice, and cookies. The real-food oatmeal cookies his mother made with honey went straight into his bloodstream. He kept loose and relaxed all morning. He hadn't found out whom he would wrestle, except that Region seconds always wrestled Region third-place finishers. He would meet a third-place finisher seeded below him in the first round. Greg took one step at a time. If a guy had lost to Mulino in his Region Semi-Final he could still be the second best wrestler in the state and out on the mat against Greg.

After completing his visualization, a prayer, and a talk with Gallo, Greg acknowledged his parents in the stands. He looked for Anthony and Pam, although he didn't expect to see either of them. Just thinking positive, Greg reminded himself: he donned his headgear and green anklet and took the mat.

The first bout of States, Round 1:

Greg felt comfortable using his backing away strategy regardless of the risk of stalling calls. One minute into the first period his backing and circling drew a whistle. "Stalling on green." Greg looked down, even though he knew he was green he couldn't help the reaction. Stalling? He knew States was different, but one minute into the bout? A few seconds later and Greg found himself in a scramble that mercifully ended off the mat.

"I've been here before," thought Greg. "I'm not going to change my strategy based on the stalling call. I can still catch him moving into me." Greg dropped in for a picture-perfect single. He easily converted it to two points as the first period ended.

Maintaining his strategy Greg rode his opponent as long as he could, riding legs and dropping to a leg on stand-up escape attempts. He gained just under a minute of riding time as his opponent escaped. He continued to back away, always prepared to take advantage of a poor shot or an overaggressive forward motion. While the first stalling call came early, no other stalling calls were made. The bout ended 3-1.

The second bout of States, Round 2:

One and one-half hours later Greg drew the Region champ from District 3. Only 16 wrestlers remained: all of the Region champs and most Region runners-up like Greg. Of the eight bouts, only two third-place finishers had won. Gallo scouted opponents during the last hour to report on Greg's Round 2 foe, Clay Findlay, a lanky guy nearly six feet tall who had counter-wrestled his way through the Region 3 tournament. During his visualization, Greg decided not to use his defensive style on the guy. It didn't seem right. Clay was a very good defensive wrestler. He wouldn't be aggressive enough to make Greg's style work.

In Greg's visualization, he ducked under into a double and picked up Clay quickly and dropped him down to his back. He didn't try to ride him or let him counter or switch. He would have put him straight down to his back. He'd let him go if he got back to his base. If he got into a scramble he would grab a leg and hold on.

He knew he was stronger but few of his moves would work well on this tall guy.

The match began and Greg played coy for but a few seconds. From a near three-point football stance, he proceeded to drive into Clay and tackled him for two. His momentum so quickly overpowered them both that Greg didn't have the balance necessary to pick him up, and Clay turned quickly so as not to go straight to his back. The ref called, "Two green," and blew the whistle as they went off the mat. Clay was dazed. Greg promptly let him up. Greg backed up for a few seconds and launched the same assault, receiving another quick two points. Clay stood up quickly and Greg dropped to pick up his leg with Clay reaching over, seeking to gain a reversal over the top.

Nearly a minute went by and the action stopped for blood on the mat. Greg waited for Clay to be attended to until the ref came to him and led him to Gallo. Greg hadn't noticed he was bleeding. One of the two double legs had caused his nose to bleed profusely. With the piece of a tissue securing Greg's nose, they resumed the match. The whistle then blew signaling the end of the first period. Greg remembered little more. Tired and bloody he had won, 6-3. Gallo picked him up in congratulation and then told him his draw in quarterfinals would be David Garris, the guy he had lost to in Region Finals. Gallo seemed so excited about it. Greg asked why.

"Why? Because you out-wrestled him in the Region Finals. You had the takedown at the end and besides the stalling call was ridiculous. You can beat him. You *did* beat him! After you beat Garris, you get Mulino in the Semis."

"Yes," said Greg. "I guess I'll only think about that after I get by David."

Shortly thereafter, Greg's dad found Greg and congratulated him on his match. He looked at Greg's nose, which must have been scary at that point, and said. "You okay? You looked good out there. That guy's a basketball player. You looked good. Just two more bouts, Greg."

"Three, Dad. First I beat Garris from Regions, then I meet Mulino."

"You mean *beat* Mulino?"

"That's right, then I *beat* Mulino!"

Mr. Gurist went back to the stands and consoled his wife who had said during the last bout that the whole thing should be stopped. She found the blood reprehensible. He assured her that it wasn't a big deal as the bleeding had stopped. This became obvious when Greg ran up the bleachers and gave his mom a big hug and a kiss. She thought, "If he can smile that mile-wide-smile, he's feeling pretty good."

She turned to her husband and said. "He looks good!"

"That's exactly what I told him."

Greg had skipped his visualization exercise when Anthony came up to him just before the match. "Greg, how are you doing? I understand you have Garris from Regions. Going with the same strategy? How was the Visualization?"

Greg said, "I'm just starting it now, we'll have to talk later." He still hoped he had enough time to warm up and complete the visualization. He usually had finished it by this time.

When Greg finally stepped on the mat 16 minutes later, he said a quick prayer and thanked the Lord for sending Anthony to remind him of the visualization. Because he had wrestled Garris before he had unthinkingly decided to forsake this part of his mental preparation. He now realized the gravity of his omission. But he was ready now.

Yes, he knew he could win, but Garris felt the same and had in fact won at Regions. Garris had been a straight-ahead wrestler.

Both had been cautious but Greg had been warned for stalling. Both had escaped. The only real action had consisted of his last second single leg. In the visualization Greg had tried to duplicate the set-up for the move but couldn't quite choreograph the actual Region Finals single. He knew however that he had been the aggressor over the last 20 seconds and it had nearly paid off. He remembered using a limp arm to release his arm from Garris' whizzer. Greg knew he would have to convert quickly to avoid a successful counter. His Visualization seemed solid and he visualized the win, even without the perfect recall of Regions.

Quarterfinals: The David Garris Match.

Garris and Gurist spent no time reminiscing Region Finals. Both seemed intent upon gaining the first takedown. David attacked first and moved Greg off the mat several times but clearly Greg attempted to circle while David moved with confidence forward, attempting a variety of single leg moves off a tie-up. Greg, in turn, saw several openings as David exposed his own legs with his aggressive attempts. Both wrestlers secured positions on singles that were fought off successfully. The first period ended with no scoring. Garris chose the down position. Greg worked hard to break David down. His tight waist had been plenty to hold down many wrestlers, but David's turning in on a switch and grabbing Greg's wrist in the stand-up kept Greg from breaking him down. Greg dropped to a leg on several stand-up attempts and stalemates were called. Finally with twenty seconds left in the period Garris, after getting off the mat for a fresh start, stood up and turned in for a switch. Greg backed off, giving up an escape rather than a reversal.

The second period ended with Garris ahead, 1-0.

With one minute and forty seconds of riding time Greg could win if he escaped in forty seconds, assuming, of course, no other scoring. Greg had escaped before in Regions in just 30 seconds or less, he remembered. He awaited the whistle feeling wound tight as a drum ready to burst to his feet. He quickly visualized a stand-up left leg first with his left hand down to block an arm that might grab his waist, or drop to his leg then his right hand to grab and control Garris' right arm as he turned back in. He saw it. He felt it. Finally, the whistle blew and Greg instantly jumped to his feet. This time Garris dropped down directly to his leg. Greg reached over to lift Garris' leg to reverse, but Garris held on. The ref called a stalemate.

Gallo yelled, "20 seconds!" Greg understood.

He got back to his feet, and anticipating the smeltsly ripped his left foot away, as Garris dropped towards it. Greg completely broke free and heard the ref call, "One point escape, red."

Greg looked towards the clock but didn't see it as the ref whistled the neutral start. Garris now started driving even more forcefully, taking several shots and working for arm control in some serious pummeling. Then the ref's whistle blew, "Timeout! Blood." Greg looked down and saw blood on the mat and on Garris. Seeing blood on Garris' arms, he knew who was bleeding. He was.

This time his nose wouldn't stop bleeding. Gallo had him lie back and got a wet cloth as the ref and others went to clean the mat that seemed to have drops of crimson all over the area where they last wrestled. Garris' pummeling had caught Greg's nose dead on. He had felt some pain but hadn't noticed the blood flow.

Gallo said, "Greg, there's 56 seconds left. You still have to wrestle or these refs will call stalling. But you do have a minute and eight seconds riding time. In the unlikely event he takes you down if you can get out quickly you can send it into overtime. But don't give it up. Circle, but you're still going to have to take a shot or two to prevent the stall."

After nearly two minutes, as Greg lay back, the ref went to Gallo, asking if Greg would forfeit. Coach Gallo shook his head no, cleared Greg's nose of clotted blood, quickly re-stuffed it with tissue, and sent Greg back in. The match would continue.

Greg backed away and refused to allow Garris' arm swing motions, pummeling, to bother him. "Warning, stalling red!" called the ref with 30 seconds to go. Greg knew he had to shoot but he was awaiting an opening that never presented itself. Garris made an excellent shot at a single and got in deep on Greg's leg. Gallo jumped to his feet as Greg threw in a whizzer and the clock ticked down. They both were fighting for position at the edge of the match. Garris attempted to step over the whizzer and cover Greg's leg so as to gain control and the takedown. Greg was attempting to drive Garris' shoulder down to the mat and keep him off balance to prevent control and move them off the mat. Finally, Garris stepped behind and pulled Greg towards him, gaining control as the ref called, "Two points green."

Greg looked up. The buzzer had rung. The time was at zero and the ref immediately retracted the call until the scorers could confer. The ref and scorekeepers declared with one point riding time: Greg won, 2-1.

"I got the call this time," Greg thought. Two matches down to the buzzer with Garris.

Garris congratulated Greg. "Good," he said. "You get Mulino."

"Mulino in Semis! Mulino in Semis!" Greg yelled at Gallo, who was jumping around as if he had been the victor.

"What happened? You win the lotto?" Greg's dad said smilingly.

Greg's mom also came down from the stands to greet Greg. "How are you, Son? I've never seen a nose bleed like that."

"Mom, I love you. I beat him. I won! Dad, my goal all year has been to face Mulino in States. Sure, I wish this were the Finals but still this is pretty close to my wish, my dream, and my plan! Have you seen Anthony?"

"No, I haven't. In fact, I called him this morning, as we had hoped he would drive with us, but I didn't get through."

"You didn't see him? I just wanted to thank him. He really helped me on my Garris bout. I almost skipped my visualization routine."

"Son, I've yet to even meet Anthony. How would I know if he were here?"

Greg's face went blank and then he felt a certain warmth and peaceful feeling as he shifted his thinking to his match with Mulino. He then looked up at his dad and said, "He came to me just a half hour ago."

"I haven't seen him, the number you gave me didn't work, and I haven't seen you with anyone but Coach Gallo."

Greg drank some cool water and ate some more of his mom's oatmeal, honey, and raisin cookies. He watched the end of Mulino's quarterfinal bout, then sat down on one of the warm-up mats and thought about Semis. He had already visualized his bout with Mulino many, many times. He wouldn't lapse like he almost had with Garris. Mulino was the real deal...

"Mulino has never wrestled me," he thought. But I've wrestled him a hundred times. Even winning a few, he chuckled to himself. Even in his visualization Greg found it hard to beat Mulino. He had talked to Anthony about that fact and he had said, "Greg, that just goes to show how good your process has become. Continue to improve your moves on Mulino in your visualization. Work on them in practice and then visualize again. One should help the other. Focus on the moves that work well in the visualization."

Greg had watched Mulino's bouts, including part of his quarterfinal bout. He could now accurately imagine how he moved. He could see and feel his strength and speed. He was impressed but undaunted. He could hear Anthony say, "A healthy respect is good; trepidation is not."

Greg continued his work on his visualization. Mulino's style depended upon guys moving towards him. Greg had been working the second half of the season, moving backwards and learning how to drop under a charging opponent who is lulled into thinking his opponent will continue to back away.

This has got to frustrate Mulino, thought Greg. Everyone seems to wrestle him straight up. No one at this tournament backed away from him. He will not get his good looks if I am moving away…and circling, he mindfully added. I can't let stalling calls lose this bout. I want to be sure the best wrestler wins. Regardless of the score, there should be plenty of excitement.

Greg knew Mulino moved very predictably. He stood in a pose for his team's photo and it wasn't just for show. He often wrestled half wound-up, liked a cocked windmill, for the inevitable pancake that he could rapidly convert into a pinning combination. Greg remembered one regional champ with a great barrel roll, Wojechowski, trying to work it on Mulino. Wojechowski would drive for a double leg and as his opponent sprawled to flatten him, he would underhook and pull the wrestler under and around for a barrel roll takedown. He had done this to many very solid wrestlers. He tried it on Mulino. Mulino let him drive for the double and simply pancaked him flat to his back for five points. Mulino was strong. Greg had no intention of driving on Mulino to have his own energy turn into points for Mulino.

Greg began his Visualization by imagining what Gallo would say during warm-up: "Greg, use your strategy. Back up and circle. Don't let him get set. Don't let him tie-up. Watch his left leg move forward as he drops his right back. You'll know when he will shoot. You need to be one step ahead of him. Keep anticipating. Be warned, Greg, he has been here before. The refs know him. They may give him the benefit of the doubt so be careful on the edge. Get off the mat when you need to but keep circling. Look at me, Greg. Mulino can be beaten. He has never faced anyone with your style. Go get him!"

As the ref handed him his green anklet, Greg pleasantly noted he could see color. He didn't often see color in his visualizations. Adjusting his headgear and listening for the ref to start the bout, the wrestling part of the visualization began. Mulino stood there in the middle awaiting Greg to come towards him. Greg didn't.

So Mulino blinked, thought Greg, now watching and creating simultaneously. Mulino's movement forward was a bit awkward as his set-up always had wrestlers moving towards him or standing still while he moved towards them. He watched Mulino's feet carefully and moved out of the way just as Mulino began his move. You could see a look of surprise come across Mulino's face. He didn't know what Greg was doing but it seemed that every time he set up, Greg moved back just enough to require a new set-up.

Greg completed the visualization, and felt good about it. The result was a 1-1 tie and overtime. Overtime only took about four minutes with only two minutes of wrestling, Greg knew that it was close to perfect with a solid result. He wasn't going to continue the visualization. He only added the conclusion of the bout with his hand being raised in victory as Mulino fell to the mat in defeat as Greg unconsciously searched the crowd for Pam and his parents. The pictures in his head were now crisp, clean, and favorable.

Greg then began his physical warm-up and listened to his new **Personal Commercial** sui generis, made just for this tournament. It was focused on Mulino, concentration, maintaining style, turning noradrenalin into power, and yes, having fun. He continued his warm-up and looked around smiling and reflecting on how perfect this tournament was. He was where he was meant to be.

This is my time. He said a prayer that he often said. Even though one could easily recognize prayers embedded in Greg's **Personal Commercial**, this prayer included thanks for all his countless blessings, his family, friends, and loved ones. He asked for strength, endurance, and a continued positive outlook. His prayer, personal to Greg, covered many of Anthony's keys and the Lord's Prayer. And he thought of Pam. He knew she would be watching.

"This one's for you, Pam. This one's for you."

Semi-Finals: The John Mulino Match.

Greg knew he couldn't be more ready. *Bring it on. Bring it on,* Greg thought. His bout called, he stood on the side and listened to Gallo.

"You can take this guy, Greg. You've come pretty far. Is it over, Greg?"

"No, Coach. It's just beginning."

"Remember to keep him out of position. Watch his left — it telegraphs his move. If you get called for stalling, you get called. Keep working your back-up and keep circling. Mulino has never wrestled anyone like you, Greg. You will frustrate him. Stick to your plan."

"Got it, Coach. Thanks."

"Go get him, Greg." Gallo added.

No surprises there. The ref handed Greg a green anklet and Greg smiled at the ref. So far both Gallo's speech and the anklet were spot on, thought Greg, but back to the here and now. The two were brought to the center and the match began. Mulino moved towards Greg as Greg backed away. Greg continued to back away as the wrestlers went off the mat and then brought back to center. Mulino stood still in the center, and Greg also maintained his position too far for either to tie-up or shoot.

The ref made a motion as to say it's okay to start. Mulino moved forward and Greg watched the left leg and saw the cake coming. Greg circled left as he had planned and Mulino was out of position to hit his move. Greg continued to circle and more confidently began to look for an opening. He had visualized a takedown halfway through the third but as Mulino seemed a little sluggish he felt he might get an earlier opportunity. Mulino began moving in more quickly and Greg continued to anticipate as Mulino moved his left leg forward before his shot. Greg felt quick and precise and exactly where he wanted to be, away and to the left of Mulino's attack.

Mulino started to anticipate Greg's leftward movement and attempted to cut him off. Greg then moved right and almost caught Mulino with a double that drove him off the mat. The ref had been preparing to warn Greg for stalling when Greg made the shot. Mulino powerfully got under Greg's attempt and the crowd made serious noise as Mulino threw him, but did so well off the mat. It would have been a four or five point move.

"Good shot," Greg thought. "I was there. I've got to finish faster, which I could with a single," he remembered from his visualization. The first period came to a scoreless end just as Greg had visualized. The match seemed to be happening somewhat in slow motion for Greg. He saw all of Mulino's moves, not that he could easily stop them. He worked harder on maintaining a position that put John out of position.

Mulino, having choice, chose down. With a big stand-up, he nearly shot to his feet as Greg lifted him off the mat and out of bounds. He stood up again and Greg dropped to a smeltsly and hung on for a stalemate call. With a fresh start he bolted up and turned, escaping in 26 seconds. *Not bad riding*, thought Greg.

Mulino, now leading by one point, wanted a lot more and upped his already formidable attack. As Greg backed away and circled, Mulino threw up his arms in disgust. The ref seemed to ignore the plea, as the second period ended.

Greg started in the down position. As he sprang to his feet Mulino picked him up and dropped him rapidly to the mat. Greg quickly stood up again and John repeated the move with even more force than before. It unsettled Greg. Mulino continued his ride until halfway through the third period. After a fresh start Greg stood up again and successfully getting his arms under Mulino's, turned in and broke free with 50 seconds left in the period. The ref yelled, "One point escape, green!"

Greg heard it as he had in his visualization. Mulino had but 44 seconds of riding time so they were truly tied at 1-1. Growing even more impatient, he threw Greg, but again they were off the mat. With just 30 seconds to go the ref blew the whistle, "Warning, stalling green." With the match tied, Mulino continued to shoot and Greg continued to stay out of range, with Mulino clearly the aggressor. There was little more action but for Greg backing and circling as the match went into overtime.

Greg felt great. No one had gone this far with Mulino in two years. Mulino was clearly frustrated and the ref saw that he was getting good shots but converting them off the mat. He also saw that Greg had made several credible attempts himself. The ref wanted the wrestlers to decide the bout. This referee had no apparent intentions to let a stalling call be the difference.

In the first overtime period Greg chose down and promptly escaped to lead 2-1. Mulino continued to pursue and Greg continued his defensive wrestling style, thwarting all of Mulino's shots. The first overtime one-minute period ended with Greg up 2-1. Mulino took down and as he stood up Greg dropped to a leg to smeltsly, but John picked up Greg's leg as his own was lifted and burst free. They had both escaped in seconds. Then Mulino totally stopped his pursuit and Greg circled and made several single shots that John countered. With the score tied, many anticipated a referee's decision. This could have cost Greg the match as his stalling call may be the deciding factor.

Gallo yelled, "Go get him, Greg! He's yours."

Greg became the aggressor. With 20 seconds left he got in on a single, picked up Mulino's leg high into the air, tripped him to the mat, and gained control, only to be called out of bounds. Gallo jumped up to complain. The ref went over and talked to him. A blown whistle could not be overturned, the call stood.

Then with only eight seconds remaining, Mulino caught Greg in a shot he made without a telltale left-foot warning. He spun Greg around landing him on his back in a perfect pancake that Greg bounced through and off the mat as time was called. Greg smiled as he awaited the outcome. The throw was so fast and Greg rolled right through that there was little question as to control. Greg assumed the refs were conferring on the criteria. *My takedown attempt was solid, not off the mat. I'll get credit for that in the referee's decision. I won! My visualization worked!*

Greg bounced up and down. "I did it. I did it!"

Gallo, kept saying, "Great match, Greg, great match, you took it to him."

The refs conferred at the scorers' table and then a point came up for Greg and two points came up for Mulino. They had given Mulino the takedown and Greg the escape.

Gallo yelled at the refs, "Where was the control?"

Mulino had won, but you wouldn't know it by either of their faces. Greg's elation didn't change although Mulino continued looking dejected.

He slowly turned to Greg and said, "Hey, great match. I couldn't do a thing."

"Hey, you did *win*. Congratulations."

Greg looked around and found his parents and brother, Allen. They all said he wrestled great and thought his takedown was on the mat and should have been called. Greg stood there talking to his parents, coach, and brother. They all congratulated him as he couldn't help but search the crowd for the two people he most wanted to celebrate with, Anthony and Pam.

Greg continued in consolations and placed third.

Greg called Anthony the day after the tournament to thank him for showing up in Atlantic City. It was Anthony's reminder to visualize that had gotten him past David Garris. The phone rang and rang. *That's strange. He always picks up on the second or third ring*. Then Greg heard, "You have reached a number that is not in service." *This is what my parents heard*. He then called an operator who confirmed the number was not in service and had not been in the last six months. Her records didn't tell her more.

Greg told his parents. They asked him who else knew or had met Anthony.

"I know that Pam did," Greg said. "But I'm not sure if anyone else had. He only came here once; when you were gone."

"When did he meet Pam?"

"Well, at the hospital they spoke."

"They spoke? Pam's parents told us she never regained consciousness. How did Anthony speak to her? Did Pam's parents see him at the hospital, Greg?"

"No, he left before they came."

"Greg, I am not questioning your honesty only my sanity, but tell me, has anyone but you ever seen or met Anthony?" Greg's father was dumbfounded. He couldn't imagine that Greg had fabricated him. Nor could he readily come up with an alternate explanation. The Gurists after many years came to view Anthony as someone or something somewhere between miracle and myth. Greg stopped talking about Anthony around his parents and never put himself in a position to be questioned about him again.

Greg knew, but couldn't say. Who would believe, he thought? *Just Pam.*

Chapter Twenty-Six
College Bound

Several days later the head coach from Lehigh University spoke with Greg's parents and set up a time for him to visit the school and meet a few of the wrestlers. This was Greg's first campus visit.

When Greg showed, several wrestlers came up to him and said they had heard he had beaten, or should have beaten, the three-time State Champ, Mulino. The coach said, "I saw a tape of the bout. It could have gone either way. Gurist wrestles with the power of a college wrestler. I think he would fit in well here."

"Especially if you teach me how to wrestle," joked Greg.

"How are your grades?" asked one wrestler.

"Pretty good," said Greg.

"Pretty good? Coach Gallo told me you were in the top 5 percent of your class, that you had made the National Honor Society, and that you had pinned the SAT."

"Well, yeah, pretty good," said Greg.

"Well," another wrestler said, "I guess you wrestle *pretty good*. So, are you coming?"

The End

[If you would like to hear from ***Anthony***… turn to page 243]

Appendices

PERSONAL GROWTH INDEX

Accept Fate, 11-14, 55, 169, 176, 212, **214**, 219, 229
Accept Death and Face Fear, 147, 156-159, 184, **224**, 230
Accomplishments, 18, 19, 22, 23, 158, 170, 215, 217
Analyze Results, 13, 14, 175, 212, **218**, 219, 229
Anger control, 24-32, 50, 85, 144, 179-180
Dating, **52-57**, 64-71, 92-102
Dieting, x, 58, 128, 142-144, 151, 226
    21 Points, **143-144**
    binging, 58, 139-147, **232**
Directed Daydream, 3D, 191, see also **Visualize Success**
Employment, 213, 227
Endorphins Corral Frissons, xi, **93-98**, 103-106, 109, 110, 190
Exercise, ix, x, xi, 31, 32, 92, 144, 185, 189, 226, 242
    Greg's workout, 64, 92-93, 113-114
    recovery, 114, 226
Fear control, 33-42, 104, 109, 182, 184, 187, 189, 224, see also Endorphins Corral Frissons
Forgive and Repent, 24-30, 51, 52, 63, 82-91, 134, 146, 147, 149, 158, **222**, 230
    reparations, making, 89-90
Have Fun, 34, 57, 81, 120, 173, 185, 186, 192, **226**, 230
Help Others, 152-155, 187, **227**, 230
Learn Who You Are, x, 169, 176, **218**, 219, 230
Live in the Present, vii, 39, 180-184, **223**, 224, 226, 230
Love Everyone, 186, **225**, 230
Measure Results, 13-14, 23, 174, 212, **217**, 218, 219, 229
Mindfulness, ix, 39, 178, 223, 226, also see **Live in the Present**
Nitric oxide, xi, 236
Nobility, poem, 149
Parental expectations, 106-109
Peak performance, 94, 96, 192, see also Zone
Personal Commercial, xi, **22-23**, 33, 34, 41, 42, 58, 63, 64, 93-95, 143, 158, 161, 170-172, 174, 179, 189, 192, 203, 212, 215, 221, 241-244
Personal Commercial Jingle, **22-23**, 41, 42, 58, 170
Personal Growth Cycle, The Seven Steps of, 11-16, 19, 22, 23, 34, 90, 166-175, **212-218**, 229, 230
Personal Journal, 23, 34, 42, 170, 171, 174-176, 189, 217-219
Pray and Meditate, 177-178, **220**, 221, 228, 230
Problem solving, 12, 29, 31, 51, see also Whys Approach
Purposive living, 171, 178, 189, 217, 223, **237**
Pursue Your Purpose, 171, 188, **228**, 230
SAT, 52, 103-110, 160, 176, 242
Serenity Prayer, **181**, 214
Set Goals, 12-16, 170-171, 174, 212, **215**, 229, 242
Seven Steps, The (see also **Personal Growth Cycle**)
Study, how to, 65, 69-70, 72, 73
Sun, get out in the, 79-80, 181
Survivor syndrome, 158, 239
Ten Keys, x, 22, 90, 166-192, 212, **219-228**, 230
To Do List, 41, 58, 171, 180, 217
Think Positive, 10-14, 34, 39, 167, 212, **213**, 224, 225, 229
Tune In to a Higher Power, 177, 178, **220**, 221, 224, 230
Visualize Success, 12, 14, 33-57, 190-208, 212, **216**, 229, 239
Vocabulary, 103, see also Glossary 231
Whys Approach, **29-30**, 175
Work Hard, 12, 14, 37, 81, 106, 120, 157, 173, 212, **217**, 219, 225, 229
Worry, 44, 167, 181-182, 213, 223-225
Wrestling benefits, 55-56, 61, 77, 80, 81, 108
Zone, in the, 49-50, 94, 96, 221

[211]

The Seven Steps of the Personal Growth Cycle and the Ten Keys

The **Seven Steps of the Personal Growth Cycle,** the **Ten Keys,** and the **Personal Commercial** combine to assist those along a path of personal growth. The **Personal Growth Cycle** begins with **Think Positive**, **Accept Fate,** and **Set Goals.** You then **Visualize Success**, **Work Hard**, **Measure Results**, and finally, you **Analyze Results**. These are **The Seven Steps** in this ongoing self-improvement cycle. The cycle then begins anew.

The Cycle helps show how **Good Things Happen to Good People Who Do Good Things**.

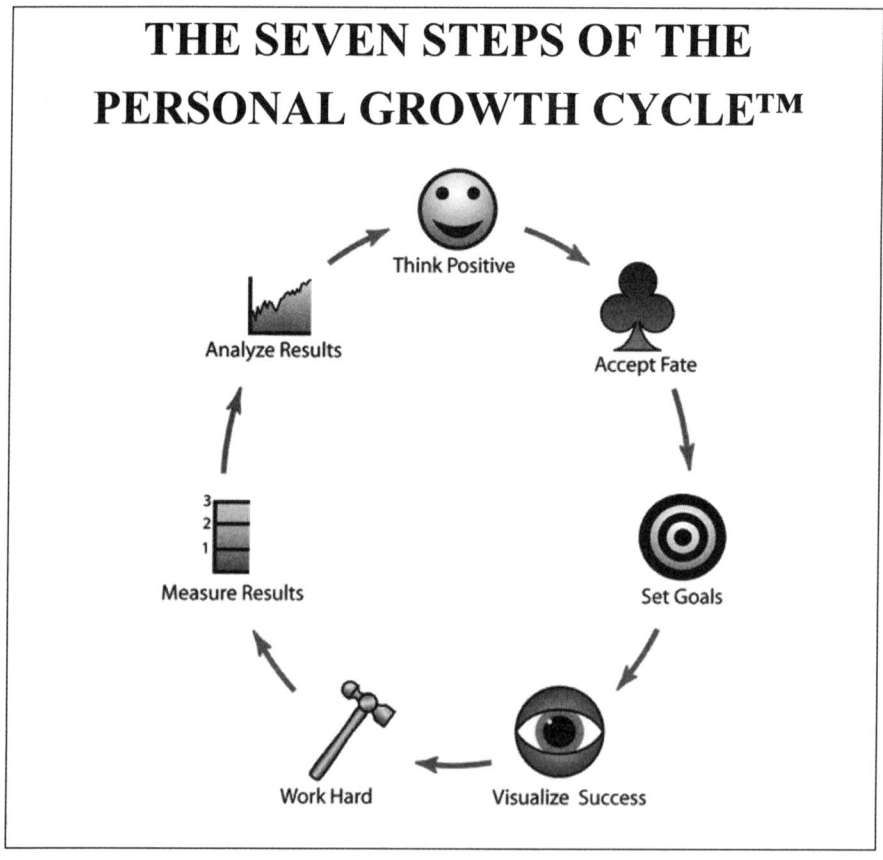

The Seven Steps of the Personal Growth Cycle

 Think Positive

Personal growth begins with thinking positive. To make this step work you must believe in yourself. This means more than having a smile on your face. This means you must always see the good and always think constructive thoughts. See the cup as half full and be worry-free. Be positive. Think Positive thoughts and do positive things. Remember to look for the good in all people and situations. *Good things happen to good people who do good things.*

Thinking about the good will bring good. The opposite is also true. Just as good things happen when you think positive thoughts, *bad things will happen when you worry*. What you think about, you create. This is the principle of Visualization. Think positively about getting good grades or a good job and you will find yourself doing things in furtherance of good grades or a good job. Worry about an illness and you risk developing that very malady.

Looking for the good in all things allows you to benefit from failure. Thomas Edison viewed failure as eliminating one thing that wouldn't work, thus bringing him closer to his goal.

Thinking positive aligns your actions so that you are prepared for good things. Being jobless and assuming people want to hire you puts your mind where it should be. Don't think you are bothering people in your search: realize you are helping someone find a great employee – you! As human beings, we all have an equal right to the wonderful benefits of this Universe.

Accept Fate

No true progress can be made until you accept your starting point and the rules of living. The serenity prayer often attributed to Reinhold Niebuhr explains it well:

> *God grant me the serenity*
> *to accept the things I cannot change;*
> *the courage to change the things I can,*
> *and the wisdom to know the difference.*

Accepting fate means to recognize who you are and where you are. Accept yourself and the Universe. Accept yourself as the miracle you are with all your faults and accept the Universe as the incredible miracle it is.

View the Universe as fair. This logic says that God is good. God is fair. Know that the Universe and God are good and fair. There are no real accidents. Even accidents happen for a reason. To know these things allows – it requires – you to accept your lot in life. If you were born with an infirmity, it is for a good purpose. Accept what you have. If you have lemons, make lemonade. Don't pine or claim your situation deplorable. Many people have struggled through infirmities that helped them become exceptional human beings. Some people have tremendous burdens. Some war prisoners suffering the horrors of the death camps still found a purpose in life and achieved spiritual growth.

You show progress by measuring advancement. You need a starting point to do so. If the starting point is inaccurate, your measurements will be futile and you won't see progress. True progress can be made when you accept your starting point and the rules of living.

 Set Goals

Properly Setting Goals is critical to creating an effective **Personal Commercial**. If you want to get somewhere you must decide where you want to go. Choosing goals requires you to learn about yourself. You must assess strengths, weaknesses, accomplishments, happy moments, sad moments, proud moments, likes, dislikes, and a no-holds-barred wish list, including all goals, desires, hopes, and dreams. After this initial self-assessment and inventory, long-term and short-term goals can be developed. After selecting a short list of one to three major goals, you then review each.

Evaluating a goal requires review of your assessment and an analysis of the goal: Why do you want the goal? Will the goal achievement make you happy and why? Why have you failed to achieve it in the past? What might block you now and what can you do to overcome these challenges? Once establishing the goal as worthy and desirable, you establish a measure for the goal and you establish strategies, tactics, and action plans to achieve it. Sometimes when you have little idea how to achieve it, your only action may be to study ways to achieve the goal and perhaps talk to those or read about those who have done it or may help you find out how to do it.

Goals should be measurable with timelines so that you know when you have met them. They must be realistic but they need only be realistic to you. Edison's light bulb looked impossible to his peers. A detailed path to achievement should be developed and those first steps to achieving it should be identified. Include in the actions the important steps related to motivation as well.

 Visualize Success

After setting proper goals you must **Visualize Success**. When you see your success, reflect upon your success, and imagine the enjoyment of your successes, you do this. When you mentally prepare for each and every important event, you create your own personal movie, scripting and performing each step toward your goal. You should visualize success from beginning to end. You see the goal as accomplished and you imagine the enjoyment of the accomplishment.

If your goal is to marry a special woman or man, make your Visualization take place at the reception, perhaps on the dance floor with your friends and family watching. Feel your reaction and see their reaction. Make it real; see it, feel it, hear it, touch it, and smell it if you can. Use all your senses in the Visualization. If your goals include a hands-only rope climb and well-defined abs, then visualize yourself moving up the rope freely with your sculpted body. Watch your peers as they praise your achievement.

The more accurate and detailed the visualization, the greater the impact. If you have trouble visualizing the achievement, use this failure as a sign you need to do more planning and analysis.

Work Hard

Work Hard means take the appropriate action. It is the last part of *Good Things Happen to Good People Who Do Good Things*. **Work Hard** means to take the actions that you planned when you set your goals. It means following a *To Do List*.

Working hard is not all about hard work. It is doing the right thing, right now. With practice all work becomes simple, less like hard work, and even enjoyable. The more purposively you live your life, the more effortless **Work Hard** becomes, ultimately leading to a self-fulfilled life.

Measure Results

Measure Results. Record the actions you take and the results of your actions each day in your Personal Journal. You may record the miles you walk, run, bike, swim, or the hours you played tennis or golf. Any convenient journal or log can work as a Personal Journal. The Franklin-Covey planners are good, as long as there's ample room for goals, action plans, the recording of comments, and a separate page to list Accomplishments.

A Personal Journal that has every week on two facing pages with additional pages to save good ideas works well. It can be notebook size or pocket-sized, whichever you prefer.

Use your Personal Journal to record facts, events, feelings, thoughts, and ideas.

Analyze Results

While measuring has benefits, the full benefits come through analysis. Analyze your results continually; minimally review your Personal Journal each month. Analyzing results should lead to modest or dramatic changes in actions and goals.

Look for trends. If you had a great day, it is important to understand why so that you may replicate the success. Likewise, a bad day, like any failure, can be a great teacher. If something isn't working, figure out why. If your actions aren't furthering your goals, decide if you need more time or need to change your actions.

As you measure results and review your Personal Journal, you may notice a trend. You may suddenly realize the goal you had no longer makes sense or needs to be revised. Be sure to use your Personal Journal to **Learn Who You Are.**

Analyze Results also means taking the time to note successes. Celebrate them.

Analyze Results comprises the information-gathering and analysis step necessary to best revise your goals.

The Ten Keys

The Seven Steps of the **Personal Growth Cycle** and the **Ten Keys** work together to promote personal growth. While they are described separately they work together and rely on each other. For example, the first key, **Learn Who You Are**, improves the quality of your goal setting. Positive thinking affects all the steps and keys and is assumed to exist when using any of the principles.

 ## Learn Who You Are

Socrates said, "Know yourself." As you work hard, measure results, analyze results, meditate, and pray, you will learn about yourself. *It is important that some time is spent specifically on getting to know yourself.* The **Accept Fate** step is critical to allowing yourself the clarity of thought to accurately see yourself. You will never see your own flaws if you don't accept yourself and your fate.

The **Personal Growth Cycle** helps you learn who you are. The better you know yourself, the better you will establish goals, measure, and analyze goals, the better the **Personal Growth Cycle** works. In much the same way, as personal growth relies on Thinking Positive, the more you understand yourself, the more you can succeed. Proper goal setting relies upon you to **Learn Who You Are**. *Lead an examined life.*

Measurements help you see yourself accurately. Grades, raises, thank-you notes, customer satisfaction levels, test scores, and the opinions of those you trust all provide valuable feedback. But Socrates would say that soul-searching best helps you understand yourself. Use all of the tools at your disposal, especially your Personal Journal.

Tune In to a Higher Power

The vast majority of the world believes in something bigger. Call it God, the Universe, or the collective unconscious. We believe. Many believe in Christ and Christianity. Regardless of who or what you believe in as a higher power, even if it be your personal group of friends, family, or associates, **Tune In to a Higher Power**. *Make a decision to listen.*

Seek and ye shall find. Ask and it shall be given to you. These words from the Bible have become both clichés and tenets.

 Pray and Meditate

The only way to **Tune In to a Higher Power** is through prayer and meditation. Both prayer and meditation are very personal and varied. There are truly googols of ways to pray and meditate. Find yours. If you search for a solution from God or the Universe, help will come. It is a two-step process: Seek help and open yourself to receive that help. Take both steps.

A powerful prayer may begin with thanksgiving and entails a request for the wisdom or strength to solve a particular problem. If one assumes that the Universe or God will do their part, then it is only the other individuals who need to do theirs in order for the world to work at its best. Praying for world peace may be beneficial. But surely seeking the knowledge and strength on your part for the wisdom and strength to contribute to world peace could be more effective.

Prayer and Meditation can be simple. Prayer may be done in solitude with a quiet mind and in a quiet environment. We can thank God for all He has done and we can ask Him for things we need. We seek His help to do things or to understand things.

Basic problem solving may be the best prayer one can offer. We can ask for things we have already begun honest efforts to bring about by ourselves. If one has a legitimate need, ask the Lord for assistance in understanding how to get it.

Meditation, much like prayer, is best done when your mind is quiet, when you can set aside distractions. More so than mere relaxation, meditation can help you hear the answer to your prayers. It can help you tap into the collective unconscious or God. Just as listening is a decision, hearing is a similar decision.

There are many good books on meditation but not as many on how to pray. A few simple thoughts may help. Wherever you can relax and calm your mind, thank God for all He has done, ask for his guidance, ask for those things you need and can't do alone, and listen very intently for answers. Sometimes this is like doing some deep thinking with God effectively holding your hand. It happens when you listen to your **Personal Commercial** and pray and think. Answers come to you, solutions to little things and big things that may have eluded you.

Meditation and prayer may be active. During a walk, when knitting, or when working, one can mentally Tune In to a Higher Power and get into the zone. The solutions to problems may appear once we have exhausted all possibilities and when we then engage in a repetitive act that may open our minds to the answer, as Benson and Proctor point out in *The Break-out Principle*. This shows how prayer can be answered. Here, it is the repetition of the mindless task that opens our minds to answers.

 **Forgive and Repent**

A proper conscience helps us determine when we have wronged people. If we have morals and do wrong, we may feel guilt and remorse. Proper atonement requires we make up for the impropriety. If you offend someone you can't very well retract that offense. You can, however, apologize, ask forgiveness of God, the offended, and from yourself, and resolve to exercise self-control in the future. If you can make amends, do so. The world is fair. What goes around comes around, so be sure to do good things so that good things will happen to you.

Forgiveness, both giving and receiving, has a powerful baggage-lifting effect. If you hate someone, the hatred you harbor will eat at you and do nothing but hurt you. When Christ said to forgive your enemies, it wasn't that you did it only for your enemies. It is something you do for yourself. Hate is a cancer that grows inside. Forgive and free the cancer. Harboring malice, hate, guilt, or other negative emotion can cause you pain and suffering. It may bring disease.

So *forgive and live.* Make peace with everyone. Even for soldiers on the battlefield, where killing may be critical to survival and preservation of one's country, hatred won't help you nor hurt your enemy. You can choose not to hate even in the worst of times.

Live in the Present

Live in the Present requires practice and the right attitude. The right attitude comes from the knowledge that every second counts. **Live in the Present** recognizes that there really are no unimportant activities. All actions are important. It is only by treating every second and resulting action or thought as precious and fully using every second can we optimize our potential.

If one participates in a sporting event where absolute concentration remains critical, one understands the importance of **Live in the Present**. In football or baseball, if you are thinking about running or passing the ball before you catch the ball you often fail to catch it. This analogy parallels life. *If you continue to anticipate what comes next, you will drop the ball.*

Living in the Present is its own reward. We are each given opportunities to contribute to our own welfare and others. If we **Live in the Present**, then we remain available to do our best and carpe diem.

The great Zen master, Thich Nhat Hanh, labels Living in the Present as mindfulness, awareness of all of your thoughts and actions as they occur. The Zen master's phlegmatic demeanor results from giving every second its due and no more. Living in the Present reduces worry as random negative thoughts have little room in a fully conscious, mindful life.

Meditation, prayer, and accepting the equal importance of each moment may all assist one in the practice of **Live in the Present**.

 ## Accept Death and Face Fear

Death is inexorable and our bodies are mortal; we die. Can one live fully with the Damocles' Sword of death hanging over our head? The sooner we accept death not as friend or foe but just a part of life, the sooner we live. The immortality of the soul may comfort believers. Accepting death allows us to accept a full life.

Accepting death requires confronting life's greatest fear. Fear of death is like most fears – irrational. There is no benefit to fear. Being positive, confident, and fearless is logical, smart, and Christian. David toppled Goliath by living the Keys; **Accept Death and Face Fear**, **Tune In to a Higher Power**, **Think Positive**, and **Live in the Present**.

Fear by definition is painful alertness caused by potentially unfavorable consequences. The initial warning your senses have given you carries all of the potential benefits of the emotion of fear. *Angst, pain, and dread of impending doom carry no benefits.* Acknowledge this feeling and let it pass. Be aware of the danger, prepare for it, but do not fear it. Worry has no value.

Live in the Present is a logical response to the fear of death. If we will die tomorrow, we should enjoy every moment as we would our last. If we will not die, then surely we will be no worse for living each moment to its fullest, like the Zen master.

We fear most the unknown and things we are unprepared for. *The best cure for fear is to prepare for all foreseeable difficulties and remember that **good things happen to good people who do good things**.* Worry, fear, and other negative emotions are unhealthy, unnecessary, and unproductive. Prevention, on the other hand, benefits and comprises the only positive response of fear. The prepared speechmaker or athlete rarely fails to perform. Be prepared for death and all fears and accept them and face them. They will soon disappear.

 ## Love Everyone

Love heals. Love allows people to grow and prosper. It warms us and protects us. The power of love can be unleashed by anyone. Love opens our hearts and minds to the infinite power of the Universe and allows us to tap into it.

You will be better, stronger, and more alive with love in your heart. You will be free to work hard and do good works. You may be free of worry and pain. **Think Positive**, the first step, is also the step that opens us to love. With love there is little room for negative emotions. Instead your body is filled with endorphins that promote health.

If one truly loves, everyone will see it and be attracted to you. Mother Teresa's love shone so bright that Catholics, Christians, and nonbelievers alike saw a very special and good person. Boundless love frees one's heart and soul. True love allows us to unclench our fists of desire, to marvel at the beauty of the Universe, to achieve all of our potential, and to recognize our true selves and true purpose.

Love, like other actions and thoughts, is under our own control and God-given free will. Choosing to love is a wise and supernal decision.

Have Fun

There are two parts to **Have Fun**. The first is to dedicate time to enjoyable activities. The second is to cherish and find joy in each second. Revel in your daily chores. Recognize the tremendous blessing of life's mundane activities, even washing dishes and folding clothes. Living in the Present and mindfulness promote **Have Fun**.

Life and living are fun and enjoyable. You can take life very seriously without taking it so seriously as to stop having fun. Some people feel that play is wrong or undeserved. Play goes hand in hand with having a positive attitude. It is critical to keeping up a good attitude so as not to lose sight of your goals, family, and purpose.

Have Fun promotes the great things that happen in your body when you smile and when you laugh. Scientists can prove smiling, being positive, and loving create endorphins that promote health and recovery from disease. We all know that smiling feels better than frowning. **Have Fun** is an excellent strategy to fitness by using one's favorite sport, such as basketball, soccer, baseball, golf, or volleyball, to make exercise fun. Choosing your favorite healthy food can make dieting fun.

Finally, finding true purpose in our work and life can help us have fun each and every day.

Help Others

Help Others when your help is wanted and needed. Helping others feels good and garners wonderful benefits. Being a positive influence and ready to assist makes one an asset to his family, friends, acquaintances, and employer. It creates positive interchanges between you and others that in turn naturally bring good things to you. *Good things happen to good people who do good things.*

When we are young, we receive much assistance, and as we mature we tend to give more. Even toddlers can help smaller children and benefit from the interaction. Teaching is a great way to learn. Give freely of yourself without strings. Give carefully and appropriately as the most sincere but unwanted advice or generosity may create problems and pain. Unwanted and unnecessary help is no help.

Those who desperately need our help are obvious and they needn't ask. But with others we need to be sure we are helping. Tying your brother's shoe when he is two years old is properly helping him. But when he gets older and more capable your help may impede in his personal growth. Wait for people to ask for your help. Only then can you be sure that those requesting will be receptive.

How you interact with your parents, siblings, teachers, classmates, peers, subordinates, and superiors shows that you are there for them. Being open and friendly encourages those with needs to seek you when they are ready.

 **Pursue Your Purpose**

We appear happiest as we increasingly satisfy our hierarchy of needs from food, shelter, and clothing, family needs, social needs, etc., to self-actualization. Finding our true purpose allows us to do exactly that. Pursuing our unique purpose assures us of the happiness, well-being, and self-actualization that we all deserve.

We all have unique skill sets, talents, and proclivities. Search for yours and you will find it. Use **The Seven Steps** and **Ten Keys**, especially **Pray and Meditate**, to help you find your purpose. Rick Warren in *The Purpose-Driven Life* has formalized a 40-day program to help you find yours. Making the search for your purpose one of your personal goals will also allow you to maintain an effective search.

Benefits to doing your life's work are unending. When you are doing the work the Universe and God intended you to do, your mind is guilt-free. As the work matches your skill set, you find it more enjoyable, you will be more productive, and you may increase if not optimize your earnings power. Once we are *living purposively,* which is leading a life with our purpose directing us, we will find that every moment of our lives can become a prayer or a state of meditation.

While we may not find our life's purpose overnight or in 40 days, once you decide to find it and follow it, you will have instantly stepped unto your path to pursuing your purpose. As each step takes you closer, then you are by definition pursuing your purpose once you make the decision to find and follow it. *Once you decide and commit to pursue your purpose and take steps toward this pursuit, you are living purposively.*

The Seven Steps of the Personal Growth Cycle
(Symbol Meanings*)

1. **Think Positive**: *The Smiling Face*

2. **Accept Fate**: *The Clover Reflecting Chance*

3. **Set Goals**: *A Target*

4. **Visualize Success**: *An Eye*

5. **Work Hard**: *A Hammer*

6. **Measure Results**: *A Chart*

7. **Analyze Results**: *A Chart With Results*

The Ten Keys
(Symbol Meanings*)

1. **Learn Who You Are**: *The Question Mark In One's Mind*
2. **Tune In to a Higher Power**: *The Greek Letters Chi and Rho Symbolizing Christ*
3. **Pray and Meditate**: *A Prayer Book*
4. **Forgive and Repent**: *A Heart Open to Forgiveness*
5. **Live in the Present**: *Symbol of Electrical Grounding*
6. **Accept Death and Face Fear**: *A Coffin*
7. **Love Everyone**: *Two Hearts*
8. **Have Fun**: *Music Notes*
9. **Help Others**: *The International Symbol of Help or Shelter*
10. **Pursue Your Purpose**: *The Maltese Cross Symbolizing the Eight Virtues of Knighthood*

The Ten Key Symbols (in Order) for Reference:

* Each symbol was chosen as the best representation of a step or key. Some were chosen from modern ideas and some date back to the earliest of recorded history.

GLOSSARY

(A didactic guide to the recondite for the logophile):

abate	to lessen in degree or amount
abode	a home or dwelling place
accost	to approach and talk to in an aggressive or hostile manner
acquiesce	to consent or comply without protest
acronym	a word formed from the initials of words
ad nauseam	to a ridiculous degree or the point of nausea
adage	a general truth or wise saying
admonition	a warning
adrenaline	epinephrine, a secretion of the adrenal medulla gland released in response to stress
affirmation	a positive statement
alacrity	speed and willing readiness, eagerness, celerity
albatross	a large bird, an obstacle to success, or a constant worrisome burden
albeit	even though, notwithstanding
ambivalence	the coexistence of two opposing feelings or attitudes
allay	relieve, lessen the severity of, ameliorate
ample	large or fully sufficient to meet needs
Ancient Eight	Ivy League: Penn, Cornell, Harvard, Columbia, Princeton, Brown, Yale, Dartmouth
anklet	something worn about the ankle
aperçu	insight or perception, also a summary
arsenal	a store or supply, often of weapons
askance	a look of disapproval, mistrust, or suspicion
assail	to attack forcefully, physically or with words
assuage	lessen the hurt, desire, suffering, doubt
atonement	expiation, to make amends or reparations for wrongdoing
banal	trite or boringly commonplace
banter	light playful remarks or teasing
barometer	an instrument for measuring atmospheric pressure
beguile	to deceive or take away by trickery or to charm

behooves	to be necessary or proper to do
bell curve	the statistical normal distribution; a bell-shaped curve
bifurcate	divide into two, separate
braggadocio	pretentious bragging, or a cocky manner
braggart	one given to boasting
bravado	a show of defiance or false bravery
brazenly	exhibiting boldness without respect or with contempt
bulimia	an eating disorder marked by binging and purging (overeating then vomiting)
calamities	events that bring significant losses or troubles
callipygian	possessing shapely, attractive buttocks
callous	unfeeling or emotionally hardened
candidly	impartially, without prejudice
candor	sincerity or openness of expression
carpe diem	seize the day
cascading	flowing like a waterfall or moving in steps like a process
catatonic	characterized by a lack of activity
cathartic	a cleansing of the emotions such as fear
catholic	ecumenical, universal in scope
cede	give, yield, or grant
celerity	speed in action
cement mixer	a front facing move where one spins and twists, bringing his opponent under him
chaff	the worthless part, the bracts that hold the wheat removed during threshing
chagrin	a feeling of embarrassment or annoyance
charley horse	a cramp or stiffness in a muscle, usually the upper leg
chastise	to whip or severely criticize, castigate
chime	to speak in accord with
choreograph	plan steps as in a dance movement
cliché	a commonplace expression or trite phrase
cloak	to hide with or cover
cognitive dissonance	psychological conflict resulting from incongruous beliefs or attitudes
columbary, columbarium	a container or housing for the dead, usually ashes
comprised	made up of, contained
condescending	acting superior to someone
condone	to overlook or pardon

[233]

confer	to give or bestow, to compare views
conflicted	having irreconcilable ideas, beliefs, or emotions
console	alleviate grief
conspicuously	doing something obvious or so as to attract notice
constraints	checks or restrictions on actions
contemporaneously	occurring or existing at same time
contraire, ma mere	(French) to the contrary, my mother
conundrum	enigma, puzzle, riddle, secret or difficult problem
convoluted	very intricate or involved
cordial	friendly in a polite way
cornerstones	a basic element serving as a foundation
coup de grace	a decisive or finishing blow, act, or event
coy	reserved, unusually flirtatiously shy or modest
crimson	red or to make vivid red
cue	a signal or act used to prompt
culpable	guilty or blameworthy
Damocles, Sword of	a sword hanging over one's head, a precarious position
daunting	something that lessens one's courage
dauntless	not feeling pressure or intimidation, brave, fearless
decimation	massive reduction in number or severe injury
demeaning	state of being lower in character or status
demeanor	behavior, how one comports oneself
demure	modest or reserved, affectedly modest or reserved
denouement	(French) the unraveling of events, outcome
deride	to make fun of, to laugh at as worthless, to speak with contemptuous mirth
détente	reduced tensions or an agreement that leads to reduced tensions between parties
devoid	completely without, destitute, totally lacking, empty
didactic	instructive, preceptive
diplomacy	the art of handling affairs without causing hostility
disdain	to despise or treat with contempt
dissemble	to disguise, to hide one's true motives
distraught	to be severely agitated or emotionally distressed
divert	to distract or to entertain
don	to put on (usually clothes), to take on, or to assume
dross	waste products
efficacious	effective, producing the desired result

[234]

effluvium	an offensive smell or outpouring of waste often gaseous
egregious	conspicuously bad
eloquent	a powerful and fluent expression
emaciated	thin through starvation
emancipated	to be free of oppression or slavery or free from parental control
empirical	based on observation or experience
enraptured	filled with delight
envisioned	pictured in the mind
eruct	to belch, violent emission
etiolated	whitened as if bleached, paled
eulogy	a speech praising someone who has died
euphemistic	the substitution of a mild term for a harsh one so as not to hurt feelings
exhilarated	excited or made cheerful
extract	to draw out, forcefully remove, to determine through calculation
familial	related to family
fatalistic	a belief that we are powerless to change events
faux pas	an error, often embarrassing; a social blunder
fester	to sore or decay, to pus or suppurate, to increasingly become a source of pain
flail	to swing around vigorously, to thrash about
fodder	feed for cattle, raw material, often lesser quality
fold	a group of people bound together
forge	to give form or shape to
formidable	arousing fear, difficult to surmount or overcome, inspiring awe
fray	a fight, dispute, or contest
frontisteria	a place to study
frisson	a thrill or a shudder, could be pleasant or unpleasant
furrowed	having wrinkles or lines as in furrowed brow
fusillade	a simultaneous or rapid discharge of firearms, an outburst
gassed	high school term for being winded or out of gas, out of energy
gaunt	thin, emaciated, lean
gauntlet	a challenge, medieval metal glove thrown down as challenge to fight.

Geneva Convention	treaty adopted in 1947 to determine rules for treating war prisoners
Gestaltian	"aha" moment - an aperçu or sudden insight of revelation, complete view
glean	to collect bit by bit, to gather, to determine through careful observation
googol	ten to the one hundredth power or the number one followed by 100 zeros
grandiloquent	using large words to impress
gravity	importance, seriousness or weight
grimace	a pained expression
hamper	to reduce the effectiveness of something
Hawthorne studies	results that occur from the mere fact of being observed
Hegira	escape to a better place or to escape danger
hematoma	a localized swelling from the rupture of a blood vessel
hubris	pride or lack of humility
huit clos	(French) no way out, dead end; also title of Sartre's famous one-act play
hyperbole	an exaggeration for emphasis
impede	stand in the way of, block
importune	ask repeatedly, plead incessantly, annoy, vex
impropriety	an unacceptable act or improper behavior
include-moi	fabricated by Allen to mean include me
incongruity	inconsistency, lacking harmony, out of place, improper
inconsolable	impossible or difficult to be consoled or soothed
incredulous	unable to be believed, arousing skepticism or disbelief
indiscretion	an act performed irresponsibly or without discretion
inexorable	inescapable, unavoidable, relentless, ineluctable
inferred	one assumes based on data received versus implied something by giving data
intercede	to plead or act in one's behalf, mediate
interjected	inserted between
intimidate	to daunt, to cause to fear, to make timid
intrepid	having no fear, courageous, brave, fearless
jaundice	a disease causing yellowness, affected with envy, jealousy, hostility or prejudice
Jobian	related to a man in the Old Testament whose faith in God survived many tests

[236]

jot	the least or smallest part, whit, speck
joust	medieval combat using lances on horseback; here a competition with multiple encounters
juxtapose	to place side by side
kudos	praise, panegyric, plaudits, encomium
lackluster	dull, vapid, jejune, torpid
laconic	concise, using few words, sententious
lament	feel or express sorrow
levity	humor, jocularity, waggery
lexicology	the linguistic field in the use and study of words and their applications
litmus test	a test with a decisive factor
living purposively	to live life with a purpose
logomania	the frenzy over words
logophile	a lover of words
loquacious	wordy, verbose, bombastic, effusive, prolix, turgid, voluble
lugubrious	overly sorrowful
lurid	gruesome, graphic, marked by sensationalism
mesmerize	to fascinate or spellbind
mete	measure, to distribute
mettle	courage, spirit
minatory	menacing, threatening
mnemonics	a memory device or code
moniker	nickname, to apply a name
morass	a swamp, marsh, something that obstructs or impedes
morbid	grisly, gruesome, gloomy, unwholesomely sick idea, diseased, stygian
moribund	near death
mortified	extreme embarrassment, shame, dulled to insensitivity, dead, religiously dead
mulino	in Italian, windmill
muster	to show one's mettle, show proof of power
neophyte	a novice, a new member, proselyte, a convert
neurosurgeon	surgeon of the nervous system; nerves, brain, spinal cord
nitric oxide	a neurotransmitter that may enhance memory and learning
nitrous oxide	a gas that when inhaled produces exhilaration, laughing gas, used as anesthetic

noncognitive comatose	in a coma
nonplussed	surprised, vexed
noradrenalin	substance secreted by the adrenal medulla, both a hormone and neurotransmitter
octogenarians	individuals in their eighties
obtuse	slow to understand, lacking intellect, blunt, not sharp
orthodox	holding currently accepted opinion
partisan	strong, often unreasoned support
patronizing	acting in a superior or condescending way
Pavlov	Russian physiologist who discovered the conditioned response
peruse	to read carefully, inspect, observe with attention
phlegmatic	indifferent, lacking energy
pine	to long for someone or something
pithy	concise, well said with few words, meaty
plaudit	praise, kudos, pleased approval
pompous	self-important and foolishly solemn
posthaste	immediately
precipitous	dangerously steep
preemptive	a first strike so as to prevent retaliation, of rights to buy first
preordained	determined in advance
proclivities	natural talents or tendencies, natural liking
profusely	in great quantities
prognosis	opinion on the course an injury or disease will take
protean	able to take various shapes, forms, or meanings
provincial and parochial	not worldly, unsophisticated
psyche out	slang; to attempt to intimidate
pummeling	hand sparring to gain an advantage for a hold or throw
purposive living	living life with a purpose
quarter	shelter
queued	formed a line
quid pro quo	something for something else
rapprochement	a reconciliation or renewed relations between parties
real McCoy	not an imitation
recondite	difficult to understand, profound, abstruse, not commonly known
reconnoitering	surveying a place for future actions, spying
relinquishes	yields, gives up, abandons

reminiscing	talking pleasantly about the past
remorse	feeling of sorrow and guilt
rent	to separate, the act of rending or splitting
reparations	payback or compensation
repertoire	a person's set of talents, skills or abilities
reprehensible	deserving blame, blameworthy
requisite	indispensable, appropriate, and necessary
revel	joyful merrymaking, rejoice, riot
reverie	daydream
Russian single	a takedown by a spin movement where one turns 360° and shoots for a leg
sabotage	intentional secret act to harm
sagacious	shrewd, showing keen judgment
sanguinity	the state of being cheerfully optimistic and confident
salubrious	good for you, promoting of health, beneficial
screed	long wordy prose
scurrility	very obscene or vulgar words
segue	an uninterrupted transition from one song, melody, subject, or idea to another
self-actualized	to fulfill one's highest potential or desire, the top of Maslow's hierarchy of needs
sesquipedalian	long words, words a foot and a half long
singlet	wrestling uniform
smeltsly	a term attributed to Fred A. Vogel, hanging onto a leg as a defense, counter, stall, or ride
soliloquy	the act of talking to oneself
solitudinarian	one who spends much time alone
somber	dark, gloomy, melancholy
sprawl	a spreading out of the limbs, keeping one's legs beyond the reach of the opponent
spry	nimble, active, alert, clever
stanchions	the upright props for support
stigma	a mark or brand
stitch	a muscle cramp
stoic	indifferent to pain or pleasure
subdural	underneath the skin
succulent	juicy
sui generis	unique, peculiar, one of a kind
supernal	high in rank, heavenly, excellent, divine

supine	to lie on one's back or to lie with one's face up
surmise	to make a reasonable guess, deduce
surreptitious	secret
Survivor syndrome	a reaction of a survivor, characterized by guilt and reduced motivation
synthesize	to combine from parts, to blend, or to make artificially
tenets	doctrine, dogma
tenuous	slim, thin, weak
tintinnabulation	the sound or music of ringing bells
tome	a large, heavy book
tort	injury or wrong; in law a breach of a duty
tortuous	twisted, curved, windy
touché	an admission of a hit in fencing, exclamation of a successful blow
transgress	to break a law, to sin
translucent	semi-transparent, so as to be partially seen through
trepidations	anxieties, fears
unbeknownst	unknown, without the knowledge of
unbridled	free of restraint or restriction, ungoverned
unconscionable	unscrupulous, extremely unreasonable, excessive
urchin	child, mischievous youngster
verbatim	word for word, in the exact words
vex	to trouble, afflict or harass, frustrate
visualization	process of forming a mental picture of something not actually present to the sight
whet	to sharpen, to put an edge on, to increase, incite
whimsical	subject to whim or momentary fancy
whirling dervish	one that possesses abundant, often frenzied, energy; named after Sufi dancing
whit	smallest speck, iota
whitewash	attempt a cover-up
Whys Approach, the	to ask *why* as many times as necessary until uncovering the real issue or root cause of a problem
wry	bent or distorted to note disgust, displeasure, a wry sense of humor, mordant

NOTES:

TO ORDER THE
PERSONAL COMMERCIAL™
TURN THIS PAGE!

Want *Anthony* to talk to you?

Have your own *Personal Commercial* just like Greg Gurist!

Seek *Anthony's* help to:

TAKE CONTROL OF YOUR LIFE

INCREASE MOTIVATION	**GAIN SELF–DISCIPLINE**
EAT PROPERLY	**IMPROVE GRADES**
REDUCE WEIGHT	**STRENGTHEN RELATIONSHIPS**
EXERCISE REGULARLY	**ACHIEVE GOALS**
PRACTICE MODERATION	**REDUCE FEARS**
REDUCE STRESS	**INCREASE SAT/GRE/GMAT SCORES**

Here's How:

1. Fill out the Order Form on the next page.
2. Order the *Personal Commercial* for $199.95.
3. Within 48 hours of receipt of your order, Anthony (your Sanguinity Coach) will contact you via e-mail.
4. We will work with you to complete a Personal Inventory, Set Goals, and develop your unique *Personal Commercial*.
5. Anthony will mail or e-mail you your *Personal Commercial* recording as either an MPEG-3 or CD recording.
6. You will listen to your *Personal Commercial* daily.
7. Your *Personal Commercial* is usually effective for three months.
8. If after one month you are not actively striving to achieve your goals, we will refund your money.

© Sanguinity LLC 2005

ORDER FORM

To order your *Personal Commercial* or copies of *Take Control of Your Life* please fill out this ORDER FORM and mail to:

Sanguinity LLC
PO Box 156
Baptistown, NJ 08803-0156
1-408-887-5127

You can also place orders online at:
www.sanguinity.org

Please remember to include a check, money order, or credit card information.

☐ Please have *Anthony* (your Sanguinity Coach) contact me immediately to begin preparing my *Personal Commercial* at the price of $199.95

☐ Please send me _____ copies of *Take Control of Your Life* at the price of $24.90 per copy ($19.95 plus $4.95 shipping and handling per copy) (International orders $27.90 per copy)

I enclose $ _____ :   ☐ Check   ☐ Money Order

Charge My Credit Card   ☐ Visa   ☐ MasterCard

Credit Card Number _____

Expiration Date Mo _____ / Year _____ Check Code _____

Name as Shown on Credit Card _____

Signature (Required for Credit Card) _____

Shipping Address
NAME _____
STREET ADDRESS _____
CITY _____ STATE _____ ZIP _____
COUNTRY _____
DAY PHONE NUMBER (_____) _____ - _____
E-MAIL ADDRESS _____

© Sanguinity LLC 2005

TO ORDER THE
PERSONAL COMMERCIAL™
TURN BACK ONE PAGE!